# Thinking he'd misheard, Devin moved closer

"Excuse me?"

Rachel beamed at him. "I'm saying yes to a date. How does tonight sound?"

Good God, she was serious. He was so flummoxed he couldn't think of an excuse. "Um..."

"Seven o'clock suit you?" Without waiting for a response, she wrote it in her diary in neat script.

"Look, this really isn't necessary. No hard feelings."

"No, I insist. And my goodness, you need a reward for all that persistence. Which is sweet of you, incidentally."

Devin winced. "The word *sweet* should only be applied to situations involving whipped cream and a supermodel," he said.

That sparked a quick frown of disapproval from her. His confusion gave way to suspicion. Wait a minute. The librarian didn't want to date him any more than he wanted to date her. This was counterterrorism.

Intrigued, he decided to play her at her own game.

Dear Reader,

My interest in writing an ex-rock-star hero came about through watching a couple of TV documentaries, including "Heavy—the History of Metal." I expected grunts and expletives; what I heard were articulate, clever and often well-educated men looking back over extraordinary achievements in music.

Alice Cooper, Johnny Rotten…great guys.

A lot of them had been through the mill with drugs, alcohol and relationships, but those who'd come out the other side were bad boys made good. Still with that self-deprecating humor and world-weary twinkle that make rogues so irresistible to romance readers.

Another profession that often gets stereotyped is the librarian. What fun, I thought, to put these two together. Drop by my Web site, www.karinabliss.com, and tell me if you thought so, too.

Happy reading.

*Karina Bliss*

# What the Librarian Did
*Karina Bliss*

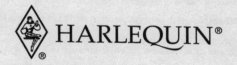

HARLEQUIN®

TORONTO • NEW YORK • LONDON
AMSTERDAM • PARIS • SYDNEY • HAMBURG
STOCKHOLM • ATHENS • TOKYO • MILAN • MADRID
PRAGUE • WARSAW • BUDAPEST • AUCKLAND

Recycling programs
for this product may
not exist in your area.

ISBN-13: 978-0-373-78367-0

WHAT THE LIBRARIAN DID

## ABOUT THE AUTHOR

New Zealander Karina Bliss was the first Australasian to win one of the Romance Writers of America's coveted Golden Heart Awards for unpublished writers, and her 2006 Harlequin Superromance debut, *Mr. Imperfect,* won a Romantic Book of the Year award in Australia. It took this former journalist five years to get her first book contract—a process, she says, that helped put childbirth into perspective. She lives with her husband and son north of Auckland. Visit her on the Web at www.karinabliss.com.

**Books by Karina Bliss**

**HARLEQUIN SUPERROMANCE**

Don't miss any of our special offers. Write to us at the following address for information on our newest releases.

Harlequin Reader Service
U.S.: 3010 Walden Ave., P.O. Box 1325, Buffalo, NY 14269
Canadian: P.O. Box 609, Fort Erie, Ont. L2A 5X3

To my sisters—
Carolyn, Janine, Deryn and Natalie.
All women supremely capable of bringing a
strong man to his knees.

## Acknowledgments

Thanks to Cheryl Castings, who suggested the name Matthew Bennett in a "Name a character" contest I ran through my Web site.

## *PROLOGUE*

*Seventeen and a half years earlier*
*Suburban New Zealand*

EVERYONE SAID ONLY a weirdo would turn down a date with Mary O'Connell's older brother, home from university for the holidays. And Rachel was sick of being a weirdo.

Tentatively, she followed Steve's lead in the kiss and wiggled her tongue. He responded with a flattering groan. Sweet sixteen and *finally* been kissed. She shivered, more from the loveliness of the thought than his gentle stroking of her bare arm. Then he touched her breast and she shied away. "Don't do that."

"I can't help it." Breathing heavily, Steve stared into her eyes. "You're so beautiful."

"Am I?" She stripped the wistful note out of her voice. "Don't be crazy." She was passable, that was all. When she wasn't in her school uniform she wore clothes that were Mom's idea of what a young lady should wear. Rachel pulled at the button-up collar of her pink blouse. She hated pink. And plaid skirts. When she left home she'd always wear bright colors.

"You *are* beautiful." Steve's voice vibrated with intensity. "And smart. And funny." He loomed closer again and her nervousness must have showed because he stopped with such an understanding smile that Rachel felt like a silly little girl.

Sure, they were a bit isolated, sitting here in his Toyota Celica, but across Hamilton Lake, suburban lights twinkled like stars.

And obviously they couldn't have a conventional date in case someone reported back to her parents. She shivered again, knowing how her father would react if he found out. But some risks were worth taking and Rachel yearned to live.

They'd drunk beer, which she'd only pretended to sip, watching Steve anxiously. But he'd stopped after one can. And he'd asked her about all sorts of subjects and listened—really listened—to the answers. As if her opinions mattered. Not even Chloe, her best and only friend, did that. Normally it was Rachel's job to listen.

His sincerity reminded her of Holden Caulfield, the hero in her favorite book, *Catcher in the Rye,* except that Steve was good-looking. Not that looks mattered; Rachel would hate to be shallow. And Steve said it was his favorite book, too. It must be a sign. Before she lost her courage, she leaned forward and initiated another kiss.

This time when he touched her breast Rachel let it linger a few seconds before she removed his hand. "I should really be getting back," she said. "I've got an exam tomorrow." She took her education very seriously. It was her way out.

Steve didn't get annoyed; he simply nodded and started the engine, and Rachel's last doubt dissipated. When he dropped her off at the end of the street he lifted her hand and kissed it, a French gesture that thrilled her all the way to the bone.

"Say we can do this again," he begged, and she nodded because her heart was too full to speak. *I'm in love.*

*Same time*
*Long Beach, Los Angeles, U.S.A.*

"GOT YOUR FAKE ID?"

Devin shouldered his bass guitar, checked his jeans pocket and nodded, but his attention wasn't really on Zander. With a sixteen-year-old's fascination, he was watching a stripper across the bar.

His brother's volatile temper had left him a bass player short an hour before a gig, and Devin was the last-minute replacement. Now he was discovering heaven had many layers. The stripper winked at him and he blushed and dropped his head.

Then caught Zander exchanging grins with the drummer, and scowled.

His brother nudged him. "And don't tell Mom I brought you here."

"You think I'm stupid?"

"Yeah."

It *was* seedy, the kind of place where people carried knives. Dimly lit, pungent with marijuana and sticky underfoot. But Devin didn't care. As they set up their secondhand equipment on the tiny platform that constituted the stage, his heart pounded harder and harder until he thought he'd pass out.

This was his chance to become a permanent member of Rage instead of the awestruck kid brother sitting in the corner of the garage. When the band let him. On the rare occasions, Devin would go up to his room afterward and create riffs on his bass or Zander's discarded electric guitar, which Devin played upside down because he was left-handed.

Zander had heard one, liked it and used it in one of his songs. After that, Devin had got more garage time. He knew every chord by heart—which was why he was here. So they didn't lose out on three hundred dollars. Devin wondered whether he could ask for a cut.

"Don't screw this up," muttered Zander as he

made his way to the microphone. Devin decided not to push his luck.

Instead he wiped his damp palms on his Guns 'N' Roses T-shirt and waited for his brother's hand signal, too scared to look around in case he caught someone's eye and got knifed, or worse, kicked out for being a kid. He couldn't lose this big chance.

Chris, the lead guitarist, gave his shoulder a friendly punch. "Breathe," he encouraged. Devin gulped as Zander grabbed the microphone and faced the band. His eyes and grin were wild and a charge crackled through the air and surged through Devin. He grinned back.

His brother raised one arm, revealing a flash of white abdomen between T-shirt and low-slung jeans. He must be the only person in L.A. without a tan, Devin thought irrelevantly, then Zander mouthed the count—*three, two, one*—and swept his arm down.

With Chris, Devin struck the first note of "Satan's Little Helper," and forgot his nerves, his hopes, forgot everything except coaxing emotion from his guitar. Lost himself in the music.

Much later, drenched with sweat, dazed from adrenaline overload, he sat at one of the scratched wooden tables in the bar. In the round of drinks, he mistakenly got a beer and drank it because he was so thirsty.

Zander noticed his empty glass. "Only one," he

warned, but he was too busy lapping up female attention to stop Devin accepting another.

After two beers he sat with a silly grin on his face, not feeling shy, not feeling anxious, not feeling anything but cocky. "Am I in, bro?" he called. Zander shrugged.

"Until we find someone better."

And Devin thought, *No one will be better than me. I'll make sure of it.*

He sneaked a glance at the stripper again and she wasn't looking at him as though he was a stupid kid anymore, because being in a band somehow changed that.

*I'm in love.*

# CHAPTER ONE

"ISN'T THIS THE SECOND marriage proposal you've turned down?" asked Trixie. "Face it, Rach, you're a heartbreaker."

"With that imagination you should be writing fiction, not shelving academia." Kneeling on the floor, Rachel Robinson snipped through the tape on the carton of books addressed to Auckland University library, then glanced at her assistant.

"I'm a thirty-four-year-old librarian, not Scarlett O'Hara, and Paul is probably breathing a sigh of relief right about now." At least she hoped he was. He'd been upset last night—and she still was. Both of them had expected her to say yes.

"That's another thing," said Trixie with the bluntness of youth. "Rejecting proposals is poor policy for a woman who wants a family. You may look twenty-nine but your ovaries are knocking thirty-five."

Normally her protégée's homespun lectures were entertaining, coming as they did from a twenty-year-old Goth-wannabe with dyed black hair and a nose stud. Today they struck a nerve. "Maybe I'm meant to devote my life to my work."

"Now that's just crazy talk."

At the other end of the counter, a student approached the help desk and pressed the buzzer. "Yours," said Rachel thankfully. The first day of the university year didn't start until tomorrow, but the smart ones were getting in early.

Trixie bent and gave Rachel a fierce, parting hug. "I hate it when you're unhappy. Go tell Paul you've changed your mind."

So much for putting on a brave face. Hauling the books out of the carton and stacking them under the counter, Rachel wished it was as simple as that. Lately her left brain didn't know what her right brain was doing. Tentatively prodding her feelings, she found no regret or remorse, only a guilty seam of rock-solid relief.

Standing, she closed her eyes, breathing in the heady smell of institutional tranquility, and tried to internalize it. *Help me,* she prayed silently. *Why do I run every time I'm close to marriage?*

Someone cleared his throat and Rachel opened her eyes. A man waited, impatiently frowning at her.

He was dressed in faded jeans with slashed knees and a too-tight olive-green T-shirt stretched over muscled biceps. Ruggedly tanned, he had sun-streaked russet-brown hair curling past his collar.

It wasn't that he had a five o'clock shadow at nine-thirty in the morning that screamed "bad boy." To Rachel's eyes, that simply made him scruffy. And most certainly his menace wasn't in his boots, butter-soft leather and, good Lord, purple?

No, it was the arrogant way he stood—feet planted wide, arms folded across his impressive chest. It was the dragon tattoo curling the length of one muscled arm. But mostly it was the sleepy sensuality in the hooded hazel eyes casually scanning Rachel as if she were part of a female buffet. She got the impression he was already very full but might possibly squeeze in dessert—if it was handed to him on a plate.

The woman in her bristled, but the librarian mustered a professional smile. "Can I help you?"

The man didn't smile back. "I heard there was a library tour for those new to the college." His voice was deep, his accent American.

Rachel reached for her timetable. "You're a day early, but if you give me your name I'll book you in for tomorrow."

There was a brief hesitation. "Devin Freedman."

"Devin. Spelled *o-n* or *i-n?*"

His mouth relaxed its tight line. *"I-n."*

"I can give you an informal look around now if you like."

For some reason his guard went up again. "I don't want any special treatment."

"You must be a student," she said drily. "If you were a lecturer you wouldn't say that."

Narrow-eyed, he assessed her, and Rachel nearly told him to lighten up. Then a thought struck her. "Oh, Lord, you *are* a new lecturer."

A smile broke through the guy's suspicion. It did strange things to Rachel's stomach. Or it could be she'd been too upset about Paul to eat breakfast.

"No," he said, "not a lecturer. And I would appreciate a tour. It's going to be hard enough tomorrow being the oldest student here."

"Don't worry, we have quite a few adult students. I assume you're part-time?"

"Full-time."

Rachel hid her surprise. Except for the boots, he didn't look as if he could afford to pay the fees without working. On the other hand, with that body, he probably made good money working nights in a male revue. She said briskly, "What degree?"

"Bachelor of commerce."

"Okay, Devin…my name's Rachel Robinson and you're in luck. I'm the subject librarian for business and finance. Follow me." She spent the next fifteen minutes walking him through the library, while he listened intently, saying little. "You're American," she commented at one point.

"No."

*Okay, we don't do small talk.* "We have a few

library tutorials of interest to you. Let me get you some brochures." She led him back to the counter and started rummaging through a filing cabinet.

"I'm *sure* I saw him come in here." The voice was female, very young and slightly breathless.

Another responded with a giggle, "Do you think he'd sign my bra?"

Startled, Rachel looked up. Devin had vanished and three teenagers milled around the entry, two girls and a boy.

"You promised you'd be cool about this if I brought you," the youth complained. Then he caught Rachel's eye and lowered his voice. "Shush, let's just go in and look."

"Can I help you?" Rachel asked in her best librarian's voice.

The boy dropped his gaze. "Uh, no, we're just looking for someone."

"Famous," added one of the girls, smoothing down her skirt and scanning the rows of books.

Rachel stepped into her line of sight. "So you're not here to use the facilities of the library?"

"No," the girl replied, "but—"

"Then it's better if you wait outside for whoever—"

"Devin Freedman." There was worship in the boy's tone.

"—you're waiting for," Rachel continued. "If you're sure he's here?"

That sowed enough doubt for them to start arguing among themselves as they left.

When they'd gone, she looked for Devin and found him leaning against a bookshelf in aisle three. He straightened at her approach, his expression wary. "As I was saying," she continued, "we have a few one-hour tutorials of interest to you. A library and resources overview, an introduction to our online library catalog…" She stopped because he wasn't listening, then added softly, "And I can show you the staff exit when you're ready to leave."

His attention snapped back to her. "Thanks."

"I'm sorry, I still have no idea who you are," she admitted.

"That makes two of us." He saw her bafflement and shrugged wide shoulders. "I was a guitarist in a band that did well."

*And now you're going back to school?* But he probably had enough of people prying into his private life. "That's why I don't know your name then. I don't keep up with contemporary pop."

He winced. "Rock."

"Excuse me?"

"We were rock."

Something in his pained tone made her smile. "Was that like comparing Gilbert and Sullivan to Puccini?"

An answering glint lit his eyes. "Sorry, I'm not

an opera buff. It's always struck me as a bunch of overemoting prima donnas going mad or dying."

"Whereas rock and roll…?"

Devin laughed. "You're right," he conceded, "no difference." He thrust out a hand. "Anyway, thanks for your help." She took the warm tapered fingers, careful to avoid the dragon's tongue flicking at the tip of one knuckle. "I'll hang around a bit longer till the coast clears," he added. "Read the brochures."

"If it's any consolation, they run a tight ship here," she said. "I doubt you'll get harassed past the first day."

"That's one of the reasons I chose this campus. I wanted fossilized conservatives dressed in…" His gaze slid over her gray pin-striped trousers and pale blue satin blouse with short puffed sleeves. "Thanks again."

Rachel felt a spike of irritation before her sense of humor kicked in. What did she care what a guy wearing purple boots thought about her vintage fetish? Still, she gave the boots a pointed look before she said kindly, "You're *very* welcome."

The edges of his irises were bright green, with copper-brown starbursts around the pupils. When he smiled with his eyes the effect was unnerving. "Ma'am," he drawled, flicked an imaginary hat brim, then strolled toward a reading nook.

*Smart aleck.* People rarely challenged Rachel and

never teased her; the world of academia was a civilized one. She sighed.

"Hell bod," said Trixie, coming up beside her. Then she started. "Hey, isn't that—"

"Devin Freedman," said Rachel knowledgeably, and went back to unpacking books and brooding on why someone who was desperate for kids couldn't cross the first threshold.

As though she'd conjured him, Paul reeled through the library's double doors. Rachel gasped. The side part that normally flipped his gray-streaked black hair rakishly over one eye zigzagged across his skull as crookedly as he now staggered across the navy carpet.

His corduroy jacket—the same soft brown as his eyes—had pizza stains on it and the blue chambray shirt that normally buttoned neatly under his chin flapped open halfway down a pale hairy chest. And the designer jeans…

Rachel rushed over and jerked up his fly. "You're drunk!"

"Are you surprised?" His voice rang loudly.

"Shush…."

She tried to drag him into the staff office, but he clutched at the countertop, swaying slightly. "You led me on!"

Heads began poking out from the aisles of books as readers took an interest. "Paul, please," she begged. Regardless of whether she deserved this humiliation, he was jeopardizing his job by showing up inebriated. She had to get him out of here. Rachel grabbed his arm again, called over her shoulder, "Trix, help me."

He flung them both off with a dramatic gesture, ruined by a loud belch. "When I've had my say."

Until last night she and Paul hadn't seen each other in six months because he'd been on sabbatical, studying some obscure Germanic dialect in Munich. Their reunion had come to an abrupt end on the way back to his apartment from the airport, when he'd proposed to her.

And Rachel had said no.

Their eighteen-month relationship had come to an even more abrupt end on his front doorstep as she'd desperately tried to explain a decision she couldn't justify except by describing her feelings. Unfortunately, terms like "panic" and "claustrophobia" didn't help him take the news any better.

Paul swallowed. "You broke my heart."

"It's not like you were crazy in love with me," she reminded him gently. In fact, they'd never been as fond of each other as when they'd been apart and their unremarkable sex life had been supplanted by romantic telephone calls and e-mails.

He refocused on her with bleary-eyed outrage. "I proposed to you, didn't I?"

"Well, yes," Rachel admitted. "Kind of."

"Guess we should think about getting married," had been his exact words. But their relationship had always been fueled by pragmatism, not passion. Paul wanted an independent, low-maintenance wife to support his brilliant career. And she wanted to start a family with a nice guy. Because Trixie was right, Rachel was running out of time. And her dating pool had always been the size of a goldfish pond. She was too self-sufficient for most guys…and too smart to pretend to be someone she wasn't.

Paul seemed to realize she wasn't reacting as she should. His face crumpled and he started to sob with a drunk's easy tears. "You really don't care, do you?"

Rachel blanched. Had his affections run deeper than she'd thought? "Of course I care." But much as she hated hurting him, she couldn't marry him. Even if only her right brain knew why. Seeing their audience growing, she tugged desperately on his arm. "Please, Paul, let me take you into the office, make you some coffee. You're doing yourself no good here."

"No!" He wiped his face with his sleeve and nearly fell over. "I don't want to."

"Oh, for God's sake." Devin Freedman appeared from out of nowhere and tipped Paul over one of his shoulders. "Where do you want him?" he asked Rachel.

## CHAPTER TWO

THE SMART-ASS LIBRARIAN looked at him with none of the self-possession she had earlier. In fact her big gray eyes were haunted. "In here," she said, ushering Devin into the office. "Trixie, take over." With trembling fingers, she pulled the venetian blinds closed, then shut the door and leaned against it.

Devin dumped the drunk on the couch and ran a professional eye over him. He'd quit bawling and was rolling his head from side to side and moaning faintly. "Some kind of container might be useful," he suggested. "He'll hurl at some point." Rachel looked at him blankly and he tried again. "Barf." Still nothing. Where was a translator when he needed one? "Throw up...vomit."

"Oh...oh!" She scanned the room, then found an empty cardboard box and bent over to pick it up. It wasn't the first time he'd noticed she had a nice ass. Rachel placed the box by the couch and backed away, her expression guilt-stricken. He suspected he knew what was worrying her. "Alcohol makes some people maudlin," he offered. Particularly those who took themselves way too seriously. "Don't worry about it."

"You don't understand," she murmured. "He proposed yesterday and I turned him down."

"That's no surprise. There must be a fifteen-year age difference."

"Seven years. I'm thirty-four." Devin's age. She didn't look it. The librarian shook her head. "Not that age matters. The important thing now is that—"

"He's acting like a wimp?"

"No!" She took a protective step toward the drunk. Anyone could see she had a conscience. That must be painful for her. "Paul had every right to expect me to say yes. I meant to say yes, only..." Her voice trailed off.

Paul sat up and grabbed the box. Rachel retreated and they both turned their backs, but couldn't escape the awful retching sounds. "Only you realized you'd be making a terrible mistake," Devin finished. Maybe the vintage clothes were an attempt to look older?

"I drove him to this." The librarian's slender throat convulsed. "And he's not the first man I've let down. I...I'm a heartbreaker."

As one who'd been given the description by the world's press, as one who'd dated and even married the female heartbreaker equivalent, Devin was hard put not to laugh. Only the sincerity in her pale face stopped him from so much as a grin. She really believed it, which was kind of cute—if a little sad. And he thought *he* was self-delusional at times.

Not that she wouldn't be pretty with a hell of a lot more makeup and a hell of a lot less clothes. The fastidious restraint of all those satin-covered buttons and dainty pearl earrings made Devin itch to pull Rachel's sleek dark hair out of its practical ponytail. Mess it up a little. Understated elegance was exceedingly bland to a man whose career had depended on showmanship.

He'd deliberately dressed down to fit in today, and thought he'd done a pretty good job until the librarian's gaze had fallen on his boots. No jewelry except one signet ring and one modest earring…hell, he was practically invisible.

The sound of retching stopped and they turned around. The drunk—Paul—had pushed up to a sitting position and was wiping his mouth on some copier paper. White-faced and sweating, he glared at Devin. "Who do you think you are, manhandling me like that?"

Devin shrugged. "Someone had to stop you making an ass of yourself."

But Paul had already turned on Rachel. "I hope you're happy reducing me to this state."

"She didn't force alcohol down your throat," Devin said quietly.

The librarian swallowed. "Paul, I'm sorry. I had no idea you cared about me this much."

"You think everyone's as lukewarm as you are?" Paul balled the paper. "I did *all* the caring in that relationship. All the work in bed. You—"

"Have really, *really* bad taste in men," Devin said, because Rachel was hugging herself and obviously taking this Paul's rant way too seriously.

The librarian seemed to remember he was there. She straightened her shoulders. "Thank you, but I can handle it from here."

"You sure?" She was obviously out of her depth. "He's likely to get more abusive. I can toss him in a cab for you."

"Thanks," she said awkwardly, opening the door, "but I'll be okay." Devin got the impression she wasn't used to accepting help. Any more than he was used to offering it. For a moment he had an odd sense of his world shifting. But it had shifted so often lately he ignored it.

Something incongruous about her appearance had been bothering him, and as she bit her lip Devin finally figured out what it was. Her mouth—lush and full—was more suited to the L.A. strippers he'd shared stages with in the band's early performing days than a prim librarian. He grinned just as Romeo grabbed the box and started hurling again.

Rachel stiffened. "I'm glad one of us finds this funny."

"Your mouth doesn't fit your profession," he explained. "It's like seeing something X-rated on the cartoon network."

He didn't think to censor himself because he'd been a rock star for seventeen years and never had to. And got a sharp reminder he was no longer in that world when she shut the door in his face.

"Lucky the librarian fantasy never made my top ten," he told the door.

DEVIN WANTED TO BE treated as normal, and yet once his amusement wore off, Rachel's reaction gave him a profound sense of dislocation.

She'd looked at him without his fame in the way and hadn't liked what she'd seen. It was a scary thought, because whoever she saw was someone he was going to have to live with for the next forty plus years.

He strode across the road from the library into Albert Park, then stopped in a stand of tall palms that reminded him of L.A.—his home before his life depended on leaving it. For a full five minutes he looked up through the fronds to the blue, blue sky, homesick. Then he started walking again, around the quaint Victorian fountain, past oaks and a lot of trees he didn't recognize.

This must be how refugees felt in a new land...displaced, wary. And yet he'd been born here, was still a citizen, though he'd left for his father's country when he was two. He breathed in the smell of fresh-mown grass, only to regret it wasn't L.A.'s smog.

"Your pancreas is shot to hell. Any alcohol and you're dead." The doctor had been blunt, and left him sitting in a private hospital room full of flowers from fans. The band had imploded at the same time as his health…. What the hell he was going to do with the rest of his life?

His car keys fell out of his hand; someone bent to pick them up. Another teenager—shit, this place made him feel like a dinosaur.

"Are you okay?" Gray eyes, intense in a pale face. Lank blond hair.

"Of course I am." The kid stepped back and Devin took a deep breath. "I'm fine…thanks." He couldn't rush the ascent, but had to stop and accli-matize, then kick up a bit more. He reminded himself that the surface was there—even when he couldn't see it.

"You're Devin Freedman, aren't you?" Ner-vously, the kid hitched up his baggy jeans. "I heard you'd be studying here this year."

Living on a remote part of Waiheke Island since his arrival in New Zealand two months earlier, Devin had got used to being left in peace. *Something else to give up.* "Yeah," he said grudgingly, "I'm him."

In his drive to take control of his life, Devin had started taking online accounting courses to decipher his financial statements. A tutor had suggested university. When Devin stopped laughing he'd thought, why not?

And already his growing fiscal knowledge had paid off. He'd appointed a new financial advisor who'd found disturbing anomalies in some of Devin's statements. It looked like someone had been ripping him off; unfortunately Devin suspected his brother. But he needed to be very sure before he acted.

"I'm a huge fan. *Darkness Fell* was a work of genius."

"Not *The Fallen* or *Crack the Whip?*" Rage's final albums.

The kid looked at his feet and shuffled. "I really liked the early stuff. I know the others sold well… I mean, not that's there's anything wrong with commercial albums…."

Devin put him out of his misery. "You're right, they were crap." By that point the band had barely been speaking.

"But you still had some phenomenal guitar riffs and—"

"You play?" Devin asked, cutting short the hero-worship. He gestured to the expensive guitar case slung over the kid's shoulder.

"Bass mainly, but also some electric and

acoustic—like you." The next words came in a rush. "Would you sign my guitar for me?" At Devin's nod, he unpacked a Gibson and scrambled in his bag for a Sharpie.

"What's your name?"

"Mark White."

Devin hesitated with his pen over the guitar.

"Your autograph will be fine," insisted Mark. "I hate phoniness, too."

Grinning, Devin signed, then handed back the bass. "See you around."

MARK MANAGED A CASUAL NOD but sank onto a bench as soon as Devin disappeared. Mark's knees were shaking. He clutched the neck of his instrument, looked at the manicured gardens of Albert Park and thought, *I imagined that. No one meets a legend, a god among bass players walking through freakin' rose beds.*

He glanced down at his guitar and for a moment panicked because sunlight was bouncing off the lacquer and he couldn't see it. But then he adjusted the angle and there it was scrawled across the maple. "To Mark, stay honest. Devin Freedman."

And Mark grinned because one part of him wanted to run back to his apartment, jump on his computer and flog it on eBay, and the other wanted to sleep with it under his pillow. *You are one screwed-up dude, Mark.*

So what was new?

Still, he let himself be happy, because it wasn't every day a guy got to meet his all-time hero. Then he looked toward the campus and his smile faded under the familiar gut-wrenching nausea, anger and terror. She was here… somewhere.

Mark had seen the University of Auckland envelope at the adoption agency when he'd asked the woman to check his file, claiming he was in an open adoption. Funny how people didn't care about hiding envelopes. The woman had been very kind, considering he'd been lying to her. "Do your parents know you're here?"

He'd lied again. "Sure."

Abruptly, Mark stood and began walking. Why had his birth mother started out wanting an open adoption, then changed her mind and severed contact? The question had been eating away at him every since he'd discovered he had a different blood type to both his parents.

He'd searched through his parents' private papers and found correspondence from an adoption agency. Mom and Dad still didn't know he knew…and Mark tried not to blame them because it was clear *she'd* made secrecy a condition of adoption.

But his anger…his alienation had spilled over into his misbehavior. It had been a tough twelve months on everybody. He'd only talked his parents into letting him enroll at a university four hundred kilometers away because "honest, Mom and Dad, I see my future now and it's all about getting an education and being normal like you want me to be."

*Like I used to be. When I knew who I was.* But Mark had another agenda. He would confront his birth mother. She would sob an apology and beg his forgiveness. He would say, "You had your chance," and walk away. Just like she had.

He'd worked out that she'd been seventeen when she had him. That made her thirty-four now.

It shouldn't be too hard to find her.

THE FADED BLUE SEASIDE cottage was one of Waiheke Island's first vacation homes, and unlike its newer neighbors, it was tiny and unpretentious. Not for the first time, Devin thought how well it suited his mother. He jumped the seaman's rope fence and strode down the white shell path, giving a cursory pat to the concrete seal balancing a birdbath on its nose. Then he caught sight of the front door and frowned.

It was wide open and a gardening trowel lay abandoned on the doorstep. His pulse quickened, and though he told himself not to panic, he shouted, "Mom!"

Three heart-stopping seconds of silence and then a faint reply. "I'm out back."

Devin walked through the dim interior to the rear garden, a sprawl of crunchy grass, lichen-covered fruit trees and roaming nasturtium. "How many times do I have to tell you to shut your damn door? Anyone could walk in."

Holding a red bucket, his diminutive mother looked down from the top of a stepladder leaning against the peach tree. "And how many times do I have to tell you this isn't L.A.?" She dropped a handful of small white peaches into the half-full bucket, then ran a hand through her short gray bob. "Any leaves in my hair?"

Devin put his hands on his hips. "Should you be doing stuff like this?"

"I'm not going to have another heart attack, honey." Katherine held out the bucket. When he took it, she climbed sedately down the ladder. "Not now they've replaced the faulty stent."

He reached out and helped her down the last couple of steps, and her hand seemed so frail in his. Briefly, her grip tightened, reassuring him with its strength.

Still, Devin said gruffly, "Is it any wonder I'm paranoid after two emergency flights in two months? If you'd listened to my advice earlier and got a second opinion—"

"Yes, dear."

Reluctantly, he laughed. "Stay with me another week." He owned the adjacent headland, sixteen acres of protected native bush shielding a clifftop residence.

"I've only just moved home. Besides, you cramp my style."

"Stop you doing what you're not supposed to, you mean," he retorted.

"Dev, you're turning into the old woman I refuse to become. I'm sure I wasn't as bossy as this when you were in recovery."

"No," he said drily, "you were worse."

She ignored that, instructing him to pick some lemon balm for herbal tea on their meander back to the house. "How was your first day at school?"

"The other kids talk funny." Ignoring the kettle, he turned on the espresso machine he'd installed.

"Make any friends?"

He gave her the Devin Freedman glower, the one that *Holy Roller* magazine had described as the definitive bad rocker look. Being his mother she simply waited. "No, but then I don't expect to."

"You know I'm on the mend now, darling, so if you want to go back to L.A.—"

"I don't," he lied. "Got anything to eat?"

"There's a batch of scones cooling on the counter."

He burned his fingers snatching a couple, but feeding him distracted his mother from the subject of his future.

Five years earlier, when he'd quit rehab for the second time, she had told him she wouldn't spend her life watching him self-destruct, and had moved back to her native New Zealand. It had been a last-ditch effort to snap him into reality. Devin had felt nothing but relief, then added insult to injury by minimizing contact. It hadn't stopped Katherine from being the first person at his hospital bed.

Now she needed him to take care of her. Whatever she said.

His older brother, still living stateside, couldn't be relied on. A keen sense of the ridiculous had kept Devin's ego in check over the last crazy seventeen years, but the planet wasn't big enough for Zander's, who still blamed Devin for the breakup of the band.

The truth was Devin had held Rage together for a lot more years than its flamboyant lead singer deserved.

So if it turned out Zander had been screwing him over…well, Devin didn't think he could put even his mother's peace of mind before his need for justice.

## CHAPTER THREE

"HE LOOKS LIKE HE NEEDS a friend," Rachel said to Trixie two days later. She'd noticed the teenager yesterday during library orientation. Now, as then, he walked around with his shoulders slightly hunched, blond fringe falling over his eyes and a scowl on his young face that did nothing to hide his apprehension. She remembered what it was to be young, alone and terrified. "Maybe I should go talk to him."

"Oh, hell, you're not starting a new collection of waifs and strays already, are you?" Trixie complained as she sorted a pile of books for reshelving. "We're not even a week into the first term."

Rachel stood up from her computer. "You were a waif and stray once, remember?" Trixie had been a scholarship kid who'd practically lived at the library in winter because she couldn't afford to heat her flat. Rachel had given her a part-time job, which turned full-time when she'd graduated last year.

"Which is why I'm protecting you now," Trixie reasoned. "You're useless at setting boundaries."

"Tell me about it. I keep getting bossed around by my junior."

The boy reached for a book on one of the shelves and the backpack slipped off his scrawny shoulder, spilling books and pens. A red apple rolled across the carpet. Rachel started forward.

Trixie caught her by the arm. "Leave some time for yourself this year. Especially now that you're single again."

Rachel freed herself, but the teenager had already fastened his backpack and was slouching out the door. She turned to Trixie. "Don't do that again," she said quietly.

Under her pale makeup, Trixie reddened. "I was only trying to look out for you."

"Thanks, but I don't need a babysitter." She needed that reminder occasionally.

Ducking her head, her assistant nodded. Was there anything more pathetic than a sheepish Goth?

"You're a good friend," she added, "but, kid, I'm bruised not broken." Trixie had no idea what Rachel could survive. "Anyway, Paul rang and apologized this morning."

Trixie's head jerked up and her kohl-lined eyes narrowed. "I hope you told him where to stick it."

"Mmm." She'd been tempted, but being in the wrong was punishment enough for Paul. Rachel knew how that felt.

"And you reckon you don't need looking after?" Disgusted, Trixie picked up a stack of books and headed for aisle three. "At least date guys who can handle their drink." She pointed one black-painted nail. "Someone like him."

Beyond Trixie's finger, Rachel saw Devin Freedman scanning titles in the business section. Instinctively, she sucked in her lips to minimize their natural pout at the very moment he chose to glance over. Amusement warmed his eyes and she froze.

Instead of politely looking away, he folded his arms and grinned, waiting to see what she'd do. Mortified, she turned her back on him and blew out a puff of irritation. Dreadful man.

When she'd recovered her composure, she turned back to find him standing right in front of the counter. "Hi, Heartbreaker," he said casually. "How'd it go with Romeo the other day?"

Rachel frowned. "It's not a subject I want to discuss with you. And please don't call me that."

"You're still pissed about the comment I made about your mouth," he guessed. "I did mean it as a compliment."

She snorted. "That I have a mouth like a hooker? Still, it's better than a sewer, I suppose."

"Actually, I was thinking stripper," he replied lazily. "But I love the outraged dignity. Put me in my place again."

"I'm a librarian, not a proctologist," she said sweetly, and he chuckled.

This guy had a thicker hide than an armadillo, and momentarily, Rachel envied him. She might have accepted Paul's apology, but it would take a long time to forget being called cold and unfeeling. She had too many feelings; that's why she protected herself. Maybe she should be grateful for any compliment, however insulting. At least Devin meant no harm.

"Look." She adopted a conciliatory tone because one of them had to be a grown-up. "I *was* annoyed the other day by your comment, but I shouldn't have shut the door on you. That must have been hurtful and I'm sorry."

"You think you hurt…" This time he laughed out loud. "You're really quite sweet under that Miss Marple exterior, aren't you?"

She realized he was referring to today's vintage outfit—a high-waisted black skirt paired with a white ruffle-front blouse, herring net tights and pewter ribbon-tie patent shoes. The man had just delivered another backhanded compliment.

Almost, almost she was amused. But Rachel's ego was still too battered. She eyed his designer stubble and rumpled roan hair. Today the boots were black and the faded jeans set off by a black leather belt, complete with a big, ornate silver buckle, that sat low on his narrow hips. "At least I don't look like a cowboy after a week on the trail. Even Trigger made more effort."

His eyes narrowed appreciatively. But before he could answer, a shocked male voice said, "Rachel!" Looking left, she saw several of the university's top staff. The vice chancellor flanked by her two deputies...one of whom was Rachel's boss. "Why are you insulting Mr. Freedman?"

In that split second she comprehended that if the vice chancellor was in attendance, Devin was donating money—lots of it. "He's..." she began, then stopped. *Arrogant and cheeky, that's why,* didn't seem like a good enough reason.

Devin decided to help her out. "Oh, Rach and I are old friends." He could read every emotion that crossed her expressive face. The smart retort she had to bite back, the irritation at being beholden to him, a begrudging gratitude. "That's why I suggested meeting in the library." He twinkled at her. "She creates such a congenial atmosphere."

She twinkled back. "So exactly how much cash are you giving us, *mate?*" Oh, she was sharp, this one. Still, Devin's appreciation was tinged with annoyance. He liked to keep his philanthropy private.

The vice chancellor looked surprised. "I thought we were all keeping this a dark secret?"

Devin's gaze pinned Rachel. "We are."

Her chin rose. "Now that's not a tone to take with an old friend."

He'd never been great with authority and it amused him that she wasn't, either—unless it was hers. On an impulse Devin leaned over and planted a light kiss on her compressed lips. "Well, see you later…old *friend*."

He could almost feel the daggers thudding into his back as he steered the vice chancellor and his deputies toward the cluster of red leather armchairs out of view.

He'd discovered this space two days ago before Paul had disturbed the peace. Each corner of the library was glassed-in with floor-to-ceiling windows. Outside, towering silver birches swayed in Auckland's constant wind, their leaves dappling light and shade across the utilitarian carpet. Sparrows peppered the branches and their noisy chirruping gave Devin an illusion of companionship.

He wanted solitude, yet when he got it, his thoughts became bleak. Too often lately he'd found himself in his mother's cottage, which only made her worry about him. And that was intolerable.

The vice chancellor introduced himself as Professor Joseph Stannaway. Like his companions, he wore a suit, his short gray hair neatly marshaled to one side, and his strong face unlined…probably because he wore an expression of permanent solemnity. "As I said to your representative," he began as they took seats, "we wanted to thank you personally for your generous donation."

"Really, there's no need—"

"And to try again," the chancellor interrupted with a smile, "to persuade you into an official ceremony. It would garner a lot of media attention, which could only be good for the university's profile. Perhaps the bank could produce one of those large checks… what do you say?"

Playfulness didn't sit well on the man—he seemed too educated for it. It must be hard, Devin thought dispassionately, to devote your career to higher learning and then have to be grateful to someone who'd made a fortune writing lyrics like "Take me, baby, before I scream, you're the booty in my American dream."

"I'm sorry." Devin deliberately shunned all publicity. Sticking his head up over the trenches for the paparazzi to take another shot at? Never again.

The delegation spent the next twenty minutes trying to change Devin's mind with flattery, which only irritated him, chiefly because in the past it might have worked. Maybe that's why he got so much enjoyment from Rachel's barbed observations—they were novel. Of course, the kiss would really stir her up; a sensible man would regret it.

He grinned as Stannaway droned on. Not, unfortunately, one of Devin's attributes.

RACHEL WAS REHEARSING her rebuke to Devin the next day when the boy she'd noticed came up to her station.

"What can I do for you?" Her smile must have had an edge because he eyed her warily as he shoved back his hair.

"I was wondering if you had any lists of all the university staff…you know, like everybody, not just the lecturers. And their ages."

"Not here. You might be able to access some information through the registrar, but there's possibly some privacy issues around their release."

His face fell. "Oh."

"What's the name? Maybe I know the person and can save you the trouble."

"Um, she's an old friend of my parents. I was just hoping I'd…recognize something when I saw the list."

Poor kid, he really was desperate for a friend if he was hunting down such tenuous connections. "Where are you from?" Rachel asked kindly. She was supposed to be leaving on her morning break but this was more important.

"A farm outside Cambridge."

"Really? I grew up in Hamilton." They were only twenty minutes apart. "Small world. First time living away from home?"

He swallowed. "Yeah."

"It's hard initially, but you'll find your feet

soon. A lot of the first years are in the same boat, all scared—"

The teen glowered. "I'm not scared."

*Damn, wrong word.* If Devin hadn't rattled her, she wouldn't have chosen it.

"I see you've got a book there…would you like me to check it out for you? It will save you joining the queue at the front desk."

It was a peace offering for hurting his pride, and he took it. "Yeah, thanks." He handed over the book along with his library card.

Which didn't work. "They do this sometimes at the beginning of term," she said. "Let me just check that all your details are filled in…." The screen came up. "Mark…nice name. Okay, one of the library's ID codes is missing."

Glancing at his address, she noticed he wasn't living in residence, which was a shame; he'd make more friends that way. She nodded at the guitar case by his feet. "You know, the university has a lot of music clubs you might be interested in."

"I'm not really a club-joining kind of guy."

About to reply, Rachel caught sight of his birth date and her breath hitched. *June 29, 1992.*

"Something wrong?"

"No." Her fingers were suddenly clumsy on the keyboard as she reminded herself of the facts. On average, there were sixty-four thousand births a year in New Zealand. Which meant around one hundred and seventy-seven people—eighty-eight boys—shared her son's birthday. But she had to ask. "So what do your parents do?"

Mark frowned. "You need that for the form?"

"No, it's processing."

"Mom's a teacher." Rachel's pulse kicked up a notch. "And Dad's a farmer."

*Not a policeman.* As always, the disappointment was crushing enough to make Rachel feel sick. Her fingers were damp on the keyboard; she wiped them on her skirt, chiding herself for an overactive imagination. She gave the teenager his card.

"Here you go. All sorted now."

Mark shoved it back in his jeans. "He used to be a cop," he added, and the smile froze on her face.

*Someone who knew how to keep her baby safe,* she'd thought when short-listing the applicants with her social worker.

"Are you okay?" Mark asked.

"Fine." Her heart was beating so hard he must be able to hear it. Rachel loosened the top button of her shirt, suddenly finding it difficult to breathe. There was only one way to know.

"You have something in your hair," she said abruptly, reaching out a trembling hand.

"Yeah?" He started flicking his fingers through the blond strands, "What is it?"

"A…an insect…let me."

Obediently, he leaned forward, and she brushed the hair away from his right ear. "Turn your head a little."

Just at the hairline behind his ear, she saw it. A birthmark the size of her thumbnail. Rachel gasped and he broke away, raking both hands through his hair. "What! Did you get it?"

She stared at him, unable to speak. Tall like his father, with his fairer hair. His eyes—shock jolted through her—were the same color as hers, but the shape was Steve's. "It's okay," she croaked, pretending to flick something away. "It was a moth."

"A moth." Shaking his head, Mark picked up his guitar case. "Jeez, the way you were going on I thought it had to be a paper wasp at least."

*No, don't leave.* "You've heard of bookworms, haven't you? Lethal to libraries." Rachel memorized his features. "The term also applies to certain moth larvae. From the family *oecophoridae.*" Outwardly she smiled and talked; inwardly she splintered into tiny little pieces. "Of the order…now what was it?" *My son, my baby. You grew up.* "Starts with *L.*"

Mark shifted from one foot to the other.

"Lepidoptera," she said brightly. "Of the order Lepidoptera." The tiny bundle treasured in her memory, gone forever. But her son—her grown son—was here, and the reality of him shredded her with love and pain and need.

"Wow," he said politely, stepping back from the counter. "That's really interesting."

"Wait!"

"Yeah?" He was impatient to get away from the crazy woman, and how could she blame him? With all her heart she wanted to say, *I'm your mother.*

But she couldn't.

Two years earlier, she'd written a letter to the adoptive parents through the agency. *If he ever wants to meet his birth mother, please give him my details.*

Their reply was devastating. *In keeping with your wishes at the time, we've never told our son he was adopted. We're very sorry at the pain this must cause you, but you must understand to do so now would be detrimental to our own relationship with him.*

"Have a good day," she rasped.

THE WOMAN WAS A WEIRDO. No doubt about it. Mark stopped outside and shifted his guitar to his other shoulder so he could tuck the book into his backpack.

He didn't have a class for another hour and he stood uncertain, glancing across the narrow, tree-lined street bisecting the university. Buildings in this part of campus were angular and geometric, to Mark's eyes, hard and unfriendly shapes for the university's social heart, holding the student union, the theater and the student commons. It was lunchtime and he was hungry, but the overflowing cafeteria was too raucous. Too…intimidating. He'd wait until later, when it cleared out somewhat before grabbing something to eat.

Coming from a small community where everyone knew everybody, he'd thought finding his birth mother would be relatively easy.

But the university employed hundreds, and trying to access lists only led to awkward questions. He certainly couldn't tell the truth.

And he missed home. He missed his parents, which he kinda despised himself for because he hadn't been all that nice to them before he'd left.

He still couldn't believe they weren't really his. That all the things he'd built his identity on—inheriting Dad's musical ability and Mom's aptitude for math—were a lie.

He wasn't from the clan of Whites whose roots in the area went back four generations. His multitude of cousins weren't his cousins and his grandparents weren't his grandparents.

A group of students swept down the footpath, laughing and horsing around, nudging him aside like he was invisible. His classes were made up of eighty to a hundred strangers in huge auditoriums…. In a week he'd never sat next to the same person twice.

And so many of them seemed to know each other. How had they made friends so quickly? What was wrong with him that he couldn't?

He'd thought staying with his air hostess cousin in her city apartment would be cool, but Suz was away two weeks out of four. And when she was home, her boyfriend was nearly always over, so Mark tended to hang out in his room. The guy was a stockbroker and a real phony.

Another bunch of kids brushed past, knocking the guitar case off his shoulder. Devin Freedman caught it before it hit the ground.

"You need to get out of the line of fire." Still carrying the case, he stepped back into the library's portico before handing it over. "It's Mark, isn't it?"

*He remembers my name.* Suddenly Mark's day got a whole lot better.

DEVIN REMEMBERED THE KID because he had a good guitar. "What are you studying…music?"

"Business…I'm in some of your classes."

"Really?" Devin hadn't noticed him, but then the teenager wasn't big on eye contact.

Mark obviously misinterpreted his surprise because he blushed and added in a rush, "But I'm not some wanker carrying his guitar case around all the time to be cool. I busk in town during lunch breaks. That's why I've got my acoustic today." He shrugged in a belated attempt to appear uncon-cerned. "The money keeps me in beer."

Devin kept a straight face. "Not something parents allow for in their budget, I guess." He looked toward the cafeteria and braced himself for stares. Having cut short the meeting, he had to hang around for his next class, and damned if he was going to go hungry because a bunch of kids would gawk at him. Delaying the moment, he asked, "Made any friends yet?"

"No. I mean I'm sure I will…."

Devin realized he'd hit a nerve. "Me, neither," he said easily. "First day everyone wanted to sit with me. The dean gave a stern lecture about harassment and now nobody does. Who'll let me copy their homework?"

The kid laughed; it sounded like he really needed to. What the hell. "Had lunch yet?" Devin had been going to ask the librarian as a peace offering, but she'd gone home sick, which was odd because she'd looked fine half an hour ago.

Color rose under Mark's pale skin. "If you're asking because you feel sorry for me—"

Devin raised his hands to the sky. "Fine, we'll sit by ourselves like a couple of geeks." He started walking across the road, heard Mark scramble to catch up, and hid a grin. "Since I'm doing you such a favor," Devin growled, "you're buying."

The kid shot him a glance. "Hey, you're the rock star," he protested.

"Which makes you the groupie," Devin drawled. "I'll have a coffee and a doughnut and it better have sprinkles."

## CHAPTER FOUR

RACHEL CAME BACK TO WORK two days later, all cried out. The aftereffects—sore eyes and red nose—led credence to her flu story, which only made her feel more guilty. A childhood of enforced deception had given her an antipathy to lying.

She was in an intolerable situation, aching to see her son but with no excuse to do so. Instead she had to depend on the occasions he chanced into the library during her shift, and not surprisingly, after her babble on Tuesday he tended to give her a wide berth.

Friday afternoon she'd just begun an informal workshop on finding and searching business resources when Mark and Devin came in together and joined the seven students already standing in a circle around her. Ignoring Devin, she smiled a welcome at Mark and summarized her intro. "Okay, everyone, let's move on to search strategies." *Act cool,* she told herself, *he needs to think of you as normal.*

As she distributed the handouts, Devin murmured provocatively, "Your hair's much nicer down."

Rachel turned her back on him. She hadn't seen him since the kiss three days earlier, and he wasn't a bit repentant. But a slap on the wrist would have to wait for privacy.

She got the opportunity twenty minutes later, when she dismissed the group. To her surprise, Devin had asked some intelligent questions, made notes, acted like a regular student right down to calling her Ms. Robinson. "Can you stay behind a moment?" she asked him.

"Sure. Mark…go ahead, buddy, I'll catch up to you."

Rachel forgot her prepared lecture on respecting people's boundaries. "How do you know that boy?"

"Who, Mark? He's one of my classmates…nice kid. But no need to be jealous. You're still my number one sparring partner." He eyed her folded arms. "I expect you want an apology for that kiss."

"That would be nice."

"I know I *should* be sorry. Will that do?"

A smile trembled on her lips. If Mark hadn't been involved she might have enjoyed this outrageous man. "About that teenager," she said. "Wouldn't you rather hang out with people your own age?"

Devin raised a hand to his impressive chest in mock horror. "Why, *Mrs.* Robinson, are you coming on to a student?"

"Are you *ever* serious?"

He considered her question. "Oddly enough, all the time I'm not teasing you. You know, maybe we should go on a date, explore this little attraction we've got going."

"So little I'm completely unaware of it," she retorted.

"Really? I thought you were a clever woman." He leaned closer. The man had charisma; she gave him that. The innate confidence that came from a lifetime of being desired. Lucky him.

Surprise came into his extraordinary eyes. Rachel thought it was because she'd held her ground. Until he sniffed. "Your perfume," he said, "it's sexy as hell."

He smelled good, too. She banished the thought. "What were you expecting, lavender water?"

Devin blinked.

"But you're right," she added coolly. "I am clever. Too clever for you."

He grinned, sending his charisma wattage through the roof, then to Rachel's relief straightened up. "Maybe you'd enjoy slumming," he offered.

"I won't lower my standards."

"The professor being such a class act."

Rachel's cheeks heated, but she held his gaze. "Speaking of classes, don't you have one?"

He glanced at his watch. "Damn, it's still hard working to a timetable. One more thing…don't mention the donation to the university to anyone."

It occurred to her that he'd bought himself a place here. Lovely.

He misread her disgust. "Please."

Before she could answer, Mark came back into the library. With a cursory nod to Rachel, he said, "Hey, Dev, we're late."

"You were supposed to go on ahead…never mind." Devin turned back to Rachel with a rueful smile. "I'd better run. I'm teaching that boy too many bad habits." With a casual wave he left.

She watched them leave with a disquiet that turned into real alarm when, on her break, she took the opportunity to research Devin on the Internet. Though his musical achievements proved substantial, Devin Freedman was a man who comfortably juggled the seven deadly sins and still found time to break a couple of commandments.

The hair rose on the back of her neck when she read he'd admitted to using recreational drugs. He was also an unrepentant drunk. When, two years earlier, a writer for *Rolling Stone* magazine had asked if he had a problem with alcohol, Devin had replied, "No, we're very happy together."

He'd collapsed on stage eighteen months ago amid frenzied rumors of a drug overdose, then effectively vanished from the media…resurfacing in New Zealand before Christmas, pulling a Marlene Dietrich "I vant to be alone."

There were a couple of pictures of him, Stetson pulled low, mirrored sunglasses hiding his eyes, palm outstretched to the camera. Otherwise nothing but speculation about the guy nicknamed the Prince of Excess.

Rachel shut down the Internet connection and stared unseeing at her screensaver, a model of the mountain bike she wanted to upgrade to. Her own experience of him did nothing to reassure her.

Beneath the banter he was self-indulgent and arrogant, a man who did what he wanted when he wanted, with no thought for other people.

And her son was under his influence.

"SO, MARK…HI!" Even to Rachel's ears, her tone was too tinny; too bright. She'd been waiting five days for this opportunity to talk.

The teenager glanced at her, startled. "Hi." He returned to scanning the library shelves.

"Need some help?"

"No, I'm okay, thanks." He'd been taught nice manners; she'd already noticed that. It warmed her…and it blistered like acid.

"Are you sure? After all, that's what I'm here for!" Rachel laughed and it was a silly, high sound. She felt like a thirteen-year-old trying to impress a crush.

"Here it is." Mark took a textbook off the shelf. "Well, see you."

She fell into step beside him. "So, how are your classes going?"

"Um, fine."

"Do you spend much time with Devin Freedman?" She hadn't intended asking so baldly, but he'd picked up speed.

He slowed at that, his gray eyes suspicious. "A bit…why?"

"What about out of school?"

He stopped at the bank of high-backed chairs that made up a study corner. "Look, if you want his autograph I think you should ask him for it yourself."

"His auto—" This time Rachel didn't have to force the laugh. "Oh, no, I'm not a fan."

"She's a friend, aren't you, Heartbreaker?"

Rachel jumped. One of the chairs swung around to reveal Devin.

"I wish you'd stop calling me that."

"What…friend or heartbreaker?"

"Both."

He chuckled and the light flashed off the heavy silver link chain around his neck. Today he'd accessorized his faded jeans, olive T-shirt and scuffed brown cowboy boots with way too much jewelry— silver hoop earrings and three rings including a skull with diamond eyes. Mark looked from one to the other, then plunked himself into a chair. "Oh, you guys know each other. That's cool, then."

About to tell Devin to take his boots off the coffee table, Rachel paused. "Sure, we're friends," she said. Advising Mark to be careful around the rocker would sound less hysterical if he thought it came from personal experience. "So, Devin—" she paused, trying to think of something "rock n' roll" to say "—how's it hanging?"

The twinkle in his eyes became more pronounced. "It's *hanging* fine, thanks for asking…. What are you up to?"

The blush she'd managed to hold back through his innuendo heated her cheeks. "The usual. Actually, I'm due in an acquisitions meeting so I'd better go." She looked at her son. "Bye, Mark."

His nod was friendly. "See ya."

She waggled her fingers at Devin, who waggled back. "Definitely up to something," he said.

Fortunately, he was gone when she came out of her meeting forty minutes later, but Mark was still there, poring over books. Hungrily, Rachel studied him, noting the way he chewed his lower lip when he concentrated.

The hand cupping his chin was big; his body still had some catching up to do. And he was boyishly thin, his bony shoulder blades sticking through the striped T-shirt as he bent over the table and took notes. Surely he was too young to be fending for himself….

With the discipline of years of practice, Rachel stopped torturing herself. She had to trust the people she'd chosen for him. Had to accept he wasn't her son—but theirs.

As though sensing her scrutiny, Mark glanced up and grinned. Something had made him happy. Encouraged by his first smile, she approached him. "Devin gone?"

"Yeah, but we're meeting later." Obviously bursting with news, he added, "I finally talked him into showing me his guitar collection."

"In town?"

"No, at his place on Waiheke. You been there?"

Rachel sat down. "No." His adoptive parents weren't here to protect him and she was. "Listen, Mark, Devin might not be the best person to hang around with. He has a history of drug and alcohol abuse…." Her voice trailed off under his look of contempt.

"Aren't you supposed to be his friend?"

"Devin knows when I disapprove of his behavior." That at least was true. "I just want to make the point that you're only seventeen years old and living away from home for the first time. That makes you vulnerable—"

"Stop right there," Mark interrupted. "Let me get this straight. I hardly know you and you're giving me a lecture?" Shaking his head, he stood up, sweeping his books into his bag. "Who the hell do you think you are—my mother?"

"SHE'S RIGHT," said Devin when Mark repeated the conversation. "I'm not the kind of person you should be spending time with."

They stood on the deck of the Waiheke ferry watching the whitecaps as the boat surged against a brisk northerly toward the island that lay forty minutes off the mainland.

Their fellow passengers were a mix of commuters holding briefcases, tourists and the alternative lifestylers who'd once had the place to themselves. Now the island's slopes were dotted with homes of the wealthy. Yet there was still a lull, a lazy charm about the place. Nearby a businessman loosened his tie, while two kids raced across the deck to the bow to point out the island to their mother.

Cool for the first time that day, Devin breathed in the salty air and felt the tension he always carried ease a little.

"You don't sound that bothered about it," Mark replied. Glancing sideways, Devin saw the kid's hurt expression. *Oh, great.* He still didn't quite know how Mark had talked him into inviting him over; it had something to do with Devin feeling he owed him.

A week and a half into university life his brain felt close to exploding under the weight of new information, and Mark had helped him out more than once, explaining concepts. The kid was bright, no doubt about it.

And so puppy dog enthusiastic about music. Devin remembered that kind of devotion; he still mourned its loss. Maybe that was really what this was about. He was warming himself at the fire of the kid's idealism. "Listen, Mark. Don't expect too much of me. You'll only be disappointed."

"I don't…I mean, it's not like… Look, I don't have to come if you don't want me to."

Devin laughed. "What are you going to do, jump in and swim back?"

MARK WAS DISAPPOINTED at his first sight of Devin's house. From watching reality TV shows on rock stars he expected some sort of mansion with white pillars, wrought-iron gates with a security keypad, a six-car garage and an entourage…definitely an entourage.

Especially since they rode from the ferry terminal to Devin's property on a customized Harley-Davidson.

But albeit secluded—and white plaster—the place was pretty simple, a long, low-lying building with no distinctive features that Mark could see. Inside was better. Mostly white with red feature walls and white leather furniture. Art covered every wall, from big canvasses of bold swirls of color to old movie posters and some hot nudes. He recognized an Andy Warhol and wondered if it was an original.

The house perched on a cliff with dramatic glass walls toward the sea. Mark stood at the window and gazed out across the expanse of water and beyond to the far horizon. Below, several seagulls hovered in the updraft. "Wow."

Musical instruments were scattered around the enormous open plan lounge—an antique snare drum, various types of guitars. A microphone in the corner and he spotted speakers so small they had to be state of the art. Memorabilia, but no Grammys or awards. Mark was disappointed.

Then his eyes fell on a bass guitar. "Is that the Fender Precision?"

"Yeah."

"Can I touch it?"

Devin smiled. "You can play it."

"No shit!" Reverently, Mark picked up the instrument, running his hands over the strings. One of rock's most distinctive riffs had been created on this very bass. He became aware of Devin watching, and froze, embarrassed to show himself up as a meager talent.

"You want a drink?" asked Devin. "Coke, Sprite, juice?"

"A Sprite would be good."

When Devin had disappeared down the hall, Mark turned on the amplifier and played the Rage anthem right through, thrilled to the bone. When he'd finished, Devin still hadn't returned, so he picked up an electric guitar and started playing his own riffs. As an only child, growing up on a farm from the age of twelve, he'd often relied on his own company. That's when he'd begun to play guitar.

He played one of his songs right through, forgetting his shyness, trailing off when he noticed Devin standing at the door holding two glasses.

"You're good."

Mark blushed. "Thanks," he said diffidently.

Devin put the drinks on the table, picked up his bass guitar and said, "Play that last one again."

Mark did, and Devin accompanied him, adding tonal qualities Mark would never have dreamed of. "I like that song," said Devin. "Whose is it?"

"Mine."

Devin looked up. For a long minute he didn't say anything. "Let's try that again," he suggested.

Mark spent the next two hours in musical heaven. He didn't ever want the day to end. But eventually Devin stopped and glanced at the clock. "I'm hungry. How about you?"

"Starving."

Mark followed him into the kitchen and sat on a stool while the rocker opened his fridge and inspected the contents. "I've got a better idea. How about we go eat with my mom."

# CHAPTER FIVE

DEVIN WAS WALKING THROUGH Albert Park en route to class the next morning when he glimpsed the librarian sitting by the circular fountain.

Her gaze immediately dropped to the open book in her lap, but he'd been around enough stalkers—and better ones than this—to know he was her target.

Her skills needed work, but her choice of location was sound. All the park's paths converged on the historic fountain, with its bronze cherubs and their water-trickling orifices.

He hid a grin. This should be interesting. Of course, she had no idea he knew she'd warned Mark to shun him. He braced himself for verbal sparks.

As he approached, she looked up in feigned surprise and Devin was conscious of another spark. One that with any other woman he would have called sexual…if she wasn't wearing a fifties-style calf-length dress in a red-and-white diamond check with a matching fabric belt. Did this woman own *any* clothes from this decade? Red suited her, though. He particularly liked the matching lipstick.

He stopped in front of her. "Of all the fountains in all the world, somehow we meet at this one."

"Isn't that a coincidence!" She looked past him—checking for Mark—then back with such undisguised relief that Devin was provoked to tease her.

"You don't happen to have any Tylenol, do you?" He put on his shades to hide his amusement. "I'm too old to keep partying this hard."

She frowned slightly and he read her thoughts. *Had Mark been with him?* But the only way to get information… She opened her bag. "Sure."

Devin sat down next to her and lifted his face to the sun. It was only eight-thirty but already humid. The scent of the park's roses was heavy in the air.

The breeze changed direction. Fountain mist drifted toward Rachel, forcing her to move closer. She wasn't wearing perfume today but she still smelled seductive. How did she do that? Maybe he shouldn't torment her by making things up. He and Mark had eaten at Katherine's, then been cleaned out in a friendly poker game with her elderly neighbor before the kid caught the 9:00 p.m. ferry.

Rachel said way too casually, "I didn't think you knew many people here." Fishing.

He took the pills she offered, shiny in their silver foil. "Heartbreaker, when you're a rock star you can always find people to party with." There was no bitterness in the observation. He'd long ago accepted that his real friends were people he knew before he'd become famous.

Except they were still treating him as fragile. Another reason to stay away from L.A. He was too close to broken to shrug off someone else's doubt. How ironic that the only person who looked at him without deference or sympathy was this woman.

"Well, the last ferry from Waiheke leaves at midnight," Rachel ventured. "So I don't suppose things got too out of hand."

She'd checked the ferry timetable? Her concern for Mark seemed a little excessive. "Oh, I have plenty of room for sleepovers and no one minds three to a bed." Her lovely mouth tightened. "But it was all pretty tame...some bourbon, coke..." Devin winked to make sure she'd make the connection to the drug, not the beverage. "A hot tub filled with twenty of my closest friends, and rock blasting over the sound system..."

He noticed as he ran out of rock star clichés that she'd slid almost to the other end of the fountain edge, and he had to bite the inside of his cheek. "It was a spontaneous thing or I would have invited you. We could have done with some classier chicks."

Devin had a sudden image of her in a hot tub, incongruous and unexpectedly appealing. It had been too long since he'd had sex, but the months of therapy and rehab had left him feeling like a peeled onion, exposed and vulnerable.

"Was Mark with you?" she asked bluntly.

"The kid? Hmm, let me just think…. We started the evening together. So hard to recognize people when they're naked and wet." He stopped when he saw the stricken look in her eyes. "I'm kidding."

"Please leave him alone."

He frowned, puzzled. "Who is that boy to you?"

For a split second Rachel looked guilty. "No one. I…I just don't like seeing minors being led astray."

Devin's sympathy evaporated. Ignoring the fact that he'd just given her reasons to be concerned, he got pissed. She was being officious, no doubt basing her assumptions on what she read in the press. Well, if she expected depravity… "If you don't want me corrupting minors, then give me someone my own age to play with." Lazily, his gaze traveled down her body, deliberately provocative.

Angry color flooded Rachel's cheeks. She stood. "Grow up!"

"Where's the fun in that?" Devin stood, too, stretched and yawned. "You know, I like a feisty woman, and this heartbreaker reputation of yours has me intrigued. Any time you want to take a ride with me—"

"I wouldn't take a walk with you, cowboy," she interrupted heatedly, "let alone a drive."

"Darlin,'" he drawled, "who said anything about a car?"

BY WEDNESDAY OF THE following week, Rachel had confronted an unpalatable truth. Mark was deliberately avoiding her. She knew he'd been into the library because his online history showed he'd been taking out books. But he was obviously timing his visits around her shifts.

She'd blown it, warning him against Devin. In hindsight, it had been a stupid thing to do. But she seemed unable to do anything except react to her emotions where her son was concerned.

The yearning to see him was terrible, as bad as giving him up had been.

Fortunately, he'd struck an acquaintance with Trixie—it seemed only Rachel couldn't make friends with him—so she was able to gather crumbs of information. It was through Trixie that she knew Mark still spent time with Devin. Apparently the rocker had become some sort of musical mentor, which Trixie thought was the coolest thing to happen to Mark, and which Rachel thought was the absolute worst.

But what could she do about it?

As she walked to the downtown parking lot after her shift, a thread of music in the city cacophony distracted her from her gloomy musings. Glancing up, she saw Mark strumming guitar with another teenager outside The Body Shop, their voices straining over the blare and honk of rush hour traffic. A meager collection of coins lay scattered in an open guitar case. Rachel stepped into a nearby doorway where she could watch unobserved.

Mark's reluctance was evident as he joined in the choruses; he obviously knew he had an indifferent singing voice. She was to blame for that. The other boy's voice was stronger and well served by a song that was both melodic and haunting.

She wasn't an expert, but Rachel could see nothing in his performance to excite a music legend into mentorship. Her fingers tightened on her bag. Was that relationship more payback from Devin?

He'd breezed into the library several times this week, always calling across the room, "Keep me posted about that ride, won't you, Heartbreaker." Rachel had fielded a lot of interested questions from fellow staff members who were agog at the thought of one of their own attracting a rocker.

As if.

She knew damn well that Devin was baiting her as punishment for sticking her nose in something that didn't concern her. What she couldn't judge was how much of that depravity was feigned to annoy her.

In her worst moments, she even considered

telling Devin the truth. But Rachel had kept this secret too long to trust it to an undisciplined rocker who probably had looser lips than Jagger.

The song finished; the buskers took a break. Flipping his hair out of his eyes, Mark caught sight of Rachel and scowled. She responded with a tentative smile and stepped forward. "Can I talk to you privately for a minute?"

"I don't need another lecture."

"I want to apologize."

He searched her face, then shrugged. "Back in a sec, Ray." They walked down the side street a few feet. It was quieter here. She steeled herself.

"I know my concern seemed intrusive—"

"It was the disloyalty that got me."

She swallowed. "Disloyalty?"

"To Devin," Mark said impatiently. "I mean, the guy's your friend."

"Oh."

"He's the one you should be apologizing to."

Rachel murmured noncommittally and Mark's expression grew even sterner.

"Especially when he agreed with you that he was a bad influence."

That surprised her. "He did?"

"At least until you read him the riot act. Then he said I could hang out with him as much as I like." Mark grinned. "Maybe I should accept your apology."

Rachel bit her lip. So she'd provoked Devin into doing the very thing she'd set out to prevent. Mark really was better off without her. Except…this was the only chance she'd ever have to know him. "So are we okay again?" *Will you stop avoiding me?*

"I guess." He was already looking beyond her as he waved to his mate. "Yeah, coming! So is that all you wanted?" He was taller than her by a few inches. *Amazing.*

Through force of will she matched his casualness. "Yes, that's all." As he walked away, Rachel knew she'd never be anything to him other than as the loopy librarian. Unless… "Mark?"

He turned back impatiently. "Yeah?"

"I will think about apologizing to Devin."

He nodded in approval; she basked in it all the way to the parking lot.

She'd always had one imperative for her son. To keep him safe. And that hadn't changed.

If the only way to Mark was through Devin Freedman, then so be it.

In the driver's seat of her Honda hatchback, she passed a hand over her face, suddenly exhausted. She felt as if she was on a teeter-totter, up one minute, down the next. For years she'd worked hard to achieve serenity. Her childhood had held no security…even the long periods of relative peace were the only uneasy calm before an impending storm.

As an adult she'd organized her life into neat compartments. Now the drawer was a jumble again.

She needed to start thinking smarter. Apologizing wasn't a fix; somehow she had to scrutinize that damn man. Then she could judge him herself.

An idea occurred to her and she grew thoughtful. If she befriended the rocker, then Mark's attitude would soften toward her, providing an opportunity to get to know her son.

Not quite the threesome Devin had had in mind when he'd tried to shock her. Rachel chuckled. She'd thought of a way to get what she wanted *and* extract a little revenge on Mr. Rock Star.

The next day when Devin called across the library, "When are you going to put me out of my misery, Heartbreaker?" Rachel smiled.

"Right now."

THINKING HE'D MISHEARD, Devin moved closer. "Excuse me?"

Rachel beamed at him. "I'm saying yes to a date. Well, really, it's a way of apologizing for hurting your feelings last week."

Hurting his… Okay, now he *knew* she was joking. "I realize I was out of line," she continued earnestly, "and this is my way of making it up to you."

Devin folded his arms, leaned on the counter and waited for the punch line. And waited.

"How does tonight sound?"

Good God, she was serious. He was so flummoxed he couldn't think of an excuse. "Umm…"

"Seven o'clock suit you?" Without waiting for a response, she wrote it in her diary in neat script.

"Look, this really isn't necessary. No hard feelings."

"No, I insist. And my goodness, you need a reward for all that persistence. Which is sweet of you, incidentally."

Devin winced. "The word *sweet* should only be applied to situations involving whipped cream and a supermodel," he said, and sparked a frown from her. His confusion gave way to suspicion. *Wait a minute.* The librarian didn't want to date him any more than he wanted to date her. This was counterterrorism. Intrigued, he decided to beat her at her own game.

"Give me your address," he drawled. "I'll pick you up."

"Maybe it's better if we meet at the restaurant."

"Except I'm still deciding where to take you."

Reluctantly, Rachel found a piece of paper and wrote down her address.

"You know, I'm kinda nervous about this," he said as he accepted it. "Given your reputation as a heartbreaker and all."

Her eyes narrowed. "Yes, I had decided not to date until I'd got that situation under control. Are you sure you want to take the risk?"

"Hmm, good point." He rubbed his chin. "Maybe I should reconsider…."

Something oddly like panic clouded her expression. It was as if she really cared about this. Then she leaned forward and said softly, "Chicken?"

Devin chuckled. There were so many lessons he could teach this woman. Specifically, never take on a hell-raiser. Even reformed ones were dangerous. "Go ahead," he dared, "break my heart."

## CHAPTER SIX

THE LIBRARIAN'S neighborhood was made up of immaculately restored colonial cottages, each with pocket-handkerchief front yards full of lavender and standard roses. *Figured,* Devin thought.

Few had garages, so everyone parked on the street, which meant he had to leave his car a mile down the road and walk. Having been raised in L.A., he bitterly resented it.

He also seriously resented being nervous. It wasn't that he was hot for the librarian, simply that this was his first date ever without the social lubricant of alcohol.

Devin found number eight. The house was the same as every other except instead of being painted cream or white like its neighbors, it was honeysuckle-yellow and the garden was a subtropical jungle of banana palms, black flaxes, and orange and red canna lilies. He was picking up way too much plant lore from his mother. A well-used mountain bike was chained to the old-fashioned porch railing.

*Sucker. She gave you the wrong address.* Why hadn't he seen that coming? He was about to turn away when the door was flung open. "You're forty minutes late," said Rachel. "I'd just about given you up."

Devin checked his Hauer. She was right. "Time-keeping's never been my strong point." He saw she expected an apology, and shrugged. "Sorry.... So your roommate owns this place?"

"I live alone. You know, I tried ringing the number you gave me—" her gaze traveled from his Black Sabbath T-shirt down to his slashed stone-washed jeans "—but there was no answer."

"The number goes to a message service. Only close friends get my direct line." She actually had to think about why. *Hello, I'm famous.* He caught himself. Channeling his egotistical brother. *Ouch.* "Ready to go?" he asked politely.

"I was beginning to think you'd stood me up," Rachel confessed. "It felt like the high school ball all over again."

So the librarian had insecurities. "Yeah? What happened?"

Her expression shut faster than a poked clam. "I'll just get my cardigan."

*Cardigan?* He might not be a hell-raiser anymore but Devin valued his reputation. "Haven't you got anything sexy?"

"Yes," said Rachel. "My mind."

Fortunately, the cardigan was a clingy black number and it did have the advantage of covering another hideous buttony blouse. It was a shame Rachel didn't do cleavage because she had great breasts. Turning from locking the front door, she caught the direction of his gaze and stiffened. Oh, great, now she probably thought he wanted her.

"Let's take my car," she said, pointing her remote.

Devin looked at the little silver hatchback emitting a high-pitched beep, and pulled out the keys of the Aston Martin he kept in town. "Let's not."

"So yours is parked close?" she inquired too damn innocently. For a moment they locked gazes.

"Fine," he conceded. "But I'm driving." He held his hand out for her keys, but her fingers tightened around them.

"I'll drive…. I don't drink."

"Neither do I." When she looked skeptical, he added, "Anymore."

An indefinable tension went out of her. She gave him the keys. "You don't know how glad I am to hear that."

"It figures you'd be an advocate of prohibition," he commented as he opened the passenger door.

"I've noticed before that you typecast li-brarians," she said kindly. "But as your experience of learning institutions is obviously quite new I'll make allowances."

Devin started to enjoy himself. "Now who's stereotyping? Besides, if you don't want to be seen as old-fashioned, you shouldn't dress like that."

He shut the door on her protest and crossed to the driver's side. "I'll have you know this is vintage," she said as soon as he opened his door.

Devin folded himself into the ridiculously small interior. "I know what it is, I just don't like it."

"Is this how you usually talk to your dates?" she demanded.

"Actually," he said, deadpan, "we don't usually talk."

Her lips tightened; she reached for her seat belt and Devin gave up on any expectation of fun. He turned the ignition and the engine spluttered into life. It sounded like a lawnmower on steroids. "I thought we'd drive into the city," he said, "and wander around the Viaduct until a menu grabs us."

"It's Thursday night. We won't get a table unless you've made a reservation. And if you'll excuse my saying so, you won't get in wearing torn jeans."

Expertly maneuvering the toy car out of its tight parking space, Devin snorted. "Watch me."


"IT'S BECAUSE YOU'RE famous, I suppose."

Rachel's luscious mouth was set in a disapproving line. "You make that sound like a bad thing," he joked. Mentally, he confirmed his game plan. Dine and dump.

They sat in a private alcove in one of Auckland's most exclusive restaurants. Through the open bifold windows, city lights reflected in the harbor and the incoming tide lapped gently against the moored yachts.

Rachel unfolded the starched napkin and laid it on her lap. "I wouldn't like to think anyone else missed out on their booking because of us, that's all."

*Loosen up, will you?* "Bread?" He passed the basket over. She took a whole wheat roll and declined the butter. "Why are you really here, Rachel?" She obviously wasn't enjoying this any more than he was.

She looked guilty and he was struck with a sudden suspicion. "Did the chancellor want you to hit me up for another donation?"

"Of course not." Her shock appeared genuine and he envied it. It must be nice not to suspect people's motives in being with you.

"So you're just punishing me then…for giving you a hard time?"

Her lashes fell, screening her eyes. "Sure."

Maybe he should have chosen his words better. "I didn't mean to imply spending time with you was a punishment," he clarified. "Just that you're not my type." Oh, yeah, that made it better. "I mean—"

"Devin." She lifted her gaze. "I'm not offended. You're not my type, either."

Perversely, he was piqued. "Not a nerd, you mean?"

Her eyes narrowed. "Not housebroken."

He chuckled. "Okay, I deserved that. Let's try and be nice to each other."

There was an awkward silence, then Rachel cleared her throat. "I understand your band produced a fusion of post punk and metal—" she paused, obviously trying to remember research "—which evolved into the grunge and later indie genres."

"And here I thought it was about playing guitar and scoring chicks." Devin dipped sourdough into herb-flavored oil. "Rachel, how the hell did you miss out on rock music?"

"I had…ill health in my teens, which forced me to drop out of school." With tapered fingers she pulled the roll into smaller and smaller pieces. "Then spent all my twenties working days and studying nights to get my library degree."

Devin was attuned to picking up wrong notes; her story was full of them. He shrugged. "Don't tell me then."

She glanced up. "What do you mean?"

"You don't have to lie, just tell me to mind my own damn business."

"You know, Devin, civility has a social purpose. It stops people from killing each other."

He grinned. "I like to live dangerously."

"That's fine," she said seriously, "as long as you don't hurt bystanders."

All alcoholics left casualties in their wake. Devin had to work to keep his tone flippant as he replied, "You say *don't* a lot, you know that? You'll make a great mother."

She said nothing. Glancing over, he saw a bleakness in her expression that shocked him. He knew that level of despair intimately. Instinctively, he laid a hand over hers. "What did I say?"

"Nothing." Sliding her hand free, Rachel gave him a small smile. "I'd have thought it would be easier studying business at an American university, considering most of your tax is paid there."

He picked up his glass and took a sip of water before answering. "My royalties come in from a dozen countries and I've got more money in tax havens than I have in the States."

"Don't tell me then," she said.

He laughed. "Touché. You're right, I don't want to talk about it."

When she dropped her guard—for about one millisecond—her smile was breathtaking. "Were you aware you have over four million Internet pages devoted to you?"

Devin leaned back in his chair. "If you've done your research there's no point trying to impress you."

"You could tell me your bio was grossly exaggerated," she said lightly.

He could have played that card. It surprised him that momentarily he wanted to. "It's not."

If there were excuses, he wouldn't make them. At sixteen he'd jumped on a roller coaster that had given him one hell of a ride for seventeen years. And if the gatekeeper had said, "Son, you'll be famous, songs you help write will be an anthem for your generation, but it will cost you. You'll all but destroy your body and soul, you'll lose your identity, and when it's over you'll lie awake at night wondering if you'll ever get it back," Devin would still have bought a ticket.

They finished their bread in silence.

RACHEL DIDN'T KNOW WHAT to think. The idea of Mark hanging around someone who could so coolly acknowledge such an appalling past made the hairs on the back of her neck rise.

But she wanted to be impartial—or at least as impartial as she could be with her son's welfare at stake. Heck, who was she kidding? She was a wreck over this. Fine, then. She'd factor in her emotional bias when weighing the evidence. Because it was important to her to be fair. God knows she'd had enough people judging her as a teenager not to jump to conclusions about someone else.

And while Devin was arrogant beyond belief, brutally honest to the point of rudeness and far too confident in his own sex appeal—flashing a charmer's grin to the waitress delivering their meals—he also had an appealing self-awareness.

He took another sip from his water glass and Rachel wondered if she was being lenient simply because he'd given up alcohol. Having been raised by a drinker, she found it was a very, very big deal to her. Surely that meant some sort of rehabilitation had taken place?

But did it extend to drugs…groupies? She didn't want Mark to be exposed to those, either, or any of the character traits she associated with rock stars—excess, selfishness, immaturity. She needed more information.

As she picked up her knife and fork, she asked casually, "Why study here…New Zealand, I mean?"

"When you're running away, the end of the earth is a good place to go." He glanced up from his steak. "I'm sure you read about my meltdown and the band's collapse on the Internet."

"Yes," she admitted. But in his business, "taken to hospital suffering from extreme exhaustion" was all too often a euphemism for drug overdose or alcohol poisoning. As she ate her fish, her gaze dropped to his fingers, long, lean and powerful—musician's hands. "Do you miss any of it?"

"I don't need the temptations of the music industry right now."

That sounded promising, but his clipped tone told her that she should change the subject. Reluctantly, Rachel backed off. "So, is your brother still in L.A.?"

"Yeah, Zander's re-formed the band, with a new lineup."

Devin's curt tone hadn't changed, but she was too surprised to notice. "Can he do that?"

He shrugged, putting down his fork. "He owns the name, and as the lead singer, he's got the highest profile. For a lot of fans that will be enough."

As Devin spoke he folded his arms so the dragon tattoo on his hand curved protectively over one muscled biceps. It struck her that he was suffering.

"But not all of them," she said gently.

Devin looked at her sharply. "Did that sound maudlin? It wasn't meant to. It was my fault as much as anyone's that the band fell apart." His mouth twisted. "Collapsing on stage disqualifies me from lectures on professional dignity. If Zander wants to try and wring a few more dollars out of the Rage brand, let him…. Shit, I *am* still bitter, aren't I?"

There it was again, the self-awareness that made him likable.

"Speaking of bitter," he added, "how's Paulie?"

It was her turn to squirm. "Back in Germany."

"You let him lay a guilt trip on you, didn't you?"

Devin picked up his fork again and stabbed a potato croquette. "I just bet he made the most of it." His gaze trailed lazily over her face. "You're too nice, Rachel. If you ever want tips on how to behave badly, come to the master."

She frowned. "What exactly do you teach your disciples?"

His gaze settled on her mouth. "That depends," he said, "on how bad they want to get." Green eyes lifted to meet hers and a jolt of sexual awareness arced between them, catching Rachel completely by surprise.

WHAT THE HELL WAS *that* about?

Devin washed his hands in the restaurant's washroom, taking his time. He'd made the comment to wind her up, and yet when she'd looked at him he'd been tempted to lean forward to taste that kiss-me mouth. Yeah, and get lacerated by that sharp tongue of hers. And he couldn't even attribute his crazy response to the demon drink. Devin smiled. Still, it had been mutual—the attraction and the immediate recoil.

"I'm glad *someone* is enjoying their evening," said a weather-beaten old man at the next basin.

"It's taken an interesting turn." Reaching for a hand towel, he glanced at the old guy in the mirror. He looked like Santa Claus in a polyester suit—

big-bellied, grizzled white eyebrows. Only the beard and smile were missing. "Your date not going well?"

Santa grunted. "I booked our dinner weeks ago and we've got a makeshift table by the bloody kitchen." The old man lathered up his hands, big knuckled and speckled with age spots. "Figure they stuffed up the booking but the snooty-nosed beggars won't admit it."

Devin experienced a pang that could have been conscience; he hadn't had one long enough to tell. Tossing the used hand towel into the hamper, he said casually, "Big occasion?"

"Fortieth wedding anniversary. Drove up from Matamata for the weekend." With arthritic slowness, the old man finished rinsing, turned off the tap and dried his hands. "We're dairy farmers, so this time of the year's a bit of a stretch for us, but the old sparrow wanted a fuss. Might as well have stayed home if we were going to eat in the bloody kitchen." He grimaced. "Sorry, mate, not your problem. Have a good night, eh?"

Devin resisted until the old man reached the door. "Wait!" *Damn Rachel.* "Let's swap tables. It's not a big night for us."

"No, couldn't put you out."

Devin said grimly, "Happy to do it."

"Why should you have to put up with clanging pots and swinging doors?" The old man's face brightened. "Tell you what, we'll join you."

"JUST CALLING TO SEE how the date's going with the rock star?"

Shifting her cell phone to the other ear, Rachel glanced in the direction of the men's room. "I told you, Trix, it's not a date. It's—" *an interrogation that's taken a disturbing turn* "—just dinner."

"Rach, the guy's been in seclusion for months. It's a real coup…ohmygod!" Rachel held the phone away as her assistant's voice rose to a non-Goth squeal. "You should be selling your story to the tabloids! I'll be your agent."

Rachel speared a green bean. "Here's your headline—I Had the Fish, He Had the Steak."

"Obviously you'll need to have sex with him to make any real money." The bean went down the wrong way and Rachel burst into a fit of coughing. Trixie read that as encouragement. "You can't deny there are plenty of women who've got famous through sleeping with a celebrity," she argued. "You could even get a place on a reality TV show…you know, celebs surviving in the Outback."

Rachel dabbed her streaming eyes with a napkin. "Tempting as the prospect is," she croaked, "I think I'll pass."

"You'll never get famous as a librarian," Trixie warned her.

"Oh, I don't know. Melvil Dewey invented the

Dewey Decimal System over one hundred and thirty years ago and everybody knows his name."

At least Trixie's nonsense was steadying Rachel's nerves. So she'd been momentarily sideswiped by the guy's sex appeal. She was female and he was prime grade male.

"For God's sake, *don't* tell him one of your hobbies is finding wacky facts on Wiki." Trixie sounded genuinely horrified. "You'll lose whatever credibility we have."

Rachel laughed. "Goodbye."

"Who was that?" Devin asked from behind her, and she jumped, her nervousness returning. Not for a minute did she believe he was seriously attracted to her, but she had an uneasy feeling he'd try anything—or anyone—once.

"Trixie, my assistant. She—" *told me to sleep with you* "—had a work query."

Devin took his seat and signaled for their waitress. "There'll be another two people joining us." He filled Rachel in. "And this is all *your* fault."

But she was impressed by his gesture—finally, signs of a conscience. And secretly relieved they wouldn't be alone.

She was starting to have doubts about her ability to manage him.

The Kincaids—Kev and Beryl—arrived. Only halfway through the introductions did Rachel realize the downside of Devin's generosity. She'd lost her opportunity to grill him further about his ethics.

"So, Devin, you're a Yank," said Beryl as they'd settled at the table. Plump and pretty, she was like a late harvest apple, softly wrinkled and very sweet.

Rachel tried to remember if Yank was an acceptable term to Americans.

"Actually, Beryl," Devin said politely, "I was born here, but moved to the States when I was two. My dad was an American, my mother's a Kiwi."

Beryl looked from Devin to Rachel. "And now you're repeating history. How romantic."

"We're not—" Rachel began.

"She's my little ray of Kiwi sunshine," Devin interrupted.

Rachel said dryly, "And he's the rain on my Fourth of July parade."

Devin chuckled. Beryl murmured, "Lovely."

Her husband eyed Devin from under beetled brows. "What do you do for a crust?"

He looked to Rachel for a translation. "Job," she said.

"Student," said Devin, after a moment's hesitation.

"You're a bit old, aren't you?" New Zealand country folk were only polite when they didn't like you. Rachel hoped Devin understood that, but the way his jaw tightened suggested otherwise.

"Changing careers," he answered shortly.

"From?" Kev prompted.

"Musician."

"How lovely," Beryl enthused. Rachel suspected she often took a peacekeeper's role. "Would we know any of your songs?"

Devin's smile was dangerous as he turned to the older woman. "Ho in Heels?" He started to sing in a husky baritone. "Take me, baby, deep…"

"Oh, Kev," Beryl clapped her hands in delight. "Don't you remember? Billy—that's the agricultural student who worked for us over Christmas—played it in the milking shed."

"Cows bloody loved it," said Kev. "Let down the milk quicker."

Rachel looked at Devin's stunned expression and had to bite her cheek. "Was it a ballad by any chance?" Her voice was unsteady.

"Slow? Yeah, not that the other bloody rubbish… sorry, mate."

Devin began to laugh.

"Did you know," Rachel said, fighting the urge to join him—one of them had to keep it together, "there was a study done at Leicester University that found farmers could increase their milk yield by playing cows soothing music."

"Is that bloody right?" marveled Kev.

Devin laughed harder.

Kev and Beryl looked to Rachel for an explanation and she dug her nails into Devin's thigh to stop him. It didn't. "Conversely," she said, hoping the effort not to laugh was the cause of her breathlessness, and not the warm unyielding muscle under her fingers, "Friesians provided *less* milk when they listen to rock music."

"Well, I never." Beryl smiled indulgently at Devin, who was wiping his eyes with a napkin. "You Yanks have a different sense of humor from us, have you noticed?"

Devin bought the restaurant's best bottle of vintage Bollinger for Beryl and Kev, who insisted that Rachel accepted half a glass for the toast.

Devin explained to the old farmer that even a sip of alcohol would kill him, then gave Beryl a ghoulish description of how his pancreas had almost exploded.

Rachel thought he was laying it on a bit thick, and told him so while Beryl and Kev debated the menu. He looked at her with a gleam in his eye. "You see right through me, don't you, Heartbreaker?"

"Heartbreaker yourself," she said tartly, but somehow it came out as a compliment.

"Frenzied Friesians," he murmured, and Rachel gave in to a fit of the giggles.

## CHAPTER SEVEN

DEVIN SAT BACK and admired her. Laughter lightened Rachel's seriousness, made her accessible. He was pretty cheerful himself. For the first time in New Zealand he didn't feel like an outsider.

However weird his life had been as a rock star, it had nothing on Beryl and Kev and the obscure facts that popped out of Rachel's luscious mouth. There was something appealing in the librarian's quirky nerdiness. She didn't give a damn about his fame or his opinion and Devin wanted her.

In a corner of the restaurant, a guitarist propped himself on a bar stool and started strumming on a Lucida. The playing was average but his voice was true enough for the flamenco ballads.

Kev thought Sinatra would be nice and requested "Blue Moon," then sang along in a surprisingly good tenor. "Played the captain in the local production of Gilbert and Sullivan's *H.M.S. Pinafore* last year," he confided to Devin. "Bloody great night this, mate. All it needs is dancing."

On the quiet, Devin handed over some bills to the management and a few now-empty tables were cleared away. Delighted, Kev and Beryl did an anniversary waltz, moving lightly around the floor. One number led to another. Touched by the elderly couple's obvious nostalgia, other diners joined them.

The effects of champagne still sparkled in Rachel's eyes. Devin held out a hand. "Shall we?"

"I haven't danced for years…you okay with a shuffle?"

She did better than that. As long as Devin distracted her with conversation, her body moved with his in perfect rhythm. She only stumbled when she concentrated on the steps. Which was unfortunate, because Devin didn't want to talk—he wanted to savor the softness of Ms. Rachel Robinson.

So he encouraged her to expand on her theory of why musicians were so often good at math. "They're both about playing with nonverbal patterns so there's a lot of commonality there."

As she warmed to her subject Devin found he could get away with an "Mmm" and a "Really?" Gradually he drew her closer, until her body was right where he wanted it.

"Mmm."

THERE WAS SOMETHING in that last "Mmm" that jolted Rachel into awareness that she was dirty dancing with Devin Freedman.

One of his muscular thighs cleaved snugly between hers, his chest was a wall of hot muscle against her breasts and his "Mmm" still vibrated on the top of her head, where he'd been resting his chin.

And the hand supposed to be around her waist was caressing the upper curve of her bottom. About to protest, she became conscious that both her hands were in exactly the same position on *his* anatomy. She jerked back. "Excuse me a minute."

In the bathroom she splashed her face with cold water and sprinkled a few drops down her neckline, appalled and ashamed. Obviously, three sips of five-hundred-dollar champagne was an aphrodisiac. Why hadn't there been a warning on the bottle?

"Remember you're here to assess his character," she admonished her guilty reflection.

Rachel put her hair up in the tight ponytail Devin hated. She'd outgrown her partiality for bad boys after the last one got her pregnant.

Back in the main restaurant, the music had stopped and a small group—which included Kev and Beryl, diners and kitchen staff—milled around Devin, who stood with his arms folded, scowling. The dragon on his forearm was a guardian across his chest.

Kev caught sight of Rachel. "Talk him into it, love…all we want is that song the cows like."

One glance at Devin, and Rachel knew not to try. "We don't have that kind of relationship," she said quietly, hoping to remind people of their own tenuous connection to him.

"We weren't trying to be pushy or anything, mate," Kev assured Devin, who raised a skeptical eyebrow.

"Of course you weren't, Kev," Rachel answered. She took Devin's arm, unconsciously patting the dragon. His hand closed firmly over hers. "I imagine if Devin picks up a guitar in public the media will start hounding him."

"I'm not going to give up my privacy." Under her hand, the muscle relaxed. "But I could have explained it better." His thumb began a gentle circuit of her knuckles. "I'm sorry for being so defensive."

Everyone apologized then, with back slaps and handshakes all around. Devin signed autographs, a camera was produced and he stood patiently while everyone had their photo taken with him. Rachel shook her head when he held out a hand for her to join them. She needed to reestablish some distance.

He closed it and her pulse sped up at the heat in his eyes. "Shall we go?"

"No," she said firmly, practicing the word. "I promised Kev a dance." Satisfied that Devin had got the message, Rachel dragged the bemused farmer to the dance floor.

SHE WANTED HIM.

That was all Devin needed to know to be patient. While Beryl went off to get a recipe from the chef, he sat at their table and ordered coffee, watching Rachel on the dance floor. In one date, he'd gone from indifference to fascination. He wasn't used to challenge in his relationships with women. He decided he liked it.

He cast his mind back to his two marriages, the first in his late teens, to an indie rock chick in an all-female band. He'd wanted a port in the storm, but Jax had proved to be as angry offstage as she was on it.

Ten years later he'd hooked up with a Swedish actress during one of his frequent blackouts. It had been a trophy marriage on both sides, the mirror over the bed reflecting two clichés going through the motions of intimacy. They'd separated after three months.

There was no point regretting a past he couldn't change; still, Devin couldn't help wincing.

He heard a muffled ringing and tracked it to a cell phone in Rachel's bag. It wasn't a model he was familiar with and a text message flashed up when he tried to answer the phone.

Dnt blow chnce 2 screw a rck str. Trix

He stared at the message, then replied, Nt tht kd of grl?

A few minutes passed. R now, rmber our tlk!

Grimly, Devin returned the cell to Rachel's bag. He was a trophy date, and the librarian was only acting hard to get. Increase her chances of banging a celebrity, he guessed. The fact that it had nearly worked infuriated him.

When Rachel arrived back at the table five minutes later, he regarded her coldly. "I've settled the bill."

"Are you sure you don't want me to contribute?"

"Let's not spoil a great evening."

"What's wrong?"

"Nothing." He pulled himself together—never let them know you care—and steered her toward Beryl and Kev. They left with a promise to visit if they ever got to Matamata. Wherever the hell that was.

"Close to Hamilton, where I grew up," said Rachel. She filled the silence on the way home with Wikipedia trivia. If Devin hadn't known better he'd have said she was nervous.

But he did know better. His anger grew hotter, barely contained. Outside her house, he handed over the car keys, shoved his hands in the pockets of his jeans and turned away. "Good night."

"I said I'd lend you that book on music and math. Wait, I'll run and get it."

Another ploy. Damn, this woman needed a lesson. "Sure," he drawled.

He undressed her with his eyes as she led the way to the house. Rachel opened the door and started groping for the light switch. "It won't take me long to find it."

Devin cut the game short. "I'll bet." He stepped inside and spun her around to face him.

"Wha—"

In the darkness, he found her mouth. She wrenched away from him. "What on—"

"Don't tell me you haven't thought about doing this?"

She hesitated too long.

He kissed her again, pulling her close, cupping the nape of her neck with one hand. With a moan, she settled into him and he forgot everything but exploring that incredible mouth—moist, full, bitable.

Following her lead, he kept it tender, reveling in the contrast between her tentative tongue and the unconscious pressing of those lush breasts against his chest.

They came up for air.

"Do you always kiss like that?" she gasped, and he struggled to remember she was using him. And then felt disgusted all over again.

"Why, are you taking notes?" Backing her up against the wall, he nudged her thighs apart and ground his erection against her. "If you want to screw a rock star, this is how we do it, babe—standing up, right here, right— Owww!" He reeled backward from a knee to the groin.

"You narcissistic bastard!"

"Okay, I get it." Devin groped for the wall behind him. "You changed your mind."

"Changed my—" The light snapped on and Rachel advanced on him. "I was never going to sleep with you!"

"Take a look at the text messages on your mobile and let's cut the crap."

"What?" Frowning, she pulled the phone out of her handbag and checked it, then looked up, exasperated. "So one of Trixie's stupid jokes allows you to treat me like a groupie, is that it?"

Devin eyed her closely. "Was it a joke? Or something to boast about?" He'd been caught before.

She drew herself straighter. "I've never met anyone with such a high opinion of himself. What gave you the idea I was even interested?"

"Oh, I don't know…. Maybe it was when your hands were on my butt." When she blushed, he folded his arms. "Quit acting coy. I even asked you if you'd thought about it."

Her mouth tightened. "Kissing you. That's *all*."

"Kissing?" Devin stared at her incredulously. "When a grown woman tells a guy she's thinking about it, Heartbreaker, he's not imagining kissing."

"I didn't give you permission to imagine anything, mate. And if you've ever dated a grown woman I'd be very much surprised." Color high in her cheeks, she opened the front door. "Now, please leave!"

"Happy to," Devin said grimly. Didn't she know how many women wanted to sleep with him? "Frankly, I'm amazed I hit on a cardigan-wearing, pass-on-the-butter, book nerd anyway."

As he walked out, he caught his shin on the serrated pedal of the mountain bike. "Sh—"

The rest of the expletive was cut off as Rachel slammed the door behind him.

Dammit, that gave her the last word.

MARK WAITED ALL MORNING for Devin to notice he had hurt feelings. By lunchtime he gave up.

Walking to the cafeteria between classes with Devin, he stopped abruptly. "I waited for you an hour at the ferry terminal last night." It was two hours but he didn't want to seem that much of a loser.

Devin looked at him blankly and Mark's sense of grievance grew.

"You invited me for a jam session, remember?"

"Did I? Sorry, buddy, I forgot." Devin continued walking, as distracted as he'd been all morning.

Mark's hurt smoldered into active resentment. "You know what?" he said to Devin's back. "Since you obviously don't even notice I'm around, I'm gonna skip lunch and catch up on some homework in the library."

Turning impatiently, Devin scowled at the last word, and Mark immediately regretted his temper. "I'm sorry, okay?" he said. The last thing he needed to do was piss off one of his few friends here. "It was just…well…never mind." He'd had a frustrating few days piecing together a staff list from old yearbooks and faculty newsletters, but it wasn't comprehensive or age-specific. He'd have to visually scan every female staffer on campus and confront anyone who seemed the right age.

"What? I'm not mad at you." Devin walked back to him and Mark avoided his eyes. Sometimes the musician saw too much. "Why don't we get food to go and I'll give you that guitar session I promised you now?" They were blocking the path through the quadrangle and Devin steered him to one side. "I've got an apartment in town and our next class isn't for a couple of hours."

"You have another place?" Mark was impressed.

"Yeah, I bought it to stay in the city during week, but found I prefer going back to Waiheke. Mom uses it more than I do." Devin hesitated. "Do me a favor? A textbook I need has come into the library. Go pick it up while I get the food?" He handed over his library card.

"Is it because you don't want to see her?"

Devin said evenly, "What makes you say that?"

Immediately, Mark knew he'd said the wrong thing. "Um, because she told me you were a bad influence? Except that…I mean…she said she was going to apologize."

"She did. Everything's sweet."

It didn't *sound* sweet. And the guy's scowl had come back. "So you don't think she's—"

"I don't think of her at all," Devin interrupted. "Let's meet back here in ten minutes, okay?"

"Okay."

He started walking to the library, then hurried back, scrambling in his pocket for change. "Dev…let me give you some money." He didn't want the rocker to think he was a leech.

For the first time that day Devin's expression softened. "My treat."

Rachel was behind the counter when Mark walked into the library, and her face lit up when she saw him. She always looked so pleased to see him that it made him feel slightly awkward. But he guessed being cool wasn't in a librarian's DNA.

Then he caught sight of Trixie in a black leather dress and kick-ass boots and revised his opinion. She'd told him she'd toned down her look for the library job…only one pair of earrings and her most conservative nose stud.

He kind of had a crush on her even though she

was three years older and scary. She was dealing with someone but called out, "Have you been to that vegetarian café I recommended?"

He nodded. In the farming community he came from, everyone ate meat. But you didn't argue with a militant vegetarian, you meekly ate your lentil stew and tried not to be on a bus when the gas hit.

"So you like vegetarian food?" said Rachel. She always sounded like she was filing away information for the FBI.

"Love it," he lied, and handed over Devin's card to collect the reserved book. Rachel looked at the name and her smile faded.

"Devin said it was okay for me to collect it," Mark stated. Maybe they had a policy or something.

"That's fine."

She found the book. "He told me what you did," Mark added, and she froze with the book over the scanner. Gray eyes lifted to his.

"Apologized," he prompted. "Good on you. Friends shouldn't fall out." It occurred to him that he'd helped smooth the way. It was nice to do something for Devin for a change.

"Have…have you seen Devin today?"

"Yeah, we're heading over to his apar—" He stopped, wondering if Devin wanted him telling his business. "We're going to hang out for a couple of hours." He really shouldn't be so proud of it, but

Mark couldn't help himself. It was such a buzz to be an icon's friend. Well, not really a friend. But then Devin was encouraging his songwriting and…

Rachel was turning Devin's library card over and over in her hand. "Did he mention we had dinner last night?"

"No." Some of his smugness at being the peacemaker dissipated, then Mark laughed. "He stood me up for you, you know that?"

HER SON'S FACE transformed when he laughed. It was like glimpsing land after spending six months in a leaky boat. Rachel swallowed hard. She'd seen him shy, angry, solemn, even a little melancholy, but she knew instantly. *This is who you are.*

She started to laugh with him, then registered the implications of what he'd said. He thought she and Devin had kissed and made up.

She'd gone to bed in a rage, tossed and turned until 2:00 a.m., thinking about the cutting things she could have said to Devin, and wishing she'd kneed him harder.

Then she got up and cleaned the grout in the shower with an old toothbrush. Labor-intensive cleaning was Rachel's cure for insomnia; generally she'd be back in bed within fifteen minutes because she hated cleaning.

This morning the shower was sparkling. So was the range hood.

Mark looked at his watch. "I'm gonna be late meeting Devin."

He took the light with him. There was no question whose side Mark would be on when Devin told him about their disastrous date.

Even mistrusting Devin, Rachel had been temporarily disarmed by the Freedman charm. She still couldn't believe she'd fallen for it. Now she would become public enemy number one.

Rachel recalled Mark's laugh, their shared moment, and tears pricked her eyes. She hurried into the staff bathroom.

Five minutes later, Trixie barged in and found her, sitting on the floor and dabbing at her face with toilet tissue.

"Rach…ohmygod, what's wrong?"

Her red-rimmed eyes made a denial stupid, so Rachel said what she needed to believe. "Nothing I can't handle." She managed a smile. "Don't worry about it."

Trixie's boots squeaked as she crouched in front of her and took her hands. "Says the woman who never cries? I don't think so."

"Don't give me sympathy, please. I'll get worse." Standing, she went to the sink and splashed her face briskly with cold water. Defeat wasn't an option.

She'd just have to think of another way to watch out for Mark. "Anyone on the counter?"

Trixie ignored her. "Didn't the date go well?"

Better for Trixie to think that. Rachel met her assistant's gaze in the mirror. "Devin saw your text message."

"About screwing a rock star?" Trixie's eyes widened. "Didn't you tell him it was a joke?"

"Egotists rarely laugh at themselves."

"What a butt-head."

Rachel remembered the feel of Devin's butt. "The misunderstanding wasn't one-sided," she admitted. "I should never have kissed him back." In the cold light of day she couldn't understand why she had.

"You kissed!"

*Damn.* "Let's get back to work, hey?" She turned the handle but Trixie leaned against the door.

"Just tell me what the kiss was like."

*Fantastic.* "Like kissing a wet dog. Look, the whole date was a bad idea, but no harm done."

"Then why were you crying?"

"Because…" Unable to tell the truth, Rachel floundered.

## CHAPTER EIGHT

"BECAUSE YOU ACTED LIKE an asshole, Rachel's really upset."

Devin looked down at the baby Goth barring his way into the lecture hall. "You're the text sender… Trixie, isn't it? And this is another one of your oh-so-funny jokes. Because Heartbreaker doesn't get upset, she gets mad."

The young woman frowned. "No, this time I'm serious. I don't know what went down, other than the fact that you kiss like a wet dog, but—"

Devin laughed. "You see? Mad."

"You made her cry."

"I doubt that." He tried to step past her; she blocked him.

"I found her in tears this morning. She tried to make light of it, but Rachel never cries. I mean never. Even when her dad died a couple of years back."

He didn't need this. It had been enough placating Mark. Devin figured he wasn't due to make another apology for at least a year. "You're making too big a deal of this."

"You mean it isn't a big deal to *you*," said Trixie. "But it must be a big deal to Rachel or she wouldn't be so upset. She's not like us. She's led a sheltered life and hasn't learned to protect herself."

Devin recalled Rachel's well-placed knee. "Trust me, she can take care of herself."

"I mean emotionally," Trixie said impatiently. "She doesn't protect herself against being hurt."

He wasn't used to being taken to task over bad behavior. The band had been on the road so much it was easy to sidestep consequences, and if they hadn't been touring…well, there was the house in Barbados to escape to if he needed to get out of L.A. for a while.

"I'll think about apologizing."

"Really?"

"Sure." But it was a tactic to get rid of her. Devin didn't "do" hurt feelings and he wasn't about to start.

So he couldn't explain how he ended up knocking on Rachel's front door at 6:00 p.m. Friday evening.

When she was feisty he could ignore her, stay pissed. But Rachel hurt niggled at his peace of mind. And that peace was too hard won to surrender lightly.

Her shadow appeared through the stained glass door

panel, hesitating as Rachel recognized him. Then she opened the door. They eyed each other warily.

Devin saw immediately that Trixie had been telling the truth. Rachel looked washed out. Suddenly an apology wasn't hard. Whatever his faults, he wasn't such an asshole that he couldn't admit when he was wrong.

"I jumped to conclusions, last night." When she didn't say anything, he forced himself to give more. "I'm still learning to give people the benefit of the doubt instead of suspecting their motives in being with me."

She glanced away. "It doesn't matter. It's not like we expected anything from the date."

"No," he admitted. "We had too many prejudices for that."

"*I* was trying to keep an open mind." Stepping back, she started to close the door.

And Devin realized his arrogance was about to lose him a friendship with the first woman to interest him in years.

"Before I go, let me give you a few more tips on bad behavior," he said brusquely. "Develop an alcohol addiction and get married a couple of times—at least once in a ceremony you can't remember because it was during one of your alcoholic blackouts.

"Try and keep the marriages short and make sure

you write a song about eternal love to play at each wedding, which will have you cringing for the rest of your life. Become an arrogant, opinionated prick because no one ever said no to you." Devin stopped, disorientated. Overhead, the sound of a distant rumble drew his gaze. A 747 glinted in the blue sky. Wishing to God he was on it, he sighed. "I'm sorry, Rachel. I guess I'm still getting the hang of normal." He started to leave.

"Normal's overrated," she said behind him, and he turned. She was staring after the jet's vapor trail. "You know how certain songs take you back to key times in your life? Times when you were happy or sad, confused or needing courage?" She looked back at him. "Writing the soundtrack to people's lives is no small thing," she said softly.

Devin cleared his throat. "What was your special song?"

"'Letting You Go.' Sam…Samantha Henwood. I was sixteen."

"I don't know it."

She started to hum, then to sing, and it was painful to hear because the librarian was tone deaf.

Devin put his hands over his ears. "You're killing me."

Rachel smiled and sang louder.

Stepping forward, he clapped a hand over her mouth. Above his fingers, her eyes were still smiling. Devin had never thought of gray as a warm color before, but now he dropped his hand before he got burned. "Will you accept my apology?"

"As long as you admit that the world doesn't always revolve around you."

"As long as you realize it has for the last decade."

"And for the record," she told him tartly, "I didn't eat butter because before Beryl and Kev joined us I intended having dessert. I wear cardigans because I like vintage. Not sleeping with a guy on the first date doesn't make me a prude, and if you *ever* call me a book nerd again I'll ram my mountain bike down your throat."

Damn, but he liked this woman. "I get it. Librarians are people, too." And because he couldn't resist teasing her he added, "Next you'll be telling me you have a vice."

"I do." She hesitated, long enough for his imagination to jump to the bait. "I don't make my bed."

Devin laughed. "Let's try another date."

Her eyes widened. "Why?"

"Admittedly, most of the time we engage in interplanetary warfare and yet…" Devin tucked a strand of loose hair behind her hair. "And yet, Heartbreaker…"

Rachel knew what he meant. There was something between them, an odd, unexpected connection. And that kiss… But it was wrong to use him as a means to Mark, and she couldn't kid herself that that wasn't the primary temptation. She shook her head. "I just broke up with someone I thought I'd marry. You'd only be a rebound."

He grinned. "See, that's what I like about you, you keep giving me firsts. I've never been the rebound guy before. What's the drill?"

He was incorrigible…and far too appealing. Rachel wavered. He was also offering her another chance to find out more about him. Wasn't that her goal? And a repentant Devin was more likely to reveal himself…. She was skirting dangerously close to her ethical boundaries. Was it fair to use him like this?

"Any sensible person would run a mile," she hedged.

"I've had a million words written about me," he said. "I don't think *sensible* was ever one of them."

Rachel remembered the other things written about him, things he hadn't denied. This wasn't about her. Or Devin. It was about protecting her son. "Maybe we could go out to formalize our peace treaty," she suggested, "but no date. Strictly platonic." Attraction only made things tougher. Her motives murkier. This way no one got hurt.

"Sure." His lopsided, sexy-as-hell grin belied his easy acquiescence. "*The Flying Dutchman* opera is coming to town, isn't it? I've been seeing billboards."

"Next weekend, but the tickets are expensive."

Which was why she hadn't booked. Most of her income went toward her mortgage. Rachel remembered who she was talking to when he laughed.

"Consider it part of the apology."

She trusted his meekness even less than she trusted that sexy grin. "As long as we're quite clear," she stressed, "that I'm only using you to get to Wagner."

"I think I can hold my own against a dead guy." Devin's expression grew serious. "So you're not upset anymore?"

How did he know that she'd been... "Wait a minute! Did Trixie make you apologize?" *I'll kill her.*

Devin frowned. "No one *makes* me do anything."

But the apology hadn't been his idea. Rachel stopped feeling guilty about her mixed motives.

"Hi, Mom, it's Rachel."

"Rachel, are you in trouble again?"

Eighteen years later, it was still the first question her elderly mother asked.

"No, everything's fine. I always call Sunday morning to see how you are."

"Well, you know, bearing up." Maureen sighed. "Still missing your father terribly, of course."

"Did you get that book on heritage roses I sent you?" Rachel swapped the phone to her other hand and wiped her suddenly damp palm on her dress.

Maureen's voice brightened. "Yes, it's wonderful,

particularly the section on English hybrids." She rattled on about cuttings and placement, and Rachel stared out the window at her wild garden. "And Peggy and I are our club reps in the regional district's floral arranging competition."

"Sounds like you've got plenty going on." Since her father's death, her seventy-nine-year-old mother had taken up a multitude of new interests. Blossomed, in fact.

"Oh, and the most exciting thing? The council is recognizing your father's years of service by naming one of the new benches in the park for him."

Rachel caught her breath. "Well, it's great to hear you're doing so well."

"Honey, did you hear what I said? Your father—"

"You know I don't want to talk about him, Mom, and you know why." She took a few deep breaths because otherwise she'd scream, *He's dead and you can stop pretending!* But it would do no good. "Please, let's just concentrate on what you and I are doing, okay?"

Her mother sighed. "Okay. I'm sorry about your attitude, though."

A familiar sense of betrayal tightened Rachel's throat. "Listen, this has to be a short call today. I've got a roast in the oven that needs basting." She always made sure she had a good reason for a short call. Because sometimes they were all she could cope with.

"Have you started your charity lunches again?"

"It's not charity, Mom," she reminded her patiently. "Just a handful of first year students desperate for a home-cooked meal." She'd been inviting strays to her first semester Sunday lunches for five years. The event had become such a fixture around campus that staff and counselors would often send lonely scholars to see her in the library. Overseas students and out-of-towners for the most part.

"Well, I'm glad to see you've retained *some* of the values we taught you."

"Take care, Mom."

Hanging up, Rachel wiped her hands on her skirt again. Her jaw ached; she unclenched it. The weekly calls she'd initiated after her father's death, following seventeen and a half years of estrangement, had been a mistake. Foolish to think that after an adult life spent in denial, her mother would break character and admit anything had ever been wrong—with anyone except Rachel, that is.

She gripped her apron in her fist and stared at it in confusion, then with an exclamation ran into the kitchen and opened the oven to a billow of smoke and heat.

Grabbing an oven mitt she hauled out the roasting pan and inspected the sizzling leg of lamb. There was a layer of scorched fat around the base, but nothing that couldn't be saved. If only everything in life was so easily salvaged.

ON WEDNESDAY AFTERNOON Mark stood outside classroom 121 of the human sciences block waiting for the tutorial to finish. A classmate had mentioned this sociology tutor had handed out cake to celebrate her thirty-fifth birthday.

Through the door Mark could hear her voice…at least the tone of it, light yet authoritative. It gave him a strange feeling in the pit of his stomach. The talking stopped, and a shuffle of chairs signaled the end of the tutorial. He moistened his lips and straightened, trying to get some oxygen in his lungs.

The door opened and students streamed out, the industrious ones first, looking at watches and picking up their pace to get to their next class, then the easygoing chatterers.

Heart kicking against his ribs, he nervously looked over every woman coming through the doorway. Too young…too young…too old.

"Excuse me." Mark forced himself to approach the most likely candidate. "Are you Rosemary Adams?"

The blonde shifted her heavy satchel to her hip. "No, the tutor's still inside."

"Thank you," he said through bloodless lips. In the classroom, a dark-haired woman stood with her back to him, vigorously clearing the whiteboard of equations. Mark tried to remember what he'd been planning to say to her but his impassioned yet aloof denunciation had fragmented into a terrified jumble in his mind.

He cleared his throat and she turned around. "Did you forget something?"

She was Maori.

Unable to speak for the crushing disappointment, Mark shook his head and backed out of the room. In the corridor he picked up his pace until he was running, heedless, through clusters of students.

A car horn honked in warning as he jumped off the curb and ran along the gutter because people weren't moving fast enough. Only when Mark reached the park did he stop, doubling over to catch his breath. His disappointment was matched by his enormous relief.

"HALLELUJAH, you're finally going out." Holding a bag of peaches, Katherine Freedman stood on Devin's doorstep and sniffed him appreciatively. "Look hot and smell gorgeous...it must be a woman."

Resigned, Devin opened the door wider and gestured her in, leading the way to the open-plan kitchen. "Okay, who told you?" Five-thirty on a Saturday evening was not the time to be delivering peaches.

"Bob Harvey at the ferry office happened to

mention you'd booked in a 7:00 p.m. vehicle crossing. As luck would have it I'm also heading over, for dinner and a meeting with the Coronary Club. How about a lift from the ferry building into town?"

In the kitchen, Devin accepted the bag of peaches and tipped them into the fruit bowl with all the others, unsettling the fruit flies. "You're not meeting her, Mom, and I'm taking the bike."

"You think I can't straddle a Harley?"

"You still look good in leather," he conceded, "and I guess a helmet hides the wrinkles."

She picked up a peach and threw it at him, but Devin was expecting it and made a neat catch.

"Fortunately for you," she continued, "I'm going across with Susan, so you won't have to think up an excuse not to take me." She tut-tutted, eyeing the fruit bowl. "You should probably stew those."

"Yeah, because I'm a 'bottling preserves' kind of guy." Devin poured her a cold drink, then turned to find her rifling through the kitchen drawers. When she pulled out a chopping board and a paring knife, he took them away from her. "And I don't need to think up excuses. I'm perfectly comfortable telling you to mind your own business. Shouldn't you be going home to get ready?"

"Unlike you, I can be ready in five minutes." Katherine took the utensils back. "Now find me a pot." Perching on a bar stool at the marble-topped island, she started peeling and chopping peaches straight out of the fruit bowl. His mom never sprayed her trees and there were spots of brown rot on some. Devin shook his head as she carefully pared away the good flesh before discarding the rest.

Only a couple of months earlier he'd thought he would lose her. "You've got a big birthday coming up." He found the pot she wanted and placed it at her elbow. "How would you like to celebrate?"

"Quietly." Katherine tipped the peaches she'd already sliced into the pot. "I intend staying sixty-nine for at least another four years."

Devin got the compost bucket she had insisted he buy, and cleared away the discarded peelings. "So dinner at the island's best restaurant with your son sound okay?"

Katherine didn't answer. Glancing over, he caught her pensive look. "No big deal if you've already made plans with girlfriends."

"Let me get back to you on that. So tell me all about your date." Katherine dropped the knife and gripped her thumb. Blood welled above her nail. "Bother!"

Grabbing a paper towel, Devin wrapped it around her thumb, then guided her to the sink, where he rinsed the cut and inspected it. "Nothing a bandage won't fix." He found the first aid kit, dug around for the right size and handed it to her.

"Your date?" she prompted.

"Technically it's not a date." No woman had ever insisted on platonic before.

"Really?" Katherine finished applying the bandage and looked up. "What is it then?"

Devin started to laugh. "Deluded."

You'd have thought a smart woman like Rachel would know better. Nothing could have stoked his interest more than her No Trespass sign. If the librarian had been genuinely indifferent, Devin could have accepted it, but she wasn't. The kiss had proved that. And the challenge inherent in her non-negotiable decree…what kind of wuss would he be if he let the gauntlet lie?

Katherine rinsed her other hand, still sticky with peach juice. "Don't tell me you've finally met a nice girl," she said hopefully.

"I'm not telling you anything," he reminded her.

"Spoilsport. In that case I might as well go."

"What about the peaches?" he teased.

She poked her tongue out at him. "I know you'll throw them out as soon as my back's turned so give them to me. I'll finish stewing them at home." Drying her hands on a tea towel, she added, "Have you heard from Zander lately?"

Devin stopped smiling. "No." When he'd raised the subject of financial anomalies, his big brother had cut the phone call short. Since then Zander hadn't returned any messages.

"Careful with those peaches, Dev," Katherine protested. "You'll bruise them."

He slowed the tumble of peaches from the fruit bowl into the bag, and glanced at her. "So, how is he?" While Zander rarely initiated contact, Katherine kept the relationship going by phone.

"I can't seem to get hold of him lately." She busied herself searching in her bag for her car keys, which Devin could plainly see near the top. "But he must be terribly busy arranging the new tour."

Running scared more like, if he was avoiding even Katherine's phone calls.

"I'm sure he'll phone soon," he told her.

"Oh, I'm not worried."

Which meant she was. Unfortunately, the mounting evidence suggested his brother had been siphoning off more than his share of royalties on the early songs they'd cowritten. But surely Zander trusted Devin not to involve Katherine? Damn it, this situation was getting more and more complicated. On impulse Devin kissed his mother goodbye, something he rarely did. "Have a great night."

For a moment Katherine looked startled, then she patted his cheek. "You, too…and I expect to hear all about it." On those ominous words she left.

All going well, he reflected as he closed the front door behind her, the evening's activities wouldn't be fit for maternal ears. Checking his watch, Devin calculated time zones, then rang Zander's cell and left another message: "Call your mother!"

Then he finished getting ready for his date, turning his mind to more pleasurable thoughts. Like teaching the librarian to forgo restraint, caution and common sense in favor of spontaneity, recklessness and instant gratification. And that was even before they reached her unmade bed. Her so-called vice perfectly complemented the only one he had left.

Sex.

## CHAPTER NINE

RACHEL DIDN'T WANT to be nervous.

It made the evening ahead feel too much like a date.

Which it wasn't.

Peering past the mottled green patches in the antique oval mirror on her dresser, she applied a shocking pink lipstick and decided she was satisfied with her appearance. She wore a tight-fitting fifties cocktail dress of pink crepe overlaid with black lace, which had a scalloped edge at the strapless bodice and a mermaid ruffle hem. After straightening the black velvet bow at the Empire waist, she hunted for the lacy tights that went with the outfit. Holding them up, she frowned. They had a run, and the ladder was long enough for a fire brigade.

Reluctantly, she settled for patterned knee-high stockings—figuring the three-quarter-length skirt would cover them. She finished the outfit with a pair of dainty black ankle boots with a high heel, and clipped on velvet bows to match the one at her waist.

Opera presented a rare chance to dress up, but she

was also trying to prove a point. Of course vintage could be sexy—look at Dita Von Teese, the famous striptease artist once married to shock rocker Marilyn Manson. Rachel hesitated, then picked up a tissue and scrubbed off the slutty lipstick, replacing it with a less provocative nude shade.

She glanced at the diamanté watch strapped to her wrist. Her car was being serviced so they'd go in his. She hoped Devin was allowing enough time for them to walk to wherever he'd parked.

The full-throttle throb of a powerful engine brought her to the door. Nervously wrapping herself in her fringed silk shawl, she stared at the leather-clad figure on the Harley-Davidson.

Devin lifted the black visor on his helmet. "No pre-car street layout defeats a red-blooded American," he said with satisfaction, then scanned her shawl-swathed figure. "I brought a jumpsuit in case you wore a dress." Reaching into a side satchel, he pulled out what looked like a pair of orange mechanic's overalls, then unclipped another helmet from the pillion.

Rachel finally found her voice. "I'm not going to the opera on a motorbike!"

"Why not? It'll be fun." His gaze dropped to her feet. "Those boots should be okay on the bike."

She tugged the shawl tighter around her shoulders. "What about my hair?" It was piled on her head, with loose tendrils softening the diamanté sparkles at her earlobes and throat.

Devin looked at it critically. "Very pretty."

She had a sudden feeling he was doing this on purpose. "We're catching a taxi."

"Okay." To her surprise, he got off the motorcycle without a murmur. "How long do they take on a Saturday night? Not that I mind missing the first half…"

Rachel held out her hand for the jumpsuit and helmet. "Wait here." Inside, she put on the offending items, knowing better than to check her appearance in the mirror. When she came out, Devin sat astride the bike, engine idling and his face hidden behind the visor again. "If you're grinning behind that…"

He raised a gloved hand holding two tickets. "Front row mezzanine, overlooking the stage."

Gingerly, Rachel approached the bike. "How do I get on this thing?"

"Put your left foot on the foot peg, then swing your right leg over the seat. Watch out for the exhaust."

She followed his instructions, trying not to touch him, and he checked the position of her feet. "You can hold on to the grab rail or me. If you haven't ridden before you'll probably feel more secure with your arms around my waist."

Rachel reached behind her for the grab rail. "This

is fine." She couldn't see his face, but it sounded as if he was trying not to laugh.

"Let's go then."

He accelerated slowly, but her knees tightened instinctively around his hips. The Harley picked up speed and Rachel dropped the grab rail and clamped her arms around his waist, hanging on for dear life. A rumble of laughter vibrated through his torso, matching the rumble of the bike's engine.

She'd never been on a motorbike before, never comprehended the delicious assault on the senses. Speed cooled the air and pushed the scents of the city under her visor. Exhaust fumes, a sizzle of food from passing restaurants, the whiff of trash from a downtown Dumpster, and from the waterfront the salty tang of the sea.

Devin knew the streets well, bypassing traffic lights to detour down narrow alleys. If she wanted to, Rachel could lean out and touch the parked cars, talk to passing pedestrians. There was no barrier between her and the pulse of the neon city, the pulse of the powerful bike vibrating beneath her.

Under the thin jumpsuit the skirt of her dress had hiked up, and Devin's legs warmed her where she gripped him, from knees to inner thighs. Her spirits soared with a heady sense of freedom. Naughtiness was addictive. She could have been a teenager again, but a teenager without responsibility, without the burden of having to make adult choices.

Rachel felt an almost overpowering urge to stand on the foot pegs with her hands on Devin's broad shoulders and yell, "Forget the opera! Let's just ride until we run out of gas." Except she had a disquieting feeling he would agree.

"Hey!"

Twisting, she saw a stranger waving and gesturing from the sidewalk. Rachel waved back. Twice more, she returned salutes—from two openmouthed kids staring out the back window of a passing car, and from an old lady waving her walking stick. Amazing who turned out to be Harley fans.

Too soon they were at an underground parking lot on Queen Street where Devin cruised into a parking bay. In the enclosed space the rumble of the Harley was deafening.

Rachel touched his shoulder and pointed to a sign, Owners Only.

He turned off the engine. "I've got an apartment here," he said over his shoulder. "We'll dump the gear first, then walk across the road to the opera house."

Standing on the foot pegs, Rachel swung her right leg up and over the seat.

That was when she noticed the rubber heel of her dainty boot was on fire.

TAKING OFF HIS HELMET, Devin turned at the sound of Rachel's gurgle of laughter, then caught sight of her smoldering boot. "Hell!" Hunkering down, he grabbed her foot with his gloved hands, wrenched down the zip and hauled off the boot, dropping it on the concrete.

"All those people—" peals of laughter escaped under the visor "—waving and yelling—" she hauled off her helmet, gasping for air "—and I—" another paroxysm of laughter shook her "—I thought they were just being *friendly.*" Leaning on the bike for support, Rachel dabbed at her eyes.

Devin inspected her ankle. The stocking wasn't touched. Dropping her foot, he stood up. "What the hell part of 'keep your feet on the foot peg at all times' didn't you understand?"

Without waiting for a response, Devin launched into a blistering reprimand. Rachel bit her lip and tried to stop laughing. It felt almost like an out-of-body experience, looking down at himself—the never-loses-his-cool Prince of Excess—ranting at his passenger on the importance of following the damn rules. Finally he ran out of steam and stopped for breath.

Holding her helmet, Rachel bowed her head. "I'm sorry. I promise to be more careful on the way home." She didn't sound contrite, she sounded as though she was still laughing. And when she raised her head, her eyes confirmed it. "But you have to admit it's quite funny."

Tomorrow it might be funny. Right now he wasn't ready to let her off the hook for giving him such a scare. Scowling, Devin picked up her boot, looked at the indentation where the rubber had melted, then waved it under her nose. "On your leg this would be third-degree burns."

Rachel's face fell. "And they were so expensive," she said, remorseful for the wrong reason. "One hundred dollars on sale." The boots he wore were worth three grand, U.S. "Will it last through the opera?"

In answer, Devin snapped off the fragile heel. "We'll knock the other one off upstairs. That will get you through the performance at least." Leading her to the elevator, he used his key to access his floor.

The elevator opened into a private lobby. Rachel stepped out and, like all his guests, immediately gravitated to the panoramic view through the hall's archway. "My God, I thought you said you had an apartment…this is a penthouse." As her gaze swung around the living room, with its rough-hewn stone columns and steel spiral staircase, Devin willed himself not to stiffen. Seeing his wealth changed some people. He didn't want the librarian to view him any differently than she did now.

"I like the casual comfort," she commented,

stroking the saddle-brown leather couch, "but I would never have picked you as a flower man." She gestured toward the orange poppies on the sideboard, ignoring the expensive cast-bronze sculpture beside it. "Those are a homey touch."

His mother did the flowers. Devin relaxed. Nothing had changed.

"Right," Rachel said briskly, dumping the helmet. "Let's take off this gear, fix my shoe and get Cinderella to the ball."

He peeled off his leathers, but when he turned around she was still in her jumpsuit, staring at him. "I should have told you to dress up," she said in dismay.

Devin looked down at his black jeans and bloodred, V-neck silk T-shirt. The pin-striped jacket had been personally tailored for him by top American designer Tom Ford. A dragon motif, the exact match of his tattoo, was embroidered in red silk down the length of one sleeve and across his shoulder. The whole ensemble, including the red snakeskin boots, cost more than her pip-squeak car. Manfully, he resisted the impulse to tell her that.

She misread his inner struggle as hurt.

"It's my fault," she said. "I should have mentioned that men wear tuxedos to the gala opening night."

He grinned. "It wouldn't have mattered."

"You'll get stared at."

The woman was a delight. "Okay," he challenged, "show me what normal people wear."

Self-consciously, Rachel wriggled out of the overalls and smoothed the skirt of her satin-and-lace dress. Devin shook his head. "As I thought, still channeling the fifties. Although—" he assessed the outfit again "—lose the bow, drop the lace to get some cleavage and Dita Von Teese would probably wear it to the Grammy's."

For some reason Rachel started to laugh. "You've got helmet hair," he said. "Let me fix that." Removing the pins, he ran his hand through the silky, shoulder-length mass to loosen it. She used a peach blossom shampoo and for a moment Devin was back in his mother's orchard, in that fleeting new state he'd come to recognize as peace.

Without conscious thought he lowered his head. His lips brushed Rachel's. They were as soft as petals, and parted in surprise, but he didn't deepen the kiss.

Something in the moment stopped him…a freshness, an innocence. A promise? Shocked, he lifted his head.

Rachel cleared her throat. "We're not doing that, remember?"

"Why?" He needed to know.

She had to think about it, which was good, because he didn't want to be the only one shaken by this. "I don't know you well enough."

"What do your instincts tell you?"

For a moment she stared at him, then shrugged helplessly, unable—or unwilling—to answer. Devin didn't push it, simply touched his lips lightly to hers and stepped back. He could seduce her; he'd had the power too long to doubt himself. But suddenly this…thing wasn't about what he wanted.

In silence, he levered the heel off her remaining boot with a screwdriver. In silence they walked to the elevator.

RACHEL FOUND her legs were trembling, and it had nothing to do with her reconstituted boots. Something odd had just happened and she felt light-headed and breathless. While they waited for the elevator she stole a look at Devin.

He was watching her in a way that made her want to kiss him. It wasn't desire, it was awareness. He attracted her. He just did.

Before she could rationalize her action, she lifted a hand to the nape of his neck, slowly drawing him down until their lips were inches apart. And stopped. They were both deadly serious. Then he closed the gap and the heat of his tongue set off a rush of sensation. They kissed, broke apart, then kissed again. Her hands roamed restlessly under his jacket and over the silky fabric delineating every taut muscle in his back.

The ping of the elevator sent them springing apart. The lift doors opened. They looked at each other. Long seconds passed and neither moved. The doors closed. Rachel moved into his arms like a woman used to indulging in spontaneous passion with unsuitable men.

She didn't think, didn't question. She didn't do anything Rachel Robinson normally did. It didn't seem to be that important. She couldn't stop. Not even when his mouth settled on hers with a possessiveness Devin wasn't entitled to, and his hands slipped under the flounces of her dress and pulled her closer to the erection under his jeans.

Tugging out his shirt, she slid her hands beneath it and across his broad chest to the tight male nipples. His body was extraordinary, every ridge and indentation a moving, living landscape for her exploring fingers. Someone was panting, and Rachel became conscious that it was her and tried to shut up. But he kept doing things that made her gasp as he steered them toward the bedroom.

When they came up for air, she saw a white bed on a black granite floor in a starkly beautiful room that overlooked a thousand twinkling city lights. Devin kicked off his boots, shrugged out of his jacket and pulled off his shirt. The dragon on his right arm glared at her. Under his right pectoral, another tattoo began—an abstract of curves and spirals in the Maori style, tracing over his ribs and disappearing into his jeans.

"You okay?" Devin asked, and Rachel realized she'd stalled.

"Yes." Trying not to feel self-conscious, she unzipped her dress and stepped out of it, remembering too late she was wearing those awful knee-high stockings.

Devin's gaze roamed hungrily over her lingerie and stopped below her knees. "What the hell are those?"

"Sex toys…you never know when you'll need ties."

"Great, let's use 'em."

"Have you no inhibitions at all?"

"None." He took her into his arms once more. When he bent to kiss her again she couldn't remember which way to turn her head, and they bumped noses.

"Sorry." Her arms were suddenly wooden around his waist. "Devin, I don't—"

"My fault," he said. "I'm overthinking this. To tell the truth, I never had sex completely sober. And I haven't had sex at all for over a year."

Rachel lost her self-consciousness. Of their own volition, her arms lifted to wrap around his neck. "I'll try and be gentle," she whispered, and Devin chuckled. This time when they kissed there was no mistiming, no awkwardness. They'd recaptured the lazy, electric ease that narrowed their world down to this room.

His fingertips were light on her face as he traced her features, watching her through half-closed lashes, a smile tugging at his mouth. By touch, she learned the slight bump in the strong bridge of his nose, the scar under his right eyebrow. Above the raspy jaw, his cheeks were baby-soft.

Her nipples tightened as his thumb dipped between her breasts in the black strapless bra and began a gentle circling under the lace. She pulled his head down for a kiss, warm, liquid, and they fell on the bed, where they bounced on the springs and broke apart, laughing.

Lifting his knuckle, Rachel kissed the dragon's head, then followed its sinuous length up Devin's arm. Under her lips, his skin broke out in goose bumps.

His fingers tangled in her hair. "Before we go too far, let me get some condoms from the bathroom."

Rachel didn't hesitate. "Yes."

He rolled over her to go get them and somehow her bra ended up at her waist and his mouth at her breast, his hands teasing circles on her inner thighs. She pushed him off. "Go!"

Sitting up, Devin cupped her face and smiled. Somehow it was a gesture more intimate than anything they'd been doing on the bed, and her throat tightened. "How did we end up here, again?" he asked.

"Wrong turn I guess," she said lightly. She'd learned a hard lesson eighteen years ago. Never confuse sex with love.

"No," he said. "Sooner or later I would have got you here."

Something in his male arrogance took her straight back to another charmer, and Rachel instantly stiffened. "You…sound like you planned this," she said, watching him closely.

She caught the telltale flicker of guilt before he smiled at her. "*This* I didn't plan." He disappeared into the bathroom.

*So good,* she thought, stunned, *at faking sincerity.* And oh, my God, she'd nearly fallen for it. Humiliated, Rachel hauled up her bra and covered her breasts.

Except she wasn't sixteen anymore and no man got away with making a fool of her. Reaching for her dress, she paused. She had an idea. Did she dare?

When Devin came back, she was lounging seductively against the pillows in her underwear. Rachel held up the stockings. "Let's use these."

He blinked, then chuckled as he rejoined her in bed, jeans tightening over muscle. "You nearly had me."

"And I want to have you." She dropped her tone to husky. "Tied up."

Half smiling, he scanned her face, and Rachel hid it against his chest, right over the place where his heart should be. His hand caressed her nape and she resisted the urge to turn her head and bite it. "I've always wanted to try it," she murmured instead, "and you're the perfect guy to do it with." Under her cheek Devin's ribs rose and fell in what felt like a sigh. But when she glanced up he gave a lazy shrug.

"Sure, babe, whatever you want."

"Lie down." All business, she looped one of the nylons around his wrist, then tied it to the bedpost.

"You put your bra back on."

Rachel grabbed his other hand. "I'm shy."

"You know," Devin said thoughtfully, "I never thought I'd say this, but I was kinda looking forward to old-fashioned sex for our first time…ouch. Maybe you could loosen the tension on that one."

She yanked his trapped wrist against the post and double knotted the second stocking. "So you're suggesting they'll be other times, then?"

His eyes narrowed. "Okay, what's really going on?"

Rachel clambered off the bed and glared at him. "This wasn't something that just happened. You had every intention of seducing me tonight, didn't you?"

"Yeah, but you changed my mind and then…"

"And then?"

"Hell, I don't know…you changed it back."

With his arms tied to the bedposts above his head he looked like every Amazon's idea of a human sacrifice, pagan, muscular and deliciously vulnerable.

Furious at the direction of her thoughts, she bent and scrambled for her dress. "You're pathetic."

"Rachel, you know we're about more than sex."

Hand frozen on her dress, she barely registered his comment. There was a pair of red stilettos under the bed. Lying on their sides at right angles, as if they'd been kicked off in a hurry.

*I haven't had sex at all for over a year.*

The son of a…Enraged, she picked them up and tossed them onto his washboard abs above the hip-hugging jeans, hoping the heels left a mark. "Next you'll be telling me you're a cross-dresser."

She waited for signs of guilt. For shame. Devin looked at the shoes and started to chuckle. The chuckle grew into a laugh that shook the bed. He laughed until his head was rolling helplessly on his shoulders.

Tears prickled the back of her eyes. It was 1992 all over again.

Rachel picked up her dress and stepped into it, reaching behind her for the zip and jerking it up. It stuck halfway and she pulled harder. Nothing. She spun the dress around to the front.

Devin's laughter subsided. With difficulty, he wiped his streaming eyes on his bare shoulder. "They're my mother's," he said.

"Spawn of Satan don't have mothers." Rachel struggled with the tab. "And funny, isn't it, that you've never mentioned her?"

"Why? I've never heard about your family…. Untie me and I'll help you with that zipper."

"Fool me once, shame on you. Fool me twice, shame on me." The zip still wouldn't budge. Her anger grew.

"Look," Devin said reasonably, "I did my growing up in public. Every stupid thing I've ever done is documented. In rehab I decided the rest of my life is private. Mom's why I'm in this godforsaken country. She's been in hospital lately with a heart condition."

"Old ladies with heart conditions don't fling their shoes under the bed in a 'I'm about to have wild sex' kind of hurl."

He started to laugh again. "Do you use that imagination in bed?" Infuriated, Rachel stopped wrestling with the zip on her dress and dragged down the one on his jeans. "I'm hoping that's a yes," he added.

"You think this is funny?" Her dress slipped and she made a grab for it.

"Rub some soap on the zipper," Devin suggested. "C'mon, Heartbreaker, get my wallet out of my pants—there's a picture of my mom."

"I don't care if there's a picture of your family dog." She yanked off his jeans and dumped them on the carpet, but lost her nerve at the boxers. "I'm leaving you here for room service to find in the morning. Maybe that will make you think twice before lying to seduce women."

Devin started to struggle against his bonds. "Okay, this has gone far enough. Untie me right now."

His panic was the sweetest revenge. "Maybe I'll even ring the media. They love bondage stories involving celebrities."

"I'm serious. Right now!"

"Go to hell." Head held high, clutching her dress under her armpits, Rachel disappeared into the bathroom.

"If you leave me here, I'll sue you!"

"I'll settle the legal bill with what the tabloids pay me!" she yelled back. He heard the sound of cabinets and drawers being opened. "Where's the bloody soap?"

Devin renewed his struggle. "As if I'm telling you!"

She slammed the bathroom door. He tried to reach the knots on his left wrist with his teeth but the librarian had strung him so tight he couldn't get close. Just as well—he'd probably kill her if he got free right now.

"Devin." A faint, familiar voice from the doorway wrenched him from his revenge fantasies.

"Mom," he rasped. "What the hell are you doing here?"

"I host the Coronary Club here Fridays." As her fascinated gaze trailed over his bonds, he heard the sound of approaching voices, then several elderly women appeared behind her.

"Oh, my Lord, Katherine," whispered one of them. "Is this one of your boys?" Everyone behind jostled for a look-see and within seconds half a dozen matrons stood at the end of the bed, checking him out with unabashed interest. And Devin discovered he did have inhibitions left.

He wiggled to try and lift the waistband of his boxers, which had gone dangerously low when Rachel had hauled off his pants, but all that did was draw the ladies' attention lower.

"Anyone getting palpitations, leave the room," said Katherine in a pained voice he recognized from his childhood. The one that usually preceded a grounding.

Devin cleared his throat to bring everybody's attention back to his face. "It's not what you think."

The bathroom door opened and Rachel came out, rubbing a bar of soap on the zip of the dress, which was lowered to her waist. "The cabinet's full of women's toiletries. You've got quite a little harem going—" She looked up and gasped so hard, her lovely breasts threatened to pop out of her lacy strapless bra. Devin didn't much like Rachel's clothes, but her underwear was fantastic.

The expression on her face made her look like a Picasso: it was all over the place. He grinned suddenly. Okay, this was worth it. "Aren't you going to introduce yourself?" he suggested kindly.

Her grip convulsed on the soap, which popped free and flew across the room. The ladies followed its trajectory, then turned back to stare at Rachel, who was zipping her dress up as fast as she could. "I'm not a groupie," she faltered. "I'm his librarian."

"And this is a new approach to chasing overdue books?" suggested Katherine helpfully.

Devin waited for the moment Rachel's eyes widened as she registered their resemblance.

Because, as any bass player knew, timing was everything.

Then he settled back on his pillows. "Meet my mother."

His date squared her shoulders and held out her hand. "How do you do." Then Ms. Grace-under-pressure crumbled. "You see, I thought he had another woman," she explained, clinging to Katherine's hand. "It was your shoes under the bed. They were kicked off as though…" Rachel finally realized she held his mother's hand in a death grip and dropped it. "Well, my mistake."

Color flooded Katherine's cheeks as if she was having a hot flash. Except she'd been through menopause. A horrible suspicion dawned on Devin, becoming certainty when his mother flicked him a guilty look. His mouth tightened.

"*Now* who's got some explaining to do?"

## CHAPTER TEN

SOMEONE UNTIED HIM. Devin got dressed, then he and Rachel made cups of tea for the Coronary Club. Because making nice, he told her when she fluttered, panicking, toward the exit, was the way you persuaded people to keep your secrets. It worked with the media…sometimes.

Rachel approached every individual and earnestly explained all the circumstances. Devin followed with a plate of low-fat oatmeal cookies and some high-octane flirting.

Devin and the ladies had a good time. Rachel and his mom skittered away whenever there was the remotest possibility of Devin being alone with them. But he didn't own a cowboy hat just because it looked good.

He corralled his first filly when his mom left the safety of the herd to say farewell to one of her cronies. The elevator doors had barely closed on her full-figured friend when he said behind her, "You had sex with someone in *my* bed?"

Katherine turned on him defensively. "I changed the sheets."

He'd hoped for a denial. "This isn't the fifties, Mom. There are STDs to worry about now, AIDS."

She tried to step past him. "I'm not having this conversation with you, Dev."

He blocked her escape. "And what about your heart condition? I mean, should you be raising your heart rate like that?"

"Orgasms are very good—"

"Oh, God!" Devin clapped his hands over his ears. His father must be turning in his grave.

Katherine pulled his hands away. "For relieving stress, which in turn reduces blood pressure." Exasperated, she surveyed him. "I did warn you not to start this conversation."

"Well, who is it?" he demanded. "I'm assuming there's only one."

She considered him. "That's none of your business, any more than what you do with Rachel is mine." Her voice softened. "She's adorable, by the way."

Rachel came into the foyer at that moment, shawl clutched around her and staring over her shoulder as though fearful of being followed. Devin waited until she was close. "Looking for me?" he asked, and she started guiltily.

"I've explained our misunderstanding and accepted total responsibility." She avoided his gaze by smoothing the fringe on her shawl. "I don't think you've got anything to worry about." Awkwardly, she held a hand out to his mother. "Nice to have met you, Katherine."

His mom clasped it in both of hers. "And you."

Devin cut short the pleasantries. "How are you intending to get home?"

"I ordered a taxi."

"I'll wait with you. Mom—" his gaze pinned Katherine's "—we'll talk when I come back."

"Devin…we won't." Her tone was equally adamant. "At least not about that. Goodbye, Rachel." She smiled. "I do hope I'll see you again."

"Oh, I'm nowhere near through with her yet," he promised his mother.

Rachel got twitchy as soon as the elevator door closed. "I'm sorry about earlier." Despite her calm tone, she kept jabbing at the elevator button to try to make it move faster. "I jumped to—"

Devin backed her into a corner and kissed her.

She broke free, surprised. "Aren't you mad at—"

He kissed her again. Harder. This time when she came up for air, she was disheveled and breathless.

"It's probably for the best. You and I aren't—"

And again. The woman would not shut up. He could feel the moment she stopped thinking "shoulds" and "shouldn'ts" and started thinking "why nots" and "maybe."

Started seeing him as he'd grown to see her—a fascinating world unexplored. This time when he lifted his head that intriguing glow was back in her gray eyes.

Devin let the warmth permeate through to his bones before he stepped back. "We're even," he said.

"INSERT THE SIXTH NOTE after the fifth to give your bass pattern a lighter, more upbeat quality…yeah, that's it."

Mark tried but he couldn't sustain concentration past a few bars. "I'm sorry." Disheartened, he stopped playing. "I guess I'm not feeling it today."

He watched apprehensively as Devin took off his acoustic guitar and walked out of the living room of his apartment. Miserably, Mark stared down at the view, his bass still hanging from his shoulder strap.

At 11:00 a.m. on a clear summer morning, all Auckland's landmarks were on display—the Sky Tower, the bridge and Rangitoto, the dormant cone-shaped volcano in the harbor. How many chances would his mentor give him, he wondered, before he wrote him off?

Devin reappeared with a couple of energy drinks and tossed one can to him, before sprawling on the couch. "What's up? And don't say keep saying nothing. You know I haven't got the patience for it."

Mark hesitated, but he needed a confidant badly.

He rolled the cold can against his forehead. "If I tell you, you have to keep it a secret."

"Scout's honor."

He was momentarily diverted. "You were in the Scouts?"

"No, just pledging their honor."

Mark put down the can and started toying with one of the frets on the guitar. "I thought I'd tracked down my mother yesterday—my real one. Only she wasn't."

Devin whistled. "You're adopted?"

"I only found out a year ago…by accident."

"That's rough." Devin swung himself to a sitting position. "Why didn't your folks ever tell you?"

Bitterness flooded Mark, as sour as old grapes. "Because my Hamilton *birth* mother made it a condition of the adoption." The letter from social welfare had been clinical. 'Our client has changed her mind about open adoption and is only willing to proceed if you agree to secrecy….'"

"Careful of your guitar, buddy."

Confused, Mark looked down; he was torturing one of the strings. Handing the bass to Devin, he plunked himself on the throw rug and hugged his knees. "You're probably thinking, well, why am I looking for her then? But she shouldn't be able to do that without giving some kind of explanation. I mean, how am I supposed to feel?"

Devin started plucking at the strings of the bass,

casual notes that somehow reached in and squeezed Mark's heart. "You tell me."

He swallowed. "I just need to know why...I mean, I'm not expecting anything."

"Are you looking because you want to heal something in you," asked Devin quietly, "or because you want to hurt her?"

Mark didn't answer. Another cascade of bitter-sweet chords; the vise around Mark's chest tightened.

"Do your parents know you're doing this?"

"They don't even know I've found out I'm adopted." He expected Devin to lecture him, but his dark head remained bent over Mark's guitar. The notes softened, the melody became gently reflective. Mark stirred restlessly. He didn't want to be soothed. "You don't think I should do it, do you? Find my birth mother."

"Would my opinion make a difference?"

"No."

"Then why," said Devin mildly, "are we having this conversation?" The tune evolved into an electric version of "Amazing Grace," languid and hauntingly beautiful.

Mark suffered through the song. He had a sudden intense longing for home, for his parents, for the tranquility of his life before this terrible knowledge had changed everything.

Tears filled his eyes. He blinked hard, but one

escaped to trickle slowly down his cheek. Mark froze, reluctant to wipe it away in case he drew Devin's attention. The salty trail stung his shaving rash—he was still getting the hang of a new razor. At last the tear touched the corner of his mouth. Surreptitiously, he caught it with his tongue.

Devin's eyes were closed, his fingers sliding over the strings. "It's okay to have second thoughts, Mark."

"I'm not."

His mentor opened his eyes. "Maybe you should take another year or two before you do this."

"I can't," he said impatiently. "The only thing I know about her is that she works at the university. If I wait and she leaves, then I'll never find her." He stood and started to pace. "And my parents won't help me. I already know that without asking. They always do the right thing and keep their word and stuff…and, well—" he hesitated, not wanting to appear soft "—if they learn I'm looking for her, they might get hurt. Which is also why I haven't told them I found out I'm adopted. Because I have to see her."

Devin struggled for the right words. He had no skill base to handle emotional pain; he'd barely mastered his own. What the boy needed was a student counselor, but Mark would bristle at the suggestion and he didn't want to alienate him.

"Devin?"

Someone who could empathize…someone with

common sense and compassion. An insider who could influence Mark toward counseling. It was Sunday. Devin glanced at his watch. Lunchtime. Rachel had turned down his lunch invitation, citing her prior commitment with students.

He put down his guitar and stood. "Let's gate-crash a party."

RACHEL WAS HUNTING through her kitchen drawer for a carving knife when the doorbell rang. "Someone get that," she called into the adjacent lounge, where conversation hummed over the muted strains of *La Bohème.*

"I'll go," answered Huang.

Hunched over the stove, Trixie stirred a pot of steaming gravy, her brow knotted in concentration. With her kohl-darkened eyes, swirling black skirt and Alien Sex Fiend T-shirt, all she lacked was a witch's hat. Rachel grinned.

"If you do the 'double, double toil and trouble' joke again, I'm letting it burn," Trixie warned. "How you can be so happy slaving in a hot kitchen all morning is beyond me."

"Because bringing people together and feeding them makes me happy." This was Rachel's favorite day of the week, the ritual an affirmation of her dreams—family, community, tradition. If one day she could get Mark here… "I only hope we have enough meat." She found the carving knife and surveyed the joint, steaming gently on the counter-top, mentally toting numbers. Jacob, Sarah, Huang, Marama, Juan, Silei, Ming, Dale, Chris…herself, Trixie and—

Devin appeared in the kitchen doorway holding a huge bunch of red gerberas, and her heart gave a queer little lurch that she wanted to be dismay but wasn't. He eyed the knife. "I can see flowers aren't enough."

"What are you doing?" she said stupidly. This morning she'd convinced herself that the man was a scenic detour down a blind alley. She needed to get back on the freeway with its speed limits and clear signs.

"I was hoping you'd have room for extras." Over the flowers he nodded hello to Trixie. "How's the intimidation racket?"

From the stove, Trixie said, "One hundred percent success rate."

"She's promised never to interfere again," Rachel said grimly.

"I might have a job for you, Trixie," Devin continued. "My brother."

Rachel glared at her assistant. "On pain of *death*," she reiterated.

Undeterred, Trixie waved the gravy spoon toward Devin. "Have your people talk to my people."

"Mark, that's you," he said over his shoulder, and Rachel dropped the knife. It hit the floor with a clatter.

Devin strolled forward to pick it up and Mark came into view behind him, blushing as he looked at Trixie.

Delighted as she was to see him, Rachel experienced a pang of regret. Why did her son have to be so irresistibly drawn to the dark side? Then Devin straightened, holding the knife in one hand, the flowers in the other—dark, gorgeous and devastatingly sexy. *Because it runs in the family.*

"You look harassed." Handing her the gerberas, Devin tucked a loose strand of hair behind her ear in an intimate gesture that made Trixie and Mark exchange glances. Too many things were happening at once and Rachel seemed to have control over none of them. "Want us to go away again?"

She gathered her wits. "No, stay! Mark, it's lovely to see you here." Her throat tightened on a rush of emotion and she busied herself finding a vase for the flowers. "Trixie, why don't you take him through to the lounge and introduce him to everybody? I'll handle the gravy. And, Devin, since you've got the knife, would you mind slicing the meat?" She gestured in the direction of the leg of roast lamb.

"Sure, if you don't mind me butchering it."

Her pulse steadied with Mark gone. "Not as long as I get twenty-six slices out of it."

"Heartbreaker, you crack me up." Devin dropped a brief kiss on her mouth and her pulse sped up again. The dragon twisted on his forearm as he began slicing meat with a showman's flair.

Rachel concentrated on stirring the gravy but couldn't resist another glance. The noon sun streamed through the window, glinted off the flashing knife and picked up the red in Devin's stubble. He dwarfed the tiny kitchen, completely out of place against the teal-and-cream cupboards of her country-style décor, with its ceramic roosters, appliquéd tea towels and battered dresser.

This crazy attraction must be affecting her ability to be impartial, because she no longer saw him as a threat—at least not to Mark. So, what…one kiss and the frog had turned into a prince? No, she'd been softened by the fact that he was looking out for his mother. Katherine had sung his praises last night.

*What do your instincts tell you?*

To jump him.

Frowning, Rachel turned off the heat and put a lid on the gravy. *Keep it simple, stupid.* Now was the time to tell him she'd had second thoughts.

Except then he might leave—and take Mark. She put the vegetables and greens into serving dishes, then returned them to the warming drawer. She'd raise the subject after lunch.

Devin brought over a platter of meat, beautifully

sliced. "Thirty-two. Damn, I'm good. You want me to carry this to the dining room?"

Rachel pointed to the two-person oak table in the corner of the kitchen. "You mean that?"

"Don't tell me. It also makes up into a bed at night."

If only he didn't make her laugh. "Put the meat in the oven with the vegetables, then come and be introduced."

"In a minute." Off-loading the meat, he took her into his arms and smiled at her. And Rachel knew it wasn't fair to let this go on any further.

"About last—"

Devin kissed her with the same arrogant confidence he had the night before, bypassing her reservations and tapping straight into the uncomfortable heat she felt for him. "I'd rather talk about tonight."

Such an innocuous statement. Such a wealth of sinful promise.

Flustered, Rachel pulled free, fixed her gaze on his belt buckle and launched into her analogy about the difference between three-lane highways and one-way streets, and knowing what kind of driver you were. Devin balanced on the edge of the table, swinging one booted foot, and listened in polite silence.

She ran out of gas and spluttered to a stop. What had started out as a good idea had ended up a six-car pileup.

"Let me see if I've got this straight." His voice

was thoughtful. "I haven't even made a layover yet and already I'm a blind alley?"

She looked up to see the slow-burn grin that always took the chill off.

"You know this road map of yours isn't even accurate," he pointed out. "Paul, the expressway, turned out to be a dead end."

Rachel bit her cheek to stop from smiling.

Hooking one arm around her waist, Devin pulled her closer. "What you need on that map is a rest stop. Somewhere to take a break from the serious business of staying on the straight and narrow, scanning side mirrors, checking GPS, watching for safety signs…"

She couldn't hold back the laugh. "You're incorrigible."

"I love it when you use librarian words." He nuzzled her neck. It felt wonderful. Maybe she was overthinking this. No one needed to get hurt. He was a rock star, for God's sake, and she hadn't lost her head over a guy since her teens. Briefly, her arms tightened around him. To hell with impartiality. By bringing her son here, Devin was top of her hit parade right now.

"Let me introduce you to everybody, and then we'll have lunch." As she pushed Devin toward the living room, Rachel said softly, "Thanks for bringing Mark…to meet other students."

"Actually, I'm hoping for advice," he replied. "I'll tell you about his cock-eyed plan when everyone's gone."

DEVIN SUDDENLY FOUND himself standing alone, amid a dozen students of various nationalities jammed together on the sofa or seated on large cushions on the floor. Conversation dried up as they recognized him. Turning around, he saw Rachel had stopped in the doorway with an anxious expression. "Something wrong?"

She smiled and moved forward. "For a moment I thought I'd left the oven on…but I didn't." She began making introductions.

As he did the rounds, Devin noticed everyone was wearing stickers starting with "Ask me about…" Trust the librarian to have an icebreaker. Shaking hands with a guy called Huang, he looked closer. *Ask me about…*

*Growing up in Taiwan.*

*What it's like to have to study in my second language.*

*Rodeo.*

"You rodeo?"

Huang nodded. "When I first come here to learn English I live in Warkworth with rodeo family."

Devin had friends in the business, and the two of

them discussed barrel racing and bull riding for several minutes.

"And where is your sticker, Dev-an?" Huang inquired politely, and those within earshot laughed. The young man's face reddened.

Talking to Mark nearby, Rachel glanced at Huang, then pulled a sticker pad and pen out of her apron, a white cotton bibbed thing covered with cherries. "I'm so sorry, Devin, I forgot."

God, she was sweet. "No problem," he said.

"Ask me about…" She tapped the pen against her teeth while she considered. Devin smothered a smile. Sex, drugs and rock and roll? Rehab? With her hair pulled back in a loose ponytail she looked only a few years older than these kids.

"Being famous," suggested Trixie, and suddenly everyone was chiming in.

"How much money you've made."

"Dating supermodels."

"What it is like," said Huang, "to live most people's dream?"

"That's a silly question," said Trixie, "because there's only one answer. Bloody fantastic."

Everyone laughed.

"Okay, let's go with that one," said Devin. "You're nineteen years old, Trixie, and a rock star— famous, rich, dating studs. Now what?"

She raised one pierced eyebrow. "What do you mean?"

"You've got another fifty to sixty years to fill and you've got nothing left to wish for. What happens when the novelty wears off?"

Baby Goth shook her head. "Never going to happen."

"Eat your favorite food for a week," he said drily, "then tell me you don't crave a change. Eventually it happens."

There was silence as people digested that.

"But you've still got your music," Huang ventured.

Devin turned to him. "And in the first rush of fame you've overcommitted to album contracts. So, yeah, you're busy. Except your record company wants more of the kind of songs that made you famous. And you want to stay famous. Making music becomes a high-pressure business instead of a creative endeavor."

"Then I'd forget about fame," Mark said confidently, "and just write original music for my hard-core fan base. They'd keep buying."

"But not in enough numbers to keep the money flowing in that you've been spending like water."

"Then I'll enjoy what I've already bought," said Trixie. "The mansion and the boy toys." She licked her lips lasciviously and the others laughed.

"Sorry, Baby Goth." Devin shook his head. "The

boy toys won't hang around if you're not famous. And how much money you've got left to play with depends on your manager and your business savvy—which has probably been addled by the drugs or alcohol you used to medicate the terror you feel at living the dream and not being happy."

He became aware of the silence, the heaviness of the atmosphere. And he used to be the party guy. Then Rachel's hand curled around his fist, encouraging him, and he intertwined his fingers with hers.

"Listen, I was too young when I got famous," he said. "I didn't know the Holy Grail doesn't exist. But you guys are smarter." They liked that; smiles dawned. He made his final point. "Just remember when you hit the big time in your chosen careers not to tie your identity to it. And leave something left to strive for."

"Life's meaning lies in the journey, not the destination," said Huang.

"Confucius?" Devin asked.

"Cereal box," said Huang.

## CHAPTER ELEVEN

"So you won't even eat gravy?" Mark was asking Trixie as Rachel approached shyly with her own plate.

"Nope," said Trixie, "Rach prepares it out of the drippings of little baby animals." As she spoke she moved over to make room for her hostess on the couch. "Sit in the middle, Mark," she added with a shudder. "I can't look at carcasses."

Used to Trixie's theatrics, Rachel sat next to her son, who cast a longing glance at her roast lamb before scraping the gravy off his vegetables. But she knew not to interfere in affairs of the heart.

"There's pavlova and ice cream for dessert," she consoled him, and he visibly brightened.

Across the lounge, Devin perched on a stool, still swamped by students, and she was grateful. It was hard enough acting natural around Mark without Devin's keen powers of observation making her nervous. Trixie noticed the direction of her gaze. "You do realize you're going to be inundated with first-years once it gets out he's been here?"

Rachel shrugged and turned to smile at her son. "I hope you'll come again, too, Mark."

"Sure," he said, looking at Trixie.

Trixie opened her mouth, no doubt to tell him she was only here because her washing machine had broken down and she needed somewhere to do free laundry. Rachel cut her off. "So how are your studies going, Mark?" Maybe his cock-eyed plan was to give up school?

"Great. Got my first A on an assignment last week." He finished his last roast potato and reluctantly speared a carrot.

"Do you know what you want to do with your degree yet?"

"Well, it's kind of a backup if a career in music doesn't go anywhere. It was a deal I made with my parents." He pulled a face, but it might have been due to the carrot.

"How cool that you've got Devin as a mentor," said Trixie.

"Yeah, but I'm trying not to take advantage of that, y'know? I think he's had enough people using him in his life."

Rachel felt a prickle of unease but dismissed it. Her relationship with Devin had moved beyond Mark. *Yeah, and into a gray area.* So she'd be more scrupulous about keeping a distinction.

"Have you and Devin done the wild thing yet?" said Trixie.

"That question's really not appropriate." Rachel concentrated on cutting her lamb.

"Why, because of Mark? I'm sure he knows the facts of life. He grew up on a farm."

Cheeks burning, Rachel tried desperately to change the subject. "What kind of farm was that, Mark?"

It was his turn to look panicky. Puzzled, Rachel watched color creep up his cheeks, then the penny dropped and she came to the rescue. "Did I tell you about this study on dairy cows they did at Leicester University?"

Within thirty seconds, Trixie's eyes glazed over and she stood up. "Run for cover," she advised Mark. "It's one of her Wikipedia anecdotes."

When she was out of earshot, Rachel looked at Mark. "It's a beef farm, isn't it?"

"Yeah." He ducked his head. "But if Trixie finds out she'll stop speaking to me…or beat me up."

"It could be worse. Imagine what she'd be like with iron in her diet." She met her son's eyes and they burst out laughing.

DEVIN WAS GETTING recommendations on Pacific hip-hop artists from a Samoan student named Selei when the sound of Rachel's laughter made him look across the room. He liked watching her laugh, liked the way it animated her face and made her eyes glow. She and Mark sat side by side sharing a joke, heads together like conspirators.

He was glad he'd had the idea of seeking her advice about… A preposterous idea entered his mind as he stared at them. Laughing, they had a striking similarity in the tilt of their chin and the way their eyes crinkled.

No. He had to be imagining things.

"I've got a compilation CD in my car, Devin," said Selei. "I'll lend it to you." He left the room in the wake of the other students, who were making a rush to the kitchen for dessert.

Casually, Devin wandered over to Rachel and Mark. "What's pavlova, that it causes a stampede?" he asked.

*Beryl and Kev's hometown was Matamata. "Near Hamilton," Rachel had said, "where I grew up." Mark's birth mother had been from Hamilton.*

"A cake-size meringue smothered in cream and strawberries," said Rachel.

*And she was thirty-four. Around the right age.*

"New Zealand and Australia still squabble over who invented it," Mark added. "It was made in honor of some ballerina who toured Down Under a couple of centuries ago."

"Actually, it was only eighty odd years ago," Rachel corrected. "Anna Pavlova, in 1926…Devin, why are you looking at us strangely?"

"I was thinking how odd it was to fight over ownership of a dessert." He reached for Rachel's empty plate, telling himself this was all coincidence. "The food was great, thanks."

"Here, I'll take that." Mark stood and stacked the plate on top of his own, still half-full with carrots and broccoli. "You want me to get you some pav? Rachel?"

"I'll come with you. Devin, stay and enjoy the peace for a few minutes. You've earned it."

He sat on the couch, trying to think. The math worked, but Rachel wasn't the type to have had a teen pregnancy. Why was he so emphatic about that? Devin smiled. Because he couldn't imagine anyone taking advantage of her.

But he was thinking of the grown woman. What would she have been like at sixteen, seventeen? The corners of his mouth lifted again. A Goody Two-shoes without a doubt. Earnest and probably naive. But still uniquely Rachel.

Devin couldn't categorize her. Yes, she was conservative, at least compared to him, but she surrounded herself with people who were outsiders, or rebels like baby Goth. Yes, Rachel was sensible and pragmatic, but last night she'd surrendered— briefly—to passion and spontaneity.

Searching his mind for facts, not feelings, Devin came up with very few. Busy protecting his own privacy, he'd never appreciated that she was doing the same. What did he know about Rachel, really? Only what she'd wanted him to.

No wonder he couldn't get her out of his head.

He remembered how opposed she'd been to his friendship with Mark a few weeks back; in hindsight, her concern had an almost hysterical quality. But then, she looked out for new students. Hell, she had a houseful right now.

Through the open doorway, Devin watched her cluck over her brood like a mother hen. This woman wouldn't have given up a child. He was wrong. Things could stay simple. Simple was how he needed them.

TWO HOURS LATER Rachel was on the doorstep saying goodbye to students when Trixie came out with Mark.

"I'm taking him to the new health food store in Grey Lynn and stocking him up on whole foods." Rachel noticed he was carrying Trixie's bag of clean laundry. Mark caught her eye and grinned self-consciously.

Whatever his cockeyed scheme was, it wasn't serious. From their conversation, she'd learned that Mark wasn't planning to leave school. He probably wanted to date Trixie, and hoped Devin would get some pointers from Rachel. Unfortunately, he was doomed to disappointment. Trixie might consider dating a younger man but she stuck to her own kind. Hopefully, the crush didn't run too deep.

"Drive carefully," she said to Trixie.

"Yes, Mom. C'mon, Mark, let's leave the love-birds to it."

Rachel blushed. Why did Trixie keep doing this to her? "Our relationship hardly warrants that description," she began, and was pulled back into a hard male body.

"Yet," said Devin. His breath on her nape sent a shiver down her spine. "Thanks, guys, we'd appreciate it."

Rachel finished waving them down the street before she turned on him. "You're taking far too much for granted, mister."

"You just don't like someone else taking charge," he said mildly. "But what's that got you in the past? Guys like Paulie you can't respect."

"I respected Paul," she said defensively.

"Notice how you put that in the past tense?" Devin rubbed his thumb between her eyebrows, making her aware that she was frowning. "Besides, if I let you dictate the pace you'll end up thinking about it for another month, laying down rules and parameters and basically taking all the fun out of it." Devin slid his thumb down her jawline, then brushed it across her mouth. "Do you really want me to let you do that?"

His broad chest was very close. In answer she stepped forward and laid her cheek against it, then felt his arms close around her. The trouble was, around this guy she couldn't think. He smelled so good—rugged, clean, masculine. "You have pheromones in your aftershave, don't you?"

A chuckle rumbled under her cheek. "I haven't shaved for a couple of days."

She checked; he was right. Funny how she'd stopped noticing him as scruffy and disheveled. Lifting a hand, she ran her fingers through the stubble. It highlighted his mouth, wide, firm and tempting.

And his hair was soft, too. Somehow all those vibrant red highlights made her expect it to be springy, but it was baby-fine. "It's getting long again," she commented. She could lose her hand in all that rich, wild color.

"You think I should get another haircut?"

She hesitated. "No."

Something started to hum between them, like the charge in the air before an electrical storm. He freed her hair from the ponytail. "You smell good, too. Like roast lamb and gardenias." He kissed her, and she closed her eyes, suddenly weak with desire. "And you taste of strawberries," he said when he came up for air.

"I might have eaten a couple in the preparation," she admitted, smiling.

"Is that why you served yourself so little, or did you go short so the fledglings could have second helpings?" He looked at her with a frank affection he didn't bother to hide. He had no business looking at her that way, as though they had the possibility of a real relationship, a future. It took her dangerously close to needing him, and Rachel had spent her life making sure she didn't need anyone.

"You have the most expressive face of anyone I've ever met," he said. "And you've just gone AWOL on me. Why?"

Rachel swallowed. "That's silly," she said, and kissed him.

The kiss was different, distant. Devin let her go. He'd had enough casual sex to last him a lifetime, and it wasn't what he wanted from her. The realization was a shock; now he was the one who needed some time to think.

"I didn't get to eat much, either," he admitted. "How about we grab a cold lamb sandwich?"

"Good idea, there's still plenty of meat on the bone." She didn't seem the least disappointed by his withdrawal, dammit, leading the way to the kitchen, hauling out the leftovers, the bread, the chutney. The librarian never reacted how he expected. It was one of the most infuriating and charming things about her.

"Put the kettle on," she said. "We'll have tea."

"I'll make iced. It's too hot for the Kiwi version."

"Trixie left some wine in the…sorry, I forgot. Yes, iced tea would be lovely." She started building the sandwich—meat, mustard, tomato. "Do you miss alcohol?"

Devin preferred to have the subject out in the open. "For years I thought alcoholism was a problem I could be cured of, so I could go back to drinking." He found ice in the freezer, a lemon in the fruit bowl. "But when it finally came down to life or death…well, it clarified my priorities. No, I don't miss it."

"And you'll always have your music."

He concentrated on stirring in the sugar. "I haven't had an idea in months. I'm beginning to think I can't write songs sober."

"Performance anxiety," said Rachel. "You'll get over it."

"Oh, will I?" Devin was torn between amusement and irritation. "As the first woman I intend to sleep with—sober—you'd better be more encouraging in bed."

She giggled.

Devin stared at her for maybe two seconds, then strode over and threw her over his shoulder. In the hall he couldn't find the bedroom, which only made Rachel giggle more. At last he chose the right door. Pushing it wide, he paused on the threshold. It was French provincial, the whitewashed furniture all spindly carved legs and ornate handles.

The bed was narrow, piled high with pillows and bolsters, the curved headboard stenciled with fat pink roses. Fortunately, the shabby gilt mirrors on the delicate dresser injected a much-needed sinfulness to the fairy-tale theme.

Dumping the librarian on the bed, he lay on top of her until her giggles subsided and she lay boneless and quiescent under his weight. He became aware of every soft curve and valley of her body. Her eyes darkened with a similar appreciation of their differences.

She wore some kind of vintage dress of pale green cotton with a simple bodice and a full skirt. Devin hadn't liked it until now, when he realized he could flip up the skirt and position his lower body between her bare, lightly tanned legs.

"Your boots are on the bed," she protested feebly. He laughed deep in his throat, then moved to nestle against the silky fabric of her underwear, applying just enough pressure to show Rachel how denim over an aroused male could work for a woman.

They were going to do this slowly, but her surprised gasp stirred a need that tipped his lust into possessiveness.

There was fierce ownership in the way his teeth grazed her nipples through the cotton, then his mouth suckled until she moved restlessly under him. "But my dress…no…don't stop."

His mouth captured her moan as he slid his fingers up her silky thigh and between their bodies. She was wet, hot and ready for him, and they'd barely started.

He'd come if he didn't slow this down. Devin started pulling away his hand and it got tangled with hers as she struggled with the clasp of his belt, then the zipper, shoving his jeans down just low enough to… Her hand closed around him.

"Rachel, wait—"

It was her turn to cut off his protest with a kiss as hot and wild as what they were doing with their hands. Breathing heavily, he grabbed her wrist.

She was beautiful, her soft hair tangled, her eyes unguarded. Devin forgot what he was going to say and kissed her back. Their bodies came together and he remembered. "We need a condom."

"Yes."

She fumbled in the drawer beside her and he noticed her hands were shaking. So were his. Between them they managed to cover him, haul off her panties. They didn't bother with his jeans. Or his boots. She whimpered as he thrust inside her, and he heard himself answer with a similar helplessness.

Then everything was Rachel, the feel of her around him, the unfocused expression on her face. Their gazes tangled, fierce and soft at the same time. The antique bed was too narrow and their clothes bunched, stalling their rhythm, but it didn't matter. Devin felt a wonder, a wonder that built and carried him to uncharted territory.

She cried out, and the sound took him over the edge. In that timeless moment of release he loved her.

He remembered that as they lay together afterward, catching their breath and staring at the ceiling, Rachel obviously as shocked as he was by the intensity of the experience.

He was faintly embarrassed, unwilling to believe it was possible that someone who'd never considered sex as anything other than fun had been temporarily caught in the emotions of a lovesick teenager.

Rachel rolled toward him with a serious expression and he panicked. If she talked about feelings…

"I think," she said carefully, "you might have one vice left."

In his relief, Devin laughed.

SHE SHOULDN'T HAVE SLEPT with him.

Pretending to be hungry, Rachel took another bite of her roast lamb sandwich, then forced it down with a swig of iced tea. Devin sat beside her on the garden bench in the tiny paved courtyard of her backyard, devouring his second sandwich.

His long legs were sprawled out in front of him; one arm was slung casually around her shoulders, and in the early summer evening his black T-shirt was a sun trap she wanted to snuggle into. Instead she sat on her side of the bench, nursing her grievance.

The man had grossly misrepresented himself as a player when he was…well, Rachel didn't know what he was. But far from feeling light-hearted and rejuvenated, she was disorientated and vulnerable.

It had taken everything she had to come up with a flippant comment after they'd had sex, when inside she'd felt like a nervy sixteen-year-old wanting reassurance that this meant something to him. She hadn't expected to care, but he'd made her care and he had no right to.

His lazy charm and her own prejudices had lulled her into seeing him as emotionally harmless, and then he'd gone and nuked her when she wasn't looking. *Bastard.* Giving up on her sandwich, Rachel ripped off pieces and tossed them to the sparrows.

"You're not throwing hand grenades, Heartbreaker."

She picked up the jug of iced tea. "Another?"

"Thanks." He held out his glass. "I never did get around to asking your advice about Mark."

The mention of her son was a welcome diversion. "Break it to him gently," she said, refilling the glass, "but between you and me, he has as much chance of dating Trixie as you do of attending Sunday service."

"Maybe God's already answered my prayers." There was a meditative quality in Devin's voice that made her skin prickle. She fumbled and tea and ice cubes skidded across the flagstones.

"Careful." Taking the jug from her, Devin put it back on the ground. "Getting his heart broken by an older woman might be good for Mark's songwriting. Look at what Rod Stewart achieved after meeting Maggie May."

"Mark's too young to start having sex," said Rachel sharply. "If I thought for one minute Trixie was interested—" She stopped, because she was overreacting and Devin's eyebrows were raised. "Of course, it's none of my business." Though she didn't want it, she picked up her iced tea and took a sip, grimacing at how sweet it was.

"You care about teenagers," he said. "That's why I want your advice. Anyway, Trixie isn't the concern."

"So if it's not Trixie…" And Rachel knew from talking to Mark that it wasn't school. She clutched Devin's arm. "Oh, God, he's sick, isn't he?"

He laughed. "Did you see how much Anna Pavlova he ate? No, he's not sick. He recently found out he's adopted, and he wants to find his birth mother."

For a moment Rachel couldn't breathe, then happiness swept over her, a joy so great she couldn't speak. She tightened her grip.

"I want you to talk him out of it," said Devin.

"Why?" The word erupted from her. She flung his

arm off and stood up. "Don't you understand how wonderful that is?"

"He hates her," said Devin, and her iridescent rainbow-colored bubble burst.

Rachel walked to a rosebush, where she started pulling at dead flowers. "He hates her," she repeated slowly.

"For giving him up," said Devin. "He's looking for a confrontation, not reconciliation, and that's not good for him. Shouldn't you be wearing gloves to do that?"

She gazed down at the shriveled rose petals in her hand, the color of dried blood, and the tiny pinlike thorns embedded in the pads of her fingers. "Probably."

"Let me see." Mechanically, she went to him, holding out her hand like a child. "For God's sake, Rachel, it's full of thorns." He started pulling them out with long, skillful fingers.

She swallowed hard. "What if she had a good reason for giving him up?"

"We don't know that—we don't even know if she's willing to see him." Pinpricks of blood welled where he'd removed the tiny thorns, shiny beads of bright red. "He's doing it behind his adoptive parents' backs, following his own crazy trail like some vigilante, seeing his mother in every woman's face. He's even got me jumpy."

Pulling the last prickles out of her thumb, he shifted his attention to the few still in her palm. "You want to hear something funny? For a few minutes today I even thought you might be a candidate."

Her insides lurched. "That is funny," she managed to say.

Devin lifted her hand higher and examined it closely. "I think that's all of them."

A teardrop splashed onto her open palm, then another. Rachel couldn't hold them back. For long seconds, they watched the tears trickle along the heart line, then Devin lifted his head, his expression one of shock.

"Or not funny," she said.

# CHAPTER TWELVE

"MY PARENTS WANTED ME to keep the baby."

Devin watched as Rachel's hands fluttered like wounded birds before she linked them in a viselike grip. Holding herself together.

"Everyone said how wonderful Mom and Dad were through the whole pregnancy, that it was so like them to turn the other cheek." Her voice was slightly winded, as though she needed more oxygen than her lungs could produce. "I became a pariah when I insisted on adoption."

"Rachel," he said helplessly. She was in agony and he didn't know how to help her. And after her first crying jag, when she'd let him hold her, she'd pulled away. He'd already made such a mess of this he didn't want to force the issue.

It had grown dark in the intervening hour. They'd moved inside and he'd made her hot tea, piling in the sugar. Now they were in the family room, Devin on the couch and Rachel standing in front of the mantel. Her tea sat untouched.

"What about the father...did the boy deny paternity?"

"Oh, no." She gave him a tight little smile. "He and his parents offered to pay for the abortion. And made it clear that keeping the baby made it solely my responsibility."

Devin said softly, "But your parents were supportive?"

"We ended up parting ways over it."

At *seventeen?* And he'd assumed her upbringing was sheltered. "Did you have anybody on your side?"

"A good social worker." Restlessly, Rachel moved things around on the mantel—two gilded candlesticks, an antique clock, a small bowl of potpourri. "So, don't you want to ask me why I gave up my baby?"

There was a brittle quality in her voice.

"No." Devin waited until she looked at him. "I already know your reason was a good one."

Her shoulders sagged. "Thank you," she whispered.

From the couch, Devin held out a hand. "Come here."

She shook her head, returned to straightening the mantel ornaments. "I'm okay."

"I'm sure when Mark finds out—"

Her head jerked up. "Promise me you won't say anything."

"Rachel, you have to tell him," Devin said gently.

"I will, only…" She swallowed. "And this will sound silly, but I want him to like me first."

Not silly, heartrending. For a moment Devin couldn't speak. "Of course he likes you."

"As your friend or Trixie's." She stirred the pot-pourri with her index finger, round and round, completely unaware of what she was doing. Faintly, Devin smelled orange peel and cloves. "If I spend a little more time with him, build a rapport, he'll be more inclined to listen to my reasons for giving him up."

"You're scared," Devin said. "That's understandable. But waiting isn't going to make it easier.

She pounced on him. "So you *do* expect fallout."

"I don't know how Mark will react," he said honestly. "But I do think he's more likely to read some conspiracy into a delay."

Stubbornly, Rachel shook her head. "It's *my* decision to make, Devin."

"Not if you're asking me to be monkey in the middle. I have a friendship to protect here, too, remember?"

"Obviously not ours."

His own temper flared. "It's because I care about you that I'm trying to get you to see sense, you obstinate woman!"

Rachel snapped on a lamp. Light flooded the room and illuminated the angry color in her cheeks, but her voice was level. "I don't need you to care about me. I need you to butt out of what's none of your damn business."

Incredulous, he stared at her. "We just slept together. I'm a mentor to your son. Of course it's my damn business."

"Exactly. We *just* slept together." She waved a finger at him, an intensely annoying gesture. "Now you're trying to muscle in on my life. I should sue you for misrepresentation."

"Oh, I get it." Devin stood up. "I'm okay to fool around with, but God forbid we achieve any real connection."

Rachel snorted. "Says the guy with two ex-wives."

"At least I got that far." He pointed his own finger to see how she liked it. "You balk before you get to the altar. And you think you don't need advice on relationships?"

They glared at each other. "I know you've destroyed a lot of brain cells," said Rachel, "so I'll say this slowly and clearly. If you tell Mark, I'll never speak to you again."

"Here's a better idea." Devin flicked his gaze over her, as cutting as rawhide. "*Never* speak to me again and I won't tell Mark."

She didn't even hesitate. "Deal!"

"Deal." This time he was the one who slammed the door.

Devin took the 8:00 p.m. car ferry back to Waiheke in a blistering rage.

As he found a seat inside the lounge he decided he was glad Rachel had clarified where they stood before he made a fool of himself. To think that this afternoon he'd understood the allure of a relationship with a normal woman. He snorted. Rachel normal? "Ha!"

The old guy sitting opposite glanced cautiously over his newspaper, then got up and found another booth. Devin barely noticed. The librarian had more baggage than Paris Hilton.

When the boat moored he was first off, opening the throttle on the Harley as soon as he hit the island's backroads. He still couldn't get his head around the fact that she was Mark's mother. What had driven her to give him up? It had to be something bad.

Devin shook off the thought as irritably as a dog with fleas. It wasn't his problem. The librarian had spelled that out loud and clear. Like he'd welcome this kind of complication in his life, anyway, when he'd just got things back on an even keel.

In his vast empty house, Devin turned on all the lights, then stripped to his boxers and pummeled the punching bag in the gym until his arms ached. Mixed with his sweat was Rachel's perfume.

He took a shower and scrubbed himself with vicious thoroughness. It didn't help. Hauling on clean clothes, he settled down to a class assignment, but shoved it aside within minutes and opened the final report from his forensic accountant. Devin read it and his mood grew even blacker.

Checking his watch, he saw it was four in the morning in L.A. Too bad. Devin dialed Zander's cell and was again routed straight through to Message.

"Hey, brother," he said pleasantly. "Just reminding you it's Mom's birthday next weekend and it would be nice if you called her. Oh, and I've had the results back on an independent audit of the band. Seems you owe me about five million bucks in royalties on four of our early hits."

He opened the sliding door and walked out onto the deck, bracing himself against the buffeting wind. "My lawyers suggest I sue, but I figure there's a rational explanation." Far below the glass balustrade, white water boiled and broke over the jagged rocks. Gripping the rail with his free hand, Devin looked down until he'd conquered his vertigo. "I mean, only a lowlife would screw over his baby brother, right, Zand?"

Devin dropped the amiability from his tone. "You've got five days to make contact before I release the hounds."

RACHEL WATCHED DEVIN walk down the path toward the fountain, his head down, brow furrowed. Nervously she stood up, smoothing her skirt against the gusty wind. From the swirling, slate-gray clouds overhead, it looked as if they were in for rain.

She'd barely slept with worrying. This was too important to hope for the best. And Devin had mentioned he had an early tutorial this morning.

Steeling herself, she waited for him to notice her. He walked right past.

Rachel blinked and called after him. "Devin!"

He glanced back, recognized her, and his frown deepened.

Now *that* she had been expecting. "Can we talk? Please?"

"No." He kept walking.

Rachel forgot her diplomatic approach. Chasing after him, she caught him by the arm. "Look, I've got everything to lose in this. So quit sulking because I decided against following your advice."

He glared down at her. "Is that what you think our fight was about?"

"Wasn't it?"

He thought about it. God, she liked him for that. Even angry he was willing to question his motives. It made Rachel examine her own more closely. This wasn't just about making Devin keep his word; she needed his understanding.

Scattered drops hit the concrete path, and one splashed cool on her face.

"Maybe my ego's involved," he admitted.

The shower became a deluge within seconds. He took her arm and they ran for cover to the vestibule of the gothic clock tower, built in the 1920s, that was the university's most striking building. Rachel always expected to see Quasimodo swinging from one of the tall spires. At this time of the morning, seven-thirty, there were few students about and their footsteps echoed on the marble floor. Devin positioned himself near one of the massive oak doors and stared out at the pounding rain. Wanting to escape as soon as possible, she thought.

"About yesterday—" she began.

"What really shocked me," he interrupted, still watching the rain sheeting onto the steps, "was how quickly I went from lover to enemy."

"I'm sorry," she said simply. Yesterday, she'd dropped her guard for the first time in years, and his dissent had felt like an attack. The thought of telling a hostile Mark the truth terrified her. She could never make him like her enough to overcome the fear of rejection. But admitting that would reveal her vulnerability. "When you questioned my decision to postpone telling Mark, it took me by surprise. I know you were only trying to help."

All she needed was a little time to rehearse, to win Mark's trust. Was that so much to ask? She was framing her argument when Devin turned his head.

"I've been trying to piece all this together… When did you find out who Mark was?"

"A couple of days into term, but I couldn't say anything to him. As far as I knew, his parents had never told him he was adopted."

"He found out on his own. They still don't realize."

That explained why they'd never contacted her. If it wasn't for Devin Rachel might never have found out Mark knew he was adopted, let alone looking for her. Thank God for him. She felt a rush of gratitude, affection.

"So the first date…it wasn't payback for teasing you. You were trying to assess whether I was a bad influence?"

Rachel swallowed. She guessed where this was leading. "Yes."

Devin said slowly, "And you agreed to a second date—?"

"It wasn't a date. Remember? I was very clear about that." The facts and nothing but the facts. "I hadn't made up my mind about you, and platonic kept things simple."

His forehead creased in a frown. "So you slept with me because…?"

It was her turn to look out into the rain, lessening now to desultory drizzle. "I'd…revised my poor opinion of you, obviously."

"Obviously?" Devin turned her to face him. "You

knew I spend a lot of time with him. Dating me meant you would, too."

That stung, but Rachel wasn't here to fight with Devin again. Far from it. "You really *don't* trust people's motives in being with you, do you?"

His gaze didn't waver from her face.

"Okay," she conceded. "The unvarnished truth. I won't say your 'usefulness' didn't bother me, which is why I held off getting romantically involved."

"Maybe you could have tried harder."

Her heart started to pound. "When I accused you of trying to seduce me the other night, you said you'd changed your mind—until I changed it back." She coaxed him with a rueful smile. "Can't I succumb to the same temptation?"

Devin wanted to smile in return, he really did. But he'd been screwed over so many times.

Rachel's tentative smile faded. She dropped her eyes, but not before he'd seen the hurt in them. Instinctively, he reached out a hand.

Head still down, she said, "I'm not asking you to lie to Mark, but…"

Devin returned his hands to the pockets of his denim jacket. "Stay out of it?"

Sun broke through the clouds, glinted off the wet trees.

"It's a lot to ask," she admitted.

"No," he said. "Staying out of it is *exactly* what I want to do."

There was a moment's silence. That was the thing about intelligent women. They didn't need things spelled out when a guy moved on. But he didn't want to hurt her. "The thing is, Rachel, I've had a complicated couple of years." Understatement.

"And you want a simple life."

He wouldn't sugarcoat this. "Yes."

"I completely understand," she said briskly. "This is my mess and I'm sorry for dragging you into it." She gestured to the open doors and they stepped from the gloom into the brighter world outside. Smiling, she held out her hand. "No hard feelings?" The woman had guts.

Devin returned the handshake. "No hard feelings."


FOR THE NEXT THREE DAYS Devin watched Rachel campaign for Mark's friendship with a desperate cheerfulness that made him grit his teeth and turn away. He wasn't getting involved.

But dear God, didn't the woman know how to play it cool? Stupid question.

Around Mark she acted like one of those annoyingly cute little terriers, all wagging tail and eager friendliness as it frisked around your ankles, getting underfoot and gazing up at you with bright eyes begging, *Pat me. Pat me. Pat me!*

Okay, that was an exaggeration—the librarian was a little taller than that and her tail was always worth watching. But it *felt* that bad to Devin. Maybe because he knew how much was at stake. Normally Rachel understood teenagers, but in her need for Mark's approval, she was doing it all wrong. And this was too important for a misstep.

On Wednesday Devin gave up and frog-marched a protesting Rachel into her office.

"What are you doing? I have inventory to clear."

Devin kicked the door shut behind him. "I'm staging an intervention before you completely screw this up with Mark."

Immediately she was defensive. "I'm not."

"Whenever he comes into the library you drop everything to fawn all over him, and giggle at his lame jokes. Hell, he just told me you even let him borrow reference books that are supposed to stay in the library."

"I'm authorized to exercise my discretion." She took refuge behind her desk, behind an attitude of polite condescension. "Was that all?"

"No." Eyeing her with exasperation, Devin sat down and rested his boots on her desk. "So you really don't think your approach with Mark is over the top?"

Frowning, Rachel shoved his boots off. "I fuss over lots of students."

"You don't offer to lend them your car."

"It was raining yesterday and he didn't have a coat, plus his bag was particularly heavy...."

"Uh-huh." Devin put his boots on her desk again. "He's worried you're looking for a boy toy."

She'd been about to shove his feet off again, instead her fingers tightened around his boots in a viselike grip. "That's ridiculous," she said faintly.

"That's what I said." Devin could feel her nails digging through the soft leather. Scratching his eight hundred dollar boots. Gently, he wiggled them free and returned them to the floor. "Fortunately, Trixie had already pooh-poohed the idea."

"Thank God."

"Trixie—" Devin paused, waiting until Rachel looked at him "—told Mark that you've only gone a little crazy since I dumped you. Apparently you miss me."

Her gaze slid away from his, then returned blazing. "Wait a minute. *Who* said you dumped me?"

He had the answer to his unspoken question. "Hey, don't blame me. All *I* said was that we had philosophical differences. It's not my fault if Trixie and Mark read that as 'Rachel wouldn't put out so Devin dumped her.'"

"I wouldn't put...Mark thought...oh, this is horrible." Her defiance spluttered and went out. "Okay, I'll try and pull back my approach." She started playing with a paper clip on her desk.

"Tell him the truth, Heartbreaker."

"His parents are coming up next Friday…. He's bound to show them around campus." Painstakingly, she pulled at the thin metal, stretching it out. "I was going to take a short leave, but we have our annual budget meeting and when it comes to lobbying for your section's textbooks, it's dog eat dog."

"It's pronounced *dawg*."

She smiled but her fingers twisted the paper clip into a tortured Z. "I know I have to tell Mark before then. It's just, well, we haven't got the friendship I'd hoped for."

Devin leaned forward and rescued the paper clip. "How about I invite you both to Waiheke for the weekend? Mark would jump at the offer and it would give you the chance to spend time together in a more natural way."

"Why would you do that?"

He'd missed her, and it seemed she'd missed him, but one of them knew how to play it cool. So he told her half the truth. "We're still friends, aren't we?"

She gave him a crooked smile. "Friends."

## CHAPTER THIRTEEN

IT SEEMED APT, thought Rachel, as the ferry docked at Matiatia Wharf on Waiheke early Saturday morning, that Devin lived on an island. She wondered if he realized the significance. With Mark beside her, she disembarked, searching for Devin's tall figure in the crowd.

"There's Katherine." Mark waved to the slight figure at the end of the pier. "Devin's mother." In white capris and a turquoise T-shirt with matching jewelry, Katherine waved back.

Rachel hadn't seen her since being discovered in a compromising position with the woman's son, and she prayed Katherine wouldn't bring it up in front of Mark. But though her eyes twinkled as he made the introductions, Katherine said nothing about meeting her before.

"Dev asked me to pick you up," she said. "He's embroiled in some business calls from the States. I'm to take you to my place and he'll meet us there in an hour."

"He should have rung me," said Rachel. "We could easily have caught a later ferry rather than put you to this trouble."

"Are you crazy? I wouldn't miss this for the world." Really, her eyes were as wicked as her son's. Walking between them, Katherine tucked her arms in theirs. "And I wanted to see Mark again. We had a fun dinner together last time you were here."

As she steered them toward a small cherry-red Fiat parked by the ferry terminal, Rachel tried to work out how these two knew each other. It must have been the night of the "orgy" Devin had teased her about. She'd been such an idiot.

Demonstrating exquisite awareness of a teenage male, Katherine asked Mark to drive "us girls." She sat in the back next to Rachel, pointing out the passing sights. The town's trendy eateries; a view through the pohutakawas down to the harbor; workers harvesting the rows of laden vines across the hills. "That's one of the island's top wineries."

Rachel tore her gaze from the back of Mark's head—how cute, he had a cowlick—and made an appropriate response. They'd had such a lovely time on the ferry. She'd taken Devin's advice and played it low-key, and Mark had filled the silences she'd left for him.

An anecdote on childhood seasickness. A request for advice on an assignment. And, disturbingly, a brief rant about phonies, after he'd read a newspaper article rating the trustworthiness of various professions. Librarians rated highly. Rock stars weren't even on the list.

"We're just coming down into my bay now." Katherine pointed out the window, and obediently Rachel looked at the curve of shingle beach and the colorful iron roofs on the settlers' cottages scattered against the lush green backdrop.

"It's beautiful." She wouldn't think about the frightening confession that lay ahead. This weekend was only about her and Mark having fun together. There would be a happy ending with her son. And in situations where happy endings were impossible—her thoughts turned to Devin—silver linings like friendship. Unconsciously, Rachel sighed.

"We're here," said Katherine.

The Fiat pulled up beside a tiny faded blue cottage so cute Rachel had to resist the urge to hug it when she got out of the car. She patted the sun-warmed concrete seal balancing a birdbath on its nose. "Devin always does that, too," commented Katherine. "Come in. Mark, you know the way."

Inside, mullioned windowpanes gleamed, and the golden kauri floor sloped downward toward the kitchen, which had an old Aga cooker and lace curtains, and smelled of baking and lemon. Mismatched armchairs with fringed cushions lent a charm to the sunlit dining room, and somewhere Rachel could hear an old grandfather clock ponderously marking time. "I love it," she said.

"Devin keeps trying to buy me a bigger place, but telling him I need grandchildren to fill it usually shuts him up. Earl Grey?"

"Thanks."

Mark asked for water. "I think he'd be a good dad," he said, accepting a piece of homemade shortbread.

"Really?" Rachel thought of Devin with Mark and the other students at her luncheon. "Well, he can be patient when he wants to," she conceded. "And the kids would always have someone to play with."

Katherine fixed her with a meaningful stare. "What he's never had is the right woman."

Rachel bit into the buttery shortbread, still warm from the oven, and diplomatically changed the subject. "Does your other son have children?"

"Zander? No. But that's probably a good thing," Katherine handed Mark another cookie. "He's far too selfish to put anyone's interests before his own."

She caught Rachel's blink of surprise and laughed. "I love Zander, but it would have been a lot better for his personal growth if he'd become a minister instead of a rock star. That was his original choice of career, you know. He was in the choir when he was a boy…though in hindsight I think it was less of a spiritual calling than imagining himself center stage in the pulpit."

The wistfulness in Katherine's voice struck a chord. "Do you see him very often?"

"No." Katherine picked up the teapot and filled two delicate china cups. The perfumed scent of Earl Grey hung in the air. Rachel had always found it slightly melancholic, like pressed flowers in an old love letter. "But I used to say that about Devin, and now he's living down the road. So I don't give up hope." She handed Rachel her tea.

Mark stood at the window, looking out to the garden. "The last of the peaches should be ripe by now. Want me to pick them while I'm here?"

"That's so thoughtful, thank you. There's a bucket on the back step." Through the window, both women watched Mark cross the grass. "Sweet boy," Katherine commented, sipping her tea. "He and Devin picked for me last time they were here, because my son gets so huffy when he finds me up the tree.

"I had a little heart trouble earlier this year," she explained, "and he still treats me like an invalid…. So, Rachel, now that we're alone, tell me how you two are getting on."

Rachel watched Mark swing up into the tree. "Much better now that I've stopped trying so hard," she said, then realized Katherine was talking about Devin.

"Yes, I think women expect rock stars to want kinky sex," said Katherine thoughtfully. "Bondage, threesomes and such, but Devin says he's always been a one-woman man. One at a time, I mean."

Fascination overcame Rachel's embarrassment. "You two talk about stuff like that?"

"Lord, no!" She laughed. "He's such a prude with his mother. And he's terribly Victorian about Matthew—my lover. Since you outed us, I've been trying to get them to meet, but Dev keeps coming up with lame excuses. Actually, I'm hoping you'll help me. It's my birthday and Devin's taking us all to a local restaurant. But he's balking at Matthew joining us."

"I'll certainly see what I can do, but I have to warn you my influence is limited," said Rachel. "We've decided that we're better off as friends rather than…anything else." She gave a self-depre-cating laugh. "I mean, a rock star and a librarian takes the 'opposites attract' theory a little too far don't you think?"

"It can work. I was a Kiwi honor student, in the States to research a thesis on symmetric matrices, and the boys' father was a Texas-born biker. I met Ray when I was working part-time at Marie Callen-der's restaurant. He was managing a Harley dealer-ship down the road in West L.A. and was the smartest man I ever knew." Tenderness lit Katherine's eyes. "Smart enough to follow me back to New Zealand, anyway." She paused then smiled sadly. "He died of cancer when Devin was twelve." She smiled sadly. "I think part of Dev's problem with Matthew is that he doesn't like to see another man in Ray's place."

"That's why Devin likes Harleys," said Rachel slowly, "and cowboy hats."

Katherine nodded. "Are your parents alive, Rachel?"

"My father passed away some years ago. My mother lives in Hamilton." She recited the facts the way she always did, without emotion.

"No siblings?"

"No. They'd pretty much given up on having a family when they had me. Mom was forty-five when I was born, my father forty-nine."

"And you were their miracle."

For a moment Rachel said nothing, looking down at her hands. Heavy expectations, heavy disappointments. "Some people aren't meant to be parents." She'd never voiced the thought before. But she needed to practice surrendering secrets.

"And some are," said Devin, behind her, resting his hands, big, warm and reassuring, on her shoulders. "Mom, how many times do I have to tell you to close the front door? Anyone can walk in. Where's Mark?"

"Picking peaches for me," said Katherine. They all looked out the window and burst out laughing. Mark was balanced precariously on a forked branch near the top of the tree, using his cell phone.

DAMN, HE'D MISSED the call.

Red bucket propped against his feet in the fork of the tree, Mark listened to the dial tone. With his left hand, he absently picked a small white peach.

He checked his messages, saw the last one was from Trixie, and got nervous. He'd told her about his birth mother and she'd immediately offered to check staff records for women aged thirty-two to thirty-seven, teenagers when he'd been born. That would really help, because it was nearly impossible to tell females' ages from looking at them.

Maybe Trixie had found something. Taking a deep breath, he listened to her message. "Just to tell you, I've printed off the list of names, and while you're enjoying yourself in the rock star's mansion, I'll be cross-referencing all afternoon. But don't feel bad about it."

Grinning, Mark replaced the phone in his pocket. She was still pissed that she hadn't been invited, but when he'd hinted as much to Devin, he'd replied, "Tough. Restful women only."

"Are you sure you wouldn't rather be alone with Rachel?" he'd asked.

"Yeah, I would, but she insisted on a chaperone." When Mark looked doubtful, Devin had laughed. "I'm joking. It's just a hang-out weekend, buddy. Good food, a little swimming, a couple of jam sessions and my mother's birthday dinner. Think you can cope?"

Mark had relaxed. "Yeah, your mom's cool."

And he was kind of relieved Trixie hadn't been invited. Although she was a goddess among women, and being in her orbit was still better than floating alone in the universe, a guy liked to be in charge occasionally. Mark had decided he preferred his love unrequited.

As he returned to picking peaches he felt a frisson of excitement along with the old familiar dread. Today could be the day he found out the name of his birth mother.

DEVIN DIDN'T KNOW WHY he was nervous showing Rachel his house. Maybe because this was his retreat, the one place he was truly himself. Maybe it was because he'd decided on the decorating, and having seen Rachel's neighborhood, he figured she'd hate modernism.

But as always, the librarian surprised him. "Vibrant, colorful, brash and in your face—it's you." She held her hands out to the cardinal-red feature wall as though it radiated heat. "I love it."

She wandered through the spacious rooms, admiring his art collection, pausing at the nudes. "Ex-wives?"

"Very funny." *The odd girlfriend maybe.*

Rachel walked to the glass wall overhanging the cliff. "I feel like I'm in an eagle's nest."

"That was the effect I wanted…. Let me show you where you're sleeping."

He'd deliberately put her in the bedroom close to his—with Mark shipped to the L-shaped wing at the other end of the house. Rachel frowned as she took in the setup, but Mark was with them so she didn't comment.

But later, as they lay on sun loungers by the pool, digesting one of Devin's Tex-Mex specials, while Mark pitted himself against the swim jets, she said, "I'm onto you, Freedman."

He'd been watching her, lazily thinking her figure was wasted in that polka-dotted one-piece, and wondering if she'd let him buy her a bikini.

He and Mark had spent the past couple of hours messing around with the teenager's songs in the music room, while Rachel made endless cups of hot tea and sat, knees curled under her, on the white leather couch reading a book and seemingly oblivious.

Except she'd tapped her pink-painted toes to the rhythm and her eyes kept raising to Mark. Devin had realized he was showboating, not his skills but the boy's. It was a present he could give her, an insight into her son's talent.

In the end she'd stopped pretending to read and simply listened as Devin fine-tuned Mark's ideas, while the teenager basked in all the attention. *One day,* Devin thought, *I want her to look at me like that.*

He hadn't had a good morning. Today was the deadline for Zander to respond to his ultimatum, and Devin hadn't heard anything.

*Happy birthday, Mom. First thing Monday, I'm initiating legal proceedings against your eldest son.*

Devin had even considered canceling the weekend, but Rachel needed this time with Mark. And now a few hours later here he was, strangely content.

"How are you onto me, Heartbreaker?" Her pale skin was reddening in the sun. He unscrewed the lid on a tube of sunscreen and dotted some on her nose. What was it about this woman that made him feel so protective?

"I can do that." She took the tube from him. Oh, yeah, her fierce independence. "And I'm onto you because underneath the rock star bluster you're a kind man—with your mom, with me, with Mark."

Devin hadn't expected that and wasn't sure how to respond. "Keep thinking of me as a selfish prick, then I won't disappoint you," he said at last.

She finished applying sunscreen to her face and slathered some onto her shoulders, skirting the apple-green halter neck of her retro bathing suit. "For an egomaniac," she said thoughtfully, "you have a lot of trouble accepting a real compliment."

He watched Mark splash around the pool. The ego was for music. In his personal life, Devin had never been sure of his identity. People saw whatever image they projected on the famous, and as much as that irked Devin, it also protected him. No one knew who he was. Then he'd stopped drinking and discovered he didn't, either. Now he was trying to find out, and Rachel's remark set the benchmark high. He wasn't used to living up to people's expectations, wasn't sure if he always could.

But she made him want to grow. Could he?

Could he reveal himself to be as vulnerable to rejection as other men? Yet he'd never lacked courage. "You asked me on Wednesday why I'm doing this. It's more than friendship, Rachel. I think I'm in love with you."

Rubbing sunscreen over her legs, she paused, then her movements became brisk. "Of course you are. I'm the first ordinary woman you've spent time with. Understandably, you're dazzled." She started screwing the lid back on the tube.

"You don't like the idea," he said flatly.

"I don't exactly fit the Devin Freedman template, do I? For a start, I'm only a B cup."

Her flippant replies were irritating the hell out of

him. Then he noticed Rachel was having trouble screwing the cap on. Taking it from her, he finished the job. "I've never met anyone who avoids risk the way you do. You chicken out if you have to. But if I want to love you, I'll bloody love you, got that?"

"Well, you can't," she retorted. "That was never our deal."

Understanding dawned on him and with it, incredulity. "You're pissed because I'm suggesting more than a fling? If I didn't have a rock star-size ego I'd be insulted by that."

"That's silly." But a telltale blush spread across her cheeks.

"Okay, you know what?" Abruptly Devin stood. "I *am* insulted."

He dived into the pool to join Mark, making damn sure she got wet.

## CHAPTER FOURTEEN

RACHEL NEARLY DIVED in after him to apologize, but something stopped her. Probably the cowardice he'd accused her of. But she was still shocked by his casual declaration.

Even her two would-be fiancés had never said the L word—and neither had she. *I love you* had always seemed too extreme somehow for the calm, steady tenor of her previous relationships. Instead they'd talked about fondness, shared interests and goals. Certainly she'd never heard the word from her parents.

The only person who'd ever said he loved her had run back to college, terrified when she'd told him she was pregnant, and left his zealous parents to clean up the mess. Not love, sex. Teenage hormones.

Picking up a striped beach towel, she dried her arms and legs and watched Devin power into a fast crawl, water rolling off his muscular tanned shoulders as his arms sliced through it. And God knows, hormones played their part here. Now Devin wanted to change the rules? Well, what if she didn't want to?

The infinity pool gave the illusion of being open-ended, and for a moment it looked as though Devin was going to swim straight over the cliff. Rachel fought the urge to stand and shout a warning. She didn't want to lose him.

That made her even more afraid.

He surfaced, water dripping from his sleek, dark head, and glanced across the diamond-blue pool. "Come play with us, Heartbreaker." Quick to anger, quicker to forgiveness. *Oh, God, I'm in trouble.*

"Yeah, come on in, Rach," Mark called. "I think I saw a beach ball in the pool shed." He climbed out and, grabbing a towel, disappeared into the small building. She hesitated on the side of the pool.

"Sooner or later, you're going to have to get your hair wet."

"Not necessarily." Rachel slid in up to her waist, felt the prickle of cool water on her sun-warmed skin. Gingerly she fanned her arms through the water. "Maybe I'll stay in the shallow end."

"The hell you will."

Devin ducked under, and the next second a muscular arm wrapped around her waist. As the water closed over her head, Rachel started to protest, then laugh. He released her and she surfaced, coughing and spluttering.

Unrepentant Devin pinned her against the side of the pool with his body, long and wet. "No wimps allowed." His gaze caressed her with the softness of a butterfly's wing. A strange helplessness came over her, as much from fear as exhilaration.

"What's wrong?" he asked.

Because she hadn't considered a future possible with him, she hadn't put any emotional safeguards in place. "I don't know if I can do this."

"Yes, you can." He cupped her chin and lowered his head, his lips cool against hers, persuasive. So very persuasive. She surrendered to the kiss, wrapping her arms around his neck.

"Man, I only left you guys for a few minutes," Mark said in disgust.

Mortified, Rachel ducked under Devin's arm and swam to the side.

"I was drowning," Devin protested, laughing. "She was bringing me back to life."

"Yeah, right."

Rachel climbed out of the pool, avoiding her son's eyes. "I'll make us some lemonade."

"*Lots* of ice," Devin suggested wickedly.

She knotted her sarong around her waist.

"Is that a yes?" he said, and she knew he wasn't talking about lemonade.

"I'll think about it."

Except she didn't want to think, she simply wanted to savor this wonderful lightness, this trembling delight. Thinking would lead to questions like

*What the* hell *do you think you're doing?* In the kitchen, Rachel hummed as she cut and squeezed lemons, stirred in sugar and added ice. Lots of ice.

The doorbell rang as she returned to the pool, and she remembered Katherine's request to ask Devin if his mother could bring a date tonight. Better get on that.

Balancing the tray in one hand, Rachel had the other on the door handle when she caught sight of her reflection in the hall mirror. Dumping the tray on a nearby table, she wiped sunscreen off her nose with one corner of her sarong. The doorbell chimed again—and whoever was there held it down.

"Okay, okay, I'm coming." Finger-combing her wet hair, she hauled open the oversize door and blinked.

A fleet of shiny black Mercedes were parked in the driveway and a dozen beautiful people spilled across the grass between the cars and the house. A burly guy moved forward, scanning first her and then the interior, before stepping aside.

Behind him, a man in his late thirties ranted on a cell phone decorated in diamonds, so dazzling in the sun that Rachel lifted her hand to shade her eyes. His teeth were almost as white, bared in a snarl. "I don't give a shit how you do it, just do it."

A handsome man, he was dressed in white jeans and a white leather waistcoat that oozed like oil over his muscled bronze torso with every irritable gesture he made. A silver chain-link necklace with a padlock hung around his broad neck.

His shaggy blond hair looked to have enough product in it to punch its own hole in the ozone layer, and below his designer sunglasses, his strong, full mouth was currently issuing a stream of obscenities into the phone.

Two gorgeous women in their early twenties, with pneumatic breasts and lips, assessed Rachel as though they were judges in the Miss World pageant and she couldn't even qualify for Miss Congeniality.

One of them stepped forward. "About time. Is Devin Freedman home?"

Before Rachel could answer, the man rang off, his gaze sweeping over her in the same quick dismissal. It stopped at the sweetheart bodice of her bathing suit. "Holy crap, I feel like I'm on Gilligan's Island."

Even if Rachel *had* been the help, these people needed a lesson in manners. She lifted her chin. "Is Mr. Freedman expecting you?"

The man raised one blond eyebrow and took off his shades to reveal laser-blue, bloodshot eyes. "Don't you know who—"

"Let me check if he's available." Closing the door in his face, she locked it, picked up the drink tray and strolled back to the pool. Devin and Mark were lobbing the ball back and forth with graceful athleticism.

Tempting as it was to dismiss the caller as an encyclopedia salesman, Rachel figured she'd probably caused enough mischief. "There are five Mercedes and approximately fourteen people at the door and on your lawn," she said to Devin. "I think one of them is your brother."

"Cool," Mark said.

"Damn." Devin absently rotated the ball in his hands, then added cryptically, "So, the SOB is guilty." With a frown, he climbed out of the pool, wrapped a towel around his waist and padded through the house, not bothering to dry off. Rachel thought it politic to stay where she was.

"What do you think *that's* all about?" asked Mark as she put the tray beside the sun loungers.

"I don't know." She glanced at her son, torn between removing him from Zander's orbit and staying to support Devin. By the grimness in his expression, he needed it. "Maybe we should catch the ferry back to Auckland and leave them to it?"

"Are you crazy?" Mark punched the ball to the other end of the pool. "Zander Freedman…wow! He might even have some of the band with him. But you can go if you want," he added generously.

Rachel sat down, committing to the role of

watchdog. "Maybe," she said, "Zander's here to surprise his mother on her birthday?"

But from the little she'd seen of him, she doubted it.

"I'M HERE TO SURPRISE Mom for her birthday," Zander said. He met Devin's eyes with that same "you question my word, I'll knock the shit out of you," expression he always had when he was in the wrong.

"Not to confess, then," Devin replied, and saw a flicker of culpability before Zander put his shades back on.

"I thought we could clear up that little misunderstanding at the same time." Stepping into the hall, he glanced around and raised his eyebrows. "You downsizing, baby brother?"

"Yep, only five bedrooms, five bathrooms." Devin looked beyond Zander to where the others stood. "You can stay, but your entourage will need to find accommodation in Oneroa. Expect to rough it—I don't have live-in staff."

"Don't panic, I've rented my own place. But there's only one comfort I really need." Without looking around, Zander held out his arm and a blonde stepped into it. "Stormy, this is my brother. Devin, my girlfriend."

Stormy—probably christened Samantha—gave him the rock chick pout. "Hi, I've heard so much about you." He, on the other hand, knew nothing about her. Not that it mattered; she wouldn't be around long. Zander was thirty-seven, but the age of his girlfriends never rose above twenty-five. It was starting to get sad.

"Nice to meet you," he said politely.

Another blonde thrust out a hand, staring at his bare wet chest like a long-lashed limpet. "I'm Zander's P.A., Dimity." Unconsciously licking her lips, she dragged her eyes to his face. "Let me introduce you to everybody."

Resigned, Devin shook hands and exchanged pleasantries with all the people who supported his brother's ego—the stylist, the personal trainer, the publicist, the bodyguard, the dietician, the chef and a couple of buddies and their girlfriends.

He didn't recognize any of them, but Zander was notoriously hard to work for. Devin did pick up some useful information, though. No lawyer in the bunch, which, considering the legal trouble Zander was facing, was either very cocky or very clever.

"We chartered helicopters from the airport." Dimity flicked back her hair. "And we're en route to the estate we're renting." She named one of the newer mansions, built as a vacation home by an Auckland banker, and disparaged by locals as "Miami Vice." "Zander, I'll go ahead and check that everything's satisfactory. I'll leave Security and one of the cars here."

Exasperated, Devin looked at his brother. "I'll give you a lift on the Harley when you want one, and you don't need a bodyguard here."

Head cocked, Zander was studying one of the nude paintings. "Really? You've left some pretty interesting messages lately." But he nodded.

Dimity clapped her hands and hollered, "Let's go, people!"

"Stormy, darlin', you go with them." Zander encouraged his girlfriend toward the door with a spank on her shapely rear. "I need to spend a little one-on-one with my baby brother."

"Actually, that's going to have to wait," Devin said. "I have houseguests."

"The uptight broad who opened the door?" Zander laughed. "Hell, you really are downsizing."

Devin grabbed his brother's waistcoat as Zander sauntered past. "If you're going to be an asshole we'll talk through lawyers."

"C'mon, where's your sense of humor?" Breaking Devin's grip, Zander draped an arm around his bare shoulders and gave him a none-too-gentle shake. "You're the poster boy for sobriety now. Make it look fun."

Shrugging off Zander's arm, Devin led him through the house to the pool, where Rachel and Mark sat on longues, reading. The teenager leaped to his feet as soon as they came into sight, awe on his face. Rachel glanced warily over the top of her book. Seemed she already had his brother's measure.

Zander walked toward her with hand outstretched and his most charming smile. "So which wife are we up to now? Four?"

Rachel put down the book. "If that's your math, you might want to consider an assistant," she suggested kindly. About to run interference, Devin grinned. His librarian could take care of herself. "And you know very well your brother and I aren't married," she added.

Zander's eyes glittered. "I'm not that great with current affairs, either," he responded, "but tell me your name anyway, babe, and I'll try and remember it."

Her smile lost none of its sweetness. "*You* can call me Ms. Robinson."

Mark gasped, but Zander only chuckled as he turned back to Devin. "I take it back, little brother. You upgraded. But holy shit, she must be hard work. I'll stick with the airheads…."

Astonished, Rachel looked at Devin. "Think of him as a three-year-old in a man's body," he advised, "and you'll know how to deal with him."

"With a spanking, I hope," said Zander. "Dev, remember that time we—"

"And this is Mark," Devin interrupted, "one of my classmates and another musician. Lot of potential as a songwriter."

"It's an honor to—to meet you," Mark stuttered, and Devin was reminded of the first time he'd met the boy. Zander looked bored and he sent him a warning frown.

"Yeah, well." Zander shook Mark's hand. "Good to meet you, too. Always a privilege to meet the fans." It was lip service, but Mark glowed.

From inside they heard a rush of footsteps, then Katherine appeared at the open sliding doors. Spying Zander, she caught the frame for support. "My God, it is true. Alexander Freedman, why didn't you come straight to your mother's?"

"Because I wanted it to be a surprise." He held open his arms. "Happy birthday, Mom."

With a choked little laugh, Katherine flew into his embrace. "This is so wonderful."

She grabbed her oldest son's face between her hands. "Let me look at you…" Deep grooves bracketed his mouth, and under the Californian tan his brother had the slightly bloated look of someone whose excesses were starting to catch up with him. But he still had a steelworker's arms and shoulders; he spent a lot of time lifting weights.

Devin saw worry flicker in Katherine's eyes as she measured the changes, then she smiled. "Still gorgeous. How long has it been? Two years. Oh, Alex, I'm so happy I could cry."

His brother's face softened. "You are crying, Mom.

Now c'mon, you'll ruin the leather." Devin tossed him a towel and gently Zander wiped their mother's eyes. "So, you okay…the heart and everything?"

"Yes, yes…Lord, don't you start. I get enough of that from your brother." Katherine caught his hands. "So how long are you here?"

"Only a couple days."

"Oh, Alex, no, why so short?"

Casually, Zander released her grip. "We're doing some early promo on the band's Australasian tour. I've got meetings in Sydney on Monday."

Of course his brother would kill as many birds with one stone as possible. Talking Devin out of a lawsuit, self-promotion and Mom. Probably in that order.

Cloaking her disappointment, their mother said cheerfully, "Well, I'll just have to make the most of you now, then."

"On that note," said Rachel, "let Mark and I give you guys some time alone." The two of them got to their feet.

"You don't have to," Katherine protested.

"That would be nice," said Zander.

"Ignore him," ordered Devin, but Rachel shook her head. Stepping closer, she murmured, "We want to buy your mom a present, anyway. The village is within walking distance, isn't it?" He nodded. "C'mon, Mark."

As soon as they'd disappeared through the sliding

doors, Zander turned back to Katherine. "How did you know I was here?"

She laughed. "Jungle drums. I know you've rented every Mercedes on the island, used helicopters to get here and have commandeered the island's best chef for a private party tonight."

"Ah, but do you know the party's for you?"

Their mother melted. "Oh, darling, you shouldn't have gone to all that trouble."

"You're worth it." He dropped a kiss on her head. "Invite whoever you like."

Devin stifled a snort. Yep, lifting his little finger must have been hard. If the prodigal son had come back repentant, fine, but his brother was serving his own agenda, not Mom's. And that was saving his ass from being sued. Besides, knowing Zander, the party would be full of music execs, a local TV news crew, a couple women's mags and a whole lot of eye candy.

With his arm around their mother, Zander looked up and obviously read Devin's thoughts, because he smiled. "Isn't this nice, the whole family together again? Come join the hug, little brother."

Disgusted, Devin shook his head. Zander was using their mom to try to guilt him into backing off.

"Yes, Dev." Katherine freed an arm and held it out. "Get in here." Looking at her radiant face, he couldn't refuse. With her frail body between them and her arms tight around their waists, Devin glared at his brother.

Zander smiled. "Family should always come first, don't you think? Which brings me to the other reason I'm here."

He paused for a dramatic effect. "I want you to rejoin Rage."

# CHAPTER FIFTEEN

"WHAT DO YOU MEAN, you can't tell me?" Mark's spirits deflated like a three-day-old balloon. He looked at his reflection in the mirrored wardrobe of the guest bedroom, where he'd been checking himself out when Trixie rang.

Since he hadn't brought party clothes, Devin had lent him a hot shirt, black with silver stitching. The material was so soft against his skin it had to be expensive. Tight on Devin, it hung loose on Mark, but he wasn't into fitted shirts anyway, at least not until his body filled out.

"It's…complicated," said Trixie.

"What's complicated about it? If there's more than one woman who qualifies, I'll ask them all. I won't squeal where I got the information from, if that's what you're worried about."

"I think I should make a few of my own inquiries first, okay?"

Was that uncertainty? Mark's fingers tightened on the cell phone. "You know one of them, don't you?"

Her voice was suddenly wary. "I didn't say that…. I gotta go. Let's leave this until Monday."

His mind started to race. Most of the university staff used the library and Trixie was the kind of person who talked to everybody. "Tell me, please. This is important to me."

"I…I can't."

"You *have to*—"

She hung up on him.

Immediately, Mark rang back, and got the message, "This cell phone is either switched off or outside the coverage area. Please try again later." *Shit.* Tossing the phone onto the bed, he put his head in his hands.

There was a knock on the door, then Rachel popped her head in. "Ready to go to this…Mark, what's wrong?"

He was so gutted, he nearly told her. But that would only put a downer on her evening, too. And enough people knew his secret. So he dropped his hands. "Nothing."

She came into the room. "You're pale. Are you sure you're well enough to go? I'd be happy to stay behind and keep you company."

Mark mustered a smile. "No, I want to. I mean how many times do you get to go to a party like this in your life, right?" Rachel was still scanning him anxiously so he made an effort. "You look nice."

She was wearing a halter-necked sundress patterned in swirls of blue, orange and green. Rachel glowed from his compliment. She always acted as if his opinion mattered. It made him feel a little better.

"It's a bit casual," she replied, "but it's all I've got."

Mark had to smile. "Rachel, you always look dressed up."

"To a teenager, maybe." She held out her arm. "Shall we?"

Mark hooked his arm through hers, but his thoughts were already elsewhere. For Trixie to suddenly get this protective, it must be someone she liked. That substantially narrowed the field.

Surely if he thought hard enough, he could work this out.

"Wow, your old lady has a lot of friends," the hippie driver said to Devin as the battered island taxi began its descent down the steep, unsealed private road.

From the back, where she sat with Mark, Rachel watched Devin's jaw tighten as he surveyed the emerging spectacle, but he made no reply.

They were catching a cab to the party because he didn't own a vehicle that seated more than two people. It was another reminder that the man was essentially a loner.

Zander's "rental" was a monstrosity of neoclassical architecture that dominated a private beach. At eight-thirty, the sunset tinted the marble exterior a Miami pink, and the giant palms accentuated the tropical glamour.

But what made Rachel smooth the skirt of her sundress were not the few hundred people dotted around the tear-shaped swimming pool, waterfall and lush gardens, but the realization that this event was way bigger than an impromptu Waiheke party.

"I'm seriously underdressed," she said faintly. Her gold strapped sandals had low heels and she hadn't brought jewelry to the island.

Devin didn't turn to look at her. "So am I. Don't worry about it."

The difference was that he made underdressed sexy.

He was wearing slashed jeans and a vermilion shirt open over a black tank. His black belt was studded with silver that picked up the toe cappers on his kick-ass black boots, and the chains around his neck. As usual, his hair was disheveled in the unstudied style that suited his strong, stubbled jaw and wide cheekbones.

He looked exactly what he was, a supremely confident handsome male who didn't give a damn what anybody thought. And right now that seemed to include her.

Devin had been distracted since Zander's arrival, but after his mother and brother left, his mood had darkened to the point that he'd excused himself and disappeared into his study.

"Maybe he misses the life," Mark had suggested as he and Rachel walked along the sandy beach below the house. "I mean, he only quit because he had to."

She'd thought the undercurrents were more complex than that, but Devin had snapped her head off when she'd asked if something was bothering him. Though he'd immediately apologized, he continued to be remote.

"Oh, hell, pull over," Devin said abruptly, and the cab driver, Tim, slammed on his brakes. They were still three hundred yards from the entrance.

"What's up?" asked Mark.

"Press." Arm on the seat back, Devin turned to Rachel. "It's probably better if we're not photographed together."

"It's okay, I have nothing to hide." Since she was telling Mark the truth tomorrow it wouldn't matter if his parents recognized her in pictures.

"Yeah, but I do." Glancing at Tim, he lowered his voice. "There's a chance I'm going to get newsworthy again soon, so it's better if my private and public worlds are kept separate. I'll walk from here and meet you both inside."

Without waiting for an answer, he handed the driver some notes and got out of the taxi.

"It's like he's ashamed of us," murmured Mark as

Devin strode away from them. Camera lights flashed as the press recognized the figure strolling down the driveway.

"That's ridiculous," said Rachel, even though the same thought had struck her.

"I wonder what he meant by newsworthy," her son speculated, ignoring her warning frown. Tim's back was rigid with feigned indifference. "Maybe he's thinking of rejoining the band? And that's why Zander's here—to get him back."

"Man, I hope so." Giving up all pretense of not listening, Tim swung around, his goatee bristling in his excitement. While they waited for Devin to clear the press, he and Mark had an animated discussion on how cool that would be. Rachel listened in growing dismay.

Of course, it made sense. Zander wasn't the type to put his mother's birthday high on the priority list, not after two years of neglect. He obviously had an ulterior motive. And Devin was acting so distant.... She watched his tall figure disappear inside.

He was probably embarrassed to tell her he was leaving, because just this afternoon he'd said he was in love with her. Except he'd only said, "I *think* I'm falling in love with you." There was a big difference.

How lucky then that she hadn't taken him seriously. She stared at her hands, white-knuckled in her lap. "It's not too late to go home," she said to Mark.

Both he and Tim looked at her as though she was crazy, so Rachel steeled herself. "Okay then, let's get this over with." Would Zander and Devin make the announcement tonight? *Happy face,* she told herself, *practice your happy face.*

As the cab pulled up to the entrance, one of the photographers peered in at them. "Relax, it's only a couple of locals," he said.

"Bloody cheek," muttered Tim. He made a great show of opening their doors and pulling at his dreads. "What time do you want a pickup, m'lady?" he asked in a fair imitation of an English accent.

Rachel found a real smile. "Eleven would be perfect, thank you, Timothy."

The photographer fell for it. "Over here, please."

Ignoring him, she propelled Mark through an arched gate set in the hedge enclosing the pool and gardens. Among the Nikau palms, chefs supervised roasts of pork and lamb turning on spits. The scents mingled with the night-blooming jasmine and gardenias.

Out of sight of the press, Mark cracked up laughing. "They thought we were important."

Around the pool, young waitresses in tight black skirts and low-cut white blouses glided through the crowd carrying silver platters of tropical cocktails. In keeping with Katherine's era, a fifties-style band in shiny black suits and narrow ties, with pompadour hairstyles, played "All I Have to Do is Dream" over by the pool shed.

"We are important," Rachel affirmed, but as she looked at all the exquisitely dressed guests she was reminded of a recurrent dream she'd had after Steve stood her up for the school ball. She learned later he'd confessed her pregnancy to his parents and all hell had broken loose. But that night she'd still been confident that he would stick by her. In the dream she'd stood naked and alone in the middle of the dance floor, dazed by mirrored balls and strobe lights, while her fellow students pointed and laughed.

Nervously, she touched her bare neck. "I wish I had some jewelry."

"An easy fix." Devin appeared beside her from out of nowhere and took off a couple of his silver chains, twining one around her wrist, the other around her neck. The metal was still warm from his skin.

Rachel started to take them off. "I'd hate to lose them."

He caught her hand to stop her. "Easy come, easy go."

"Is that your philosophy on everything?" She couldn't keep the tartness out of her voice.

But he was distracted, watching Zander, who was holding court with Katherine by the pool. "Sometimes you don't have a choice," he replied. Then he looked down at her and Mark, and his expression softened. "Sorry, guys, this wasn't the weekend I'd planned. Listen, if Zander gives either of you any grief tonight—"

"We'll throw him in the pool," she promised. Privately, Rachel thought Zander wouldn't even notice they were there. She, for one, intended to avoid him. Just as she intended to avoid Devin, at least until she recovered her equilibrium. He still held her hand; she tried to pull free but his grip tightened.

"I'm sorry for ditching you so abruptly earlier. As I said, I wasn't expecting press. Zander swore this was a private party."

Smiling, Rachel broke his hold. "Don't give it another thought." At thirty-four she might be no better at protecting her heart than she was at sixteen, but she'd become an expert at hiding her feelings.

"Zander's signaling us over," said Mark, waving an acknowledgment.

As they started weaving their way through the crowd, Rachel's cell beeped from her clutch bag. "Hang on a second." Pausing, she retrieved it and opened a text from Trixie.

Call me. It's URGENT!!!

Mark caught sight of the message and scowled. "Can I phone her back?"

"Sure." She handed her cell over. He dialed Trixie's number and waited until she picked up. "Oh, so you'll answer when Rachel calls but not me, is that fair?"

Rachel bit back a smile. How was Trixie torment-ing him now?

"Does she know this person, too?… Fine, have it your way." Snapping the cover closed, Mark handed the cell back to Rachel. "She says phone her when you've got some privacy."

"You two have a falling-out?" Devin asked Mark.

The teenager shot Rachel a sideways glance. "I'll tell you later. I need to go find a bathroom." He loped out of sight.

"Seems everyone's got secrets tonight," she said lightly.

Accepting two nonalcoholic cocktails from a passing waitress, Devin didn't even try to deny it.

They started making their way through the crush of people, but everyone wanted to talk to Devin, and—if they were female—to touch him. Within five yards he and Rachel were separated. Through the press of bodies, he held out a hand to her but she shook her head.

"Traitor," he murmured, but let her go.

On the sidelines, she sipped her cocktail and watched him greet his admirers. Nearby, two of Zander's entourage were discussing the upcoming tour. "I heard it direct from Zander," said one. "Devin's rejoining Rage." For the first time in her life Rachel wished her drink had alcohol in it.

Across the crowd, Zander's assistant tapped

Devin's shoulder and he bent his head to listen. They made a striking couple—Dimity in a silver mini-dress, impeccably made up with long highlighted hair and even longer tanned legs; Devin in profile, all cheekbones and dark menace. As the blonde leaned forward, she teetered on her stilettos and he steadied her with a hand around her upper arm. Strands of her golden hair brushed his dragon tattoo.

And all the confidence Rachel had spent years re-building seeped away until she was sixteen again, awkward, weird and an outsider. She looked down at her 1970s sundress, bought for twenty-five dollars. Vintage was a way of being stylish on the cheap, a way of being individual without compet-ing with other women. Now she simply felt shabby.

And in that moment, she hated Devin for making her forget their differences—the nerd and the cool guy. Hated him for making her feel special when he didn't mean it.

Self-disgust quickly followed. For God's sake, he'd been married and divorced twice. How long would his "love" have lasted, anyway? Five minutes. His entire lifestyle lent itself to easy emotions. And she was a fool for ever thinking otherwise.

What had he said? Easy come, easy go.

"Isn't this fun!" Katherine called, waving for Rachel to join her circle of friends. To her relief, Zander had left his mother's side, the crowd parting before his minders like the Red Sea before Moses. Rachel couldn't like him; aside from his monumental conceit, there was something reptilian in Zander's light eyes, as though he was calculating his next strike.

His mother, however, was charming. As she returned Katherine's hug, Rachel was overwhelmed by a deep homesickness for something she'd never had. With an effort she released the older woman. Dressed as she was in a blush-pink chiffon dress with matching pearl earrings, it was obvious tonight where Katherine's sons had got their looks.

"You're radiant," Rachel commented as she handed over the hastily bought present.

"That's because I've drunk too much champagne," Katherine said, laughing. But when she turned to the man by her side, Rachel saw the real reason for her sparkle. "Matthew, this is Devin's sweetheart, Rachel."

*Sweetheart.* The old-fashioned poignancy of the term struck Rachel like a blow, but she kept the smile on her face. "Not sweetheart," she corrected, shaking Matthew's hand. "Friend."

HEARING THE AMENDMENT as he extricated himself from the crowd and joined them, Devin scowled. His nerves were strung tight since Zander's arrival, and he really needed an ally tonight, but Rachel persisted in keeping him at arm's length. Okay, he'd snapped at her earlier, but he'd apologized and meant it.

Frankly, if anyone needed to cut anybody some slack here, it was the librarian. He'd laid his feelings on the line this afternoon, a difficult thing to do, and she wanted to think about it. Any other woman… He stopped himself. But wasn't that the point? Rachel wasn't any other woman.

Still, sooner or later she needed to meet him halfway, and tonight—especially after what Dimity had just told him—would be a good start. Particularly when Devin was doing his best to protect Rachel and Mark from the media. If he ended up suing Zander, everybody close to them would be embroiled in a media circus.

He'd hedged this afternoon when Zander had asked him to rejoin the band, partly out of shock, mostly because he wouldn't have a showdown in front of their mother. Did Zander honestly think he could placate Devin by waving Rage in front of him? It was a goddamn insult.

Devin looked at the grizzled man with his arm wrapped possessively around Katherine, and found a target for his anger. "So you must be Matthew Bennett, the guy who's banging my mother?"

He regretted the words as soon as they were out of his mouth. Katherine's face fell and both Rachel and Matthew looked disgusted. Devin wanted to hit something, preferably Zander. As he opened his mouth to apologize, Matthew said quietly, "I think your mother deserves more respect than that."

Devin didn't need to be told how to treat his mother. "Yeah, well, when I want advice from a five-minute fling I'll let you know."

Out of the corner of his eye he saw Rachel flinch, but then Matthew murmured to Katherine, "You haven't told him," and a tingle ran down Devin's spine.

"Told me what?"

"Matthew asked me to marry him today." With apologetic defiance Katherine put her arm around her lover's middle-age spread. "I said yes."

Devin nailed the older man with a hard look. "She hasn't got any money of her own, you know. And everything I've bought for her is in a trust."

Matthew held his gaze. "Not even the boorish behavior of her younger son is enough to put me off. I love your mother."

"How touching. Mom, I'll set you up with a prenup lawyer, first thing Monday."

"Devin, please," Rachel said in a low voice. "This isn't L.A."

All his frustration boiled over. "It's amazing how easy it is for you to care about everyone's feeling but mine."

"You're the one who shuts me out when it's convenient," she snapped.

"We'll talk about this in private." He couldn't discuss his dilemma with Zander in front of his mother.

"Oh, that's right, public and private are kept separate." As Devin tried to work out what that crack meant, Rachel turned her back on him and lifted her glass of orange juice in a toast. "Congratulations to you both. Katherine, I'm sure what Devin is *trying* to say is that he only wants your happiness." With a last glare at him, she stalked off, her dress a swirl of moving color around her legs.

Devin saw his mother looking at him anxiously. "Of course I want you to be happy," he growled. "But I also want to protect you from gold diggers." He shot the man a cursory glance. "No offense, Matthew."

"This works both ways, you know." Matthew's authoritative tone dragged Devin's gaze back to him. "I'm a retired cop and your reputation hardly enhances my good name." With a glint in his eyes, the older man added politely, "No offense, Devin."

He started to like this guy. "That makes for some interesting family dynamics, I grant you." Devin held out his hand. "Maybe we should get acquainted before we jump to conclusions."

The lines on his mother's face deepened as she smiled.

"Sure." Matthew returned the handshake. "I can see why you'd suspect everyone's motives," he conceded. He gestured to Zander's entourage. "It's obvious that hangers-on come with the lifestyle."

"If that's a polite way of saying who the hell are all these people…I don't know. Sorry, Mom."

"I'm enjoying it," she said loyally. "Now go make up with Rachel."

Across the crowd, Zander beckoned. Devin ignored him. Mom was right. Right now, he had a more important priority. His gaze gravitated to Rachel, who was standing near the hors d'oeuvre table with Mark. Between mouthfuls, the kid was gesticulating with a passion that suggested they were talking about music. At least those two had bonded, so one good thing had come out of this weekend. Devin wished he'd told Rachel about Zander earlier.

He realized abruptly that he suffered when he was out of favor with her; the librarian's opinion had become that important. With every other woman, it had always been easy to walk away. But if Rachel wouldn't—couldn't—love him back, he was in deep trouble.

He was heading over to join them when the background music stopped. The vacuous Dimity clapped her hands. "Zander Freedman would like to say something." Oh, hell, *now* what? Frustrated, Devin turned.

His brother leaped onto the half wall that ran around the courtyard and separated the raised beds of canna lilies and native ferns from the paved courtyard and pool. It was fully dark now and the flaming torches around the garden flickered shadows over his face, making him look every one of his thirty-eight years. "Welcome, everyone. It's great to be hosting Mom's birthday and wonderful to be visiting the country I consider my spiritual home."

A smatter of applause muffled Devin's snort. His brother used that line or something like it in every city and country they ever toured.

*You're the rockingest city in the U.S. of A., Pittsburgh!*

*I've always felt a kinship with the Irish!*

*Tokyo is my favorite place in the world!*

And people bought it. Maybe it was the break in the husky voice, the soulful look in those deep-set eyes, the hand over his heart. Scanning the crowd, Devin saw they were buying it now…. Except Rachel, who stood with her arms folded, frowning slightly. *That's my girl.*

Quietly, Devin resumed weaving through the crowd toward her.

"So, Mom, come up here," Zander called. "Your sons want to sing to you."

Devin stopped dead as the crowd erupted into ecstatic applause.

"And who knows—" Zander winked at the par-tygoers "—maybe you'll be seeing us performing together more often in future."

*I'll kill him.*

The Everly Brothers tribute band bowed out, leaving their instruments free. Dimity opened the gate to the driveway and the press started shoving to the front with cameras. Maximum pathos, maximum publicity and—with a sinking heart Devin saw his mother's delight—impossible for him to refuse.

Accepting the inevitable, he made his way to Zander, smiling and waving. "You manipulative son of a bitch," he muttered when he got there.

Zander held out a Washburn electric-acoustic guitar. "It's called marketing, bro." Dammit, Devin should have guessed it was a setup from the instruments, too high-spec for a tribute band. Accepting the guitar, he lovingly imagined bringing it down on his brother's thick skull. Zander's triumph turned to dismay as he read his intent. For a long moment Devin let him sweat, then he put the strap over his shoulder and bowed in Katherine's direction. "Only for you, Mom." As one professional to another he said to Zander, "How do you want to do this?"

His brother's face sagged with relief. " 'Love Me Tender' segues into 'Happy Birthday' after the second chorus. I'm thinking the Marilyn Monroe version, but replace the sex with gutsy blues."

Devin nodded. Musically, they'd always been in perfect harmony.

Zander raised his voice. "We'll start with a hit from the decade of your birth, Mom. Something from the King." He nodded his cue; Devin struck the first note. Held it.

Beside Rachel, Mark twitched with barely suppressed excitement. "We're gonna remember this our whole lives."

She didn't respond. Another note joined the first, resonating through the hot night. She closed her eyes. As yet, the melody sounded nothing like "Love Me Tender" except in the mood it evoked—slightly melancholic, heartfelt, deeply emotional. After first meeting Devin, she'd listened to one of Rage's later albums, but was immediately alienated by the hard rock style. Now with this simple solo she understood. Devin didn't play the guitar, he prayed with it.

The tune changed and became familiar. Rachel opened her eyes. Zander began to sing, his deep, powerful voice lifting and falling in a duet with the guitar. Elvis's ballad drew to a close, and seamlessly, Devin changed instruments to a bass, seamlessly transitioned into "Happy Birthday." Together, the brothers sang it like a spiritual, made the old familiar tune both new and extraordinarily moving. Rachel saw her own awe reflected in other people's faces.

Her disappointment over Devin rejoining the band suddenly felt petty and trivial. Who was she to hold him back? She heard the answer in her father's voice. *Nobody.*

The notes faded, the audience stirred. Then the applause started, rapturous. Wiping her eyes, Katherine stood and embraced her sons. As media and well-wishers swamped them, Devin glanced up, obviously searching for her. Rachel stepped deeper into the shadows. They were done.

# *CHAPTER SIXTEEN*

AT TEN O'CLOCK, when Mark found himself alone with Zander Freedman, he officially upgraded an amazing evening to the best night of his entire life.

It happened by accident. He'd been on his way back from the bathroom when he'd caught the glow of a cigarette, then spotted a shadowy figure alone on a terrace. "Hey, kid," Zander called in his distinctive voice, "Do me a favor and bring me another bottle of Scotch."

Mark didn't need to be asked twice. "Sure." Within a minute, he was back with a bottle. Propped against the glass-and-chrome railing, Zander held out his crystal tumbler and, as he started pouring, Mark registered two things simultaneously. Zander was drunk and the cigarette wasn't tobacco.

"Whoa, careful there, you're spilling it. You know how much this stuff costs?"

Embarrassed, Mark shook his head. At least the half-moon wasn't bright enough to reveal his blush. Somewhere close, the sea hissed against the shoreline.

"Me, neither." Zander's laugh turned into a cough. "Jeez, this local weed is strong." Blowing a smoke ring, he studied Mark through the fragrant cloud. "You're the kid staying at Dev's, aren't you? What's the deal again?"

Mark tried to answer without inhaling. "We're classmates."

Zander laughed until tears ran down his cheeks. "Yeah," he gasped, "that still cracks me up…. Hold this for a sec, will you?" Handing over the joint, he wiped his eyes on the tail of his black shirt, then took it back. "I thought the novelty would have worn off by now and he'd be back where he belongs."

In his excitement, Mark forgot his shyness. "I *knew* that was why you're here!"

"Right on the money," said Zander. "You want some of this?" He held out the joint. Mark wavered, delighted to be asked and reluctant to offend. Having a cop as a dad gave him a healthy respect for consequences. As he hesitated, Zander peered at him through bleary eyes. "Oh, no, you're a kid. Forget I said that." He took a long drag, held it in his lungs. "So you and Dev are friends, huh?"

"I like to think so," Mark said awkwardly. "I play bass and acoustic, too, and Devin's kinda my mentor."

"Yeah?" Exhaling, Zander looked at him with real interest. "You must be good then. Dev's got a great track record of picking talent. In fact, the guy

I replaced him with was once his protégé. I'd hoped it would make my little brother jealous but…" Frowning, he tapped the ash off the end of his joint.

"So…you did ask him back?" Mark ventured timidly.

Zander slugged some Scotch before answering. "Didn't I say that? But on my terms. Devin seems to have forgotten who runs the show. No one has loyalty anymore, kid." He held out his tumbler for a refill. "Exactly how old are you, anyway? You look about twelve."

Mark tried not to look insulted as he refilled Zander's glass. "Seventeen."

"Older than Dev when we started." Zander stared into his drink, silent for a moment. "I used to have to protect him, you know. He's forgotten that."

"No, I haven't." Devin climbed the two steps that separated the paved terrace from the garden. How long had he been there? "Which is why it hurts so much that you've been screwing me over. And you shouldn't be smoking pot in front of a teenager."

"It's fine. I mean, he didn't offer me any," Mark lied. No, that sounded as if Zander was a tightwad. "Not like I'd ever accept." He turned back to Zander. "I'm not trying to sound judgmental or anything," he finished miserably.

The older man laughed. "I like you, kid. You ever need a start in the music business, you come to me.

I'll find something for you. Now scram while I talk sense into my little brother."

Mark left, grinning from ear to ear.

*God,* thought Devin tiredly, *what I'd give for that naïveté again, that faith.* He frowned at his brother. "You're damn lucky Matthew and Mom have left. The guy's an ex-cop."

"I might be reckless, but I'm not stupid." Zander gestured after Mark. "You were like that kid, wet behind the ears…trying to be cool but so not. Jeez, I must've been crazy to let you into the band."

"You were only twenty yourself," said Devin, responding to the ache of nostalgia in his brother's voice. "No more equipped to deal with what happened to us than I was."

"That's where you're wrong." Zander grinned with his old bravado. "I was born to be famous. Yeah. It's all I ever wanted. And I knew how to brand before the cowboys." Flinging back his head, he drained the liquor, then hurled the tumbler into the dark, where they heard it shatter against the rock wall. "Shame your alcoholism screwed everything up for us."

"Drunk, stoned and talking shit as usual." Devin took the joint from Zander's nerveless fingers and ground it out under the heel of his boot. "You might have started by taking care of me, but the reins changed hands a long time ago and you know it. The only way my drinking affected the band was when

I couldn't be your buffer anymore, smooth things over with all the people you alienated. That's the real reason you want me back. That and to bribe your way out of a lawsuit."

As usual his brother tuned out what he didn't want to hear. "And to add insult to injury you're turning on me with this legal crap." Patting his breast pocket, Zander produced another joint and a lighter. He lit it and the tip glowed red as he sucked on it angrily. "I made you and I made the band. Without me you'd all be nothing."

Devin leaned against the handrail and folded his arms. "Yeah, so what's happened since we all left, Zander? If you're so pivotal, then why are you having to work so damn hard to sell Rage with new band members? But you made me believe that for a lot of years, the bullshit you spun. Like we'd be laughed out of the studios if they thought a sixteen-year-old had cowritten our songs."

Zander waved a hand. "It was the only way I could force the record label to sit up and take notice. And dammit, you *agreed* I should take sole writing credit to help us get ahead—"

"I was a kid, Zander."

"*And* I've been slipping you royalties on those songs for years."

"But as it turns out," said Devin softly, "not anywhere near my share."

Zander turned away, searching for his glass, obviously forgetting he'd smashed it. "You wanted to be famous, you wanted to go where only I could take you," he said irritably. Giving up on the glass, he took another toke. "Maybe legally you have a case, but morally I deserve the lion's share of royalties. That's why you've never challenged me before."

"I never challenged you before because all I cared about was the next drink. Even sober it took a long time to believe you'd screw me over. Dammit, I trusted you." Anguish threaded his voice. "You were my big brother."

"I'm still your big brother," Zander insisted. "I needed the money, Dev, or I'd never have cut back your payments." He proffered the joint. Devin accepted it to slow Zander down. "This comeback tour is costing me a frickin' fortune."

"Is that why you're considering letting our two biggest hits be used as soundtracks for commercials?"

His brother glanced over sharply. "Dimity told me," said Devin. "'Sweet Stuff' and 'Summer Daze' will flog luxury cars and—wait, let's savor the irony—vodka."

"They're my songs to do what I like with."

"No, Zander, they're *our* songs. And I want my name on them as cowriter so I can stop you destroying all we have left—our legacy. I can't trust you anymore as a custodian."

"And if I refuse?"

*Sorry, Mom.* "Then I'll sue you and you'll lose the deal, anyway. No one's going to touch songs in dispute. And I'll win, Zander, you know I will. I have original music scores, notes about suggested changes."

"Dev," his brother's voice grew petulant, "if you do that then I can't pay back what I owe you."

Devin looked down at the joint in his hand. He wanted to stub it out, but that would only prompt Zander to light up another. The habit of looking out for his older brother would probably never die. "I'll let you off the back payments if you commit to visiting Mom once a year. She misses you...I miss you." *I've missed you for ten years or more.*

"Then why the hell are you trying to ruin me?"

"This isn't about you...or me. Some of our songs are anthems—" he remembered what Rachel had called them "—the soundtrack of people's lives. You want to be proud of something, then be proud of that. You can have Rage, you can promote the illusion that our band was all about you, but you're not prostituting our musical legacy. I'll fight for that, Zander. And I'll fight for your sake as much as mine."

Devin thought he saw a flash of comprehension, then his brother shook his head. "Still a frickin' dreamer." He took the joint from Devin. "Come back," he said quietly, and Devin knew he understood all too well.

"The magic's gone, Zand. We're done." He laid a hand on his brother's shoulder. "Move on."

"I can't." Zander looked out to the black horizon, the joint forgotten in his hand. "You're right, in the end it's not about the money. What would my life be if I never heard the roar of a full stadium screaming for me? Never again felt that loved? Some addictions can't be cured."

This was the first evidence of self-awareness Devin had ever seen. Even Peter Pan, it seemed, eventually had to acknowledge a world beyond Neverland. He tightened his grip on his brother's shoulder.

Zander straightened, moved away. "I'll get my lawyers onto it, but it's my idea. Hell, I need the publicity if this tour's ever going to get off the ground."

"And Mom?"

"You weren't the only reason I came home."

"Good."

Zander handed him the joint. "Now if you excuse me, my public awaits."

Devin could see him take on the rock star's mantle as he walked away, the shoulders back, the swagger coming into his stride. The rocker grin, the lovable rogue…the self-destructive ego.

He became aware of moisture on his cheeks; it must have started drizzling. But lifting his face, he saw the sky was still clear, brilliant with stars.

AT ELEVEN, Rachel tracked Mark to the lounge, an ostentatious space characterized by strong angles, vaulted ceilings and tubular-chrome-framed black couches, artfully placed on a pale marble floor that echoed with conversations.

He was sitting on the curved steps leading to the private quarters, eavesdropping on a couple of musicians. To her intense relief, Devin was nowhere in sight. "The cab driver's here," she said. "Ready to leave?"

He stood. "Let me go get Dev."

Rachel laid a hand on his arm. "I'm sure he and Zander have a lot to finalize…and they can't really talk with us around, can they?" As the only person at the party who didn't want to spend time with Devin, she'd found it easy to evade him. And on the couple of occasions he'd run her to ground, she'd avoided a tête-à-tête by staying close to Mark or Katherine and her fiancé.

She might have accepted that Devin was rejoining Rage—the only topic of conversation for most of the partygoers—but Rachel wanted to perfect her happy face before he told her. From the reaction of the photographer on their arrival, that was going to take a lot more practice. And she couldn't bear to give Devin even a hint of how much his impending departure hurt.

"Then I'll just go tell him we're leaving," said Mark.

Rachel's grip tightened on his sleeve. "It's okay, I told Dimity to…" Her voice trailed off; she stepped closer and took another sniff, then recoiled. That smell. Acrid and unmistakable. "You've been smoking marijuana."

"Shhh! Keep your voice down." Mark pulled her up the stairs and into the corridor. "I haven't."

If anything, the smaller space only intensified the odor. The music faded away, the sound of conversation. Rachel's gaze telescoped to Mark's face, taking in each rapid blink, the guilty sideways shift of his eyes. "Who gave it to you?"

Instinctively, he glanced down the corridor toward the back of the house. "Rachel, you're wrong—"

"Never mind." Stalking down the hall, she wasn't surprised to meet Zander coming the other way, a bottle of Scotch in his hand. "If it isn't Ms. Robinson."

He reeked of it. Rachel slammed him against the wall. "Did you give Mark a joint?"

Zander gaped at her in surprise, then flung back his head and laughed. And just like that, seventeen years of repressed maternal instincts were released in a tidal wave of anger. She lifted her fist.

Mark grabbed it. "Rachel, no."

She'd spent the evening feeling sorry for herself when she should have been looking out for her son.

Zander read her expression and sobered. Augmenting Mark's grip on her fist with his own, he held up his free hand to placate her. "I don't offer drugs to children." He gestured outside, beyond the French doors. "Ask Dev. He was with us."

"No," she said automatically. "He wouldn't..." She turned in time to see Devin drop a joint on the stone patio and grind it under his boot. Inarticulate with shock, Rachel put a hand out to the wall to steady herself.

*Why wouldn't he?* Because falling in love with him had blinded her to his flaws.

Zander shook his head. "Let me guess... You think you're the woman to change him?"

Rachel pushed off the wall and he stepped behind her son. "C'mon, Mark, the grown-ups need to fight." Half staggering, he steered the teenager back toward the party.

Devin was looking at the sky. He glanced her way when Rachel opened the French doors. "This is a nice surprise." He sounded happy again. Not hard to figure out why. The son of a bitch hadn't just pulled the wool over her eyes; he'd trussed her up on a spit and slow-roasted her over a burning fire.

"You smoked dope with Mark." Her voice trembled with fury.

"Whoa, there." He held up a hand. "Zander smoked. Mark and I were bystanders."

She gestured to the stubbed joint at his feet, still

releasing a coil of telltale smoke. "So, you were just *holding* it for your brother?"

Devin's mouth twitched. "Actually, yes."

His amusement only added fuel to her anger. "You really think I'm that gullible." Like she didn't already know the answer to that.

His grin faded. "Heartbreaker, you know me better than that."

"Do I?" Or had she let herself be beguiled into seeing what was never there?

"Yes. You *do*." An edge came into his voice. "I was cleaning up after Zander. Mark didn't want any, and even if he had, neither of us would have given it to him." His voice low and persuasive, Devin came closer. So did the smell of weed.

"Even if Mark didn't smoke, how can you act like it's okay when the stuff's illegal? What kind of message is that sending him?"

"If he's going to have a career in the music industry, the sooner he learns how to resist temptation the better. But he does know."

But not from her, not from his mother. And tonight she hadn't protected him. Guilt lacerated her. Teenagers, even sensible ones, made errors of judgment...who understood that better than Rachel? And yet she'd let her feelings for Devin cloud her own judgment. Even when Zander's arrival rang warning bells she hadn't taken Mark home. When she should have been looking out for her son's interests, she'd put romance first.

"This isn't his world. He shouldn't be here," she exclaimed.

"Are we still talking about Mark...or you?"

"Both." All her anguish, all her self-disgust, went into the next words. "You're a bad influence."

His face lost all expression. "Because I don't hide my past like you do? At least I don't keep secrets from people I care about."

"So Zander didn't ask you to rejoin the band?"

"He did, but I'm not going anywhere, Rachel."

She tamped down her relief. "It's no longer important." It was time she got her priorities straight. "After what just happened with Mark, *you're* no longer important."

She saw him take the hit, his shock, the closure. Like a door slamming on an opportunity she'd never had, merely imagined. "So it *was* always about Mark."

She didn't answer. Everything came back to her son. It always had. And she'd made the mistake of forgetting that for a while. Well, no longer.

Moving toward the house, he paused beside her. She'd never seen such cold contempt. "The last ferry back to Auckland leaves at midnight," he said. "Take it."

RACHEL COLLAPSED into a nearby deck chair. Slowly, the noise of the party returned, faint laughter, the underlying bass beat of the music—like the harsh throb of a migraine.

If only she'd trusted her first impression. Instead, she'd let herself be seduced by Devin's charm, disarmed by his honesty. She buried her face in her hands. How could she have been so naive?

She'd been dazzled by his sex appeal and— Rachel squirmed—by his interest in her. And this time she didn't have youth as an excuse. She was pathetic. But she was through being pathetic. She'd tell Mark the truth as soon as they had privacy…tell him and accept the consequences.

*If Devin doesn't tell him first.*

The thought propelled her to her feet. Oh, God, he was angry enough to. Rachel ran.

Back in the lounge, the music had been cranked up and the lights dimmed for dancing. Rock, loud and discordant, jangled her shattered nerves. Through the shadowy gyrating forms she could see Tim at the door. She'd forgotten all about the taxi driver.

Holding up her fingers, she mouthed, *"Five minutes."*

The cabbie jerked his head in consent. But where was Mark?

Hurrying out to the pool, Rachel scanned the surrounding gardens. Party debris was everywhere, some of it human. Shrieking with laughter, two young women frolicked in the pool, expensive gowns ballooning around their legs.

A hand slid down her bare back. "You look hot when you're mad," said Zander in her ear, his breath sour with whiskey. He fingered the halter bow of her dress. "One tweak and this unties, right?"

Skin crawling, Rachel stepped away. At least Mark was no longer with him. "You don't care who you hurt, do you?"

"Devin can take care of himself. In fact, he's about to do that right now in the spa with a few women. That frees you and me to play."

From the other side of the swimming pool, Stormy watched them, her beautiful face miserable. "And what about your girlfriend?"

"Stormy knows there's plenty to go around." Lazily, Zander ran a thumb down Rachel's cleavage. "So what do you say, you open to sharing the love?"

She shoved him into the pool and headed for the spa.

"COME ON IN, Devin, the water's steaming."

Ignoring the women in the hot tub to his right, Devin stood on the deck overlooking the ocean, letting the wind cool his temper. As soon as the proverbial hit the fan, Rachel had defaulted to what she really believed. That he was irredeemable, an evil influence.

"Yoo-hoo, Devvvin."

What hurt most was that she didn't trust him with Mark—the kid he'd helped her bond with, the kid he'd kept her secret from—against his better judgment.

She'd exploited his feelings in order to access her son, and later to manipulate him into keeping his mouth shut. Devin felt used, disgusted. And bitter.

"Devin, are you listening? We want to make room for you."

Turning his head, he saw Dimity lounging in the spa with a couple of other women—he recognized Zander's stylist and dietitian—sharing a bottle of Moet.

They were up to their necks in bubbles, inside as well as out. This was the third time his brother's P.A. had hit on Devin tonight. He was about to shut her down once and for all when Rachel spoke behind him.

"Where's Mark?"

Devin pivoted. "I told you to go."

"No more girls," Dimity called petulantly from the spa. "We want Devin to ourselves."

"Not without Mark." Rachel's anxiety gave her away.

Devin leaned back against the railing. "Worried I'll tell him?"

"Tell me what?"

Rachel froze, her expression stricken as she held Devin's gaze. Another painful reminder that she'd never trusted him.

"Dev?" It was natural for Mark to turn to him first. Guilt twisted in Devin's gut. He was supposed to be the boy's mentor, his friend, and he'd put a stupid infatuation before that.

Mark stood by the side of the house, exposed to the northerly wind, his borrowed shirt whipping behind his skinny body like a superhero's cape. His fair hair tangled over his eyes, and he swept it back as he looked past Devin to Rachel.

"What's going on?"

"Nothing," Rachel said hoarsely.

Devin laughed. Behind him, Rachel murmured, "Please."

The three women in the hot tub were whispering among themselves. "*You* can come in, Devin's friend," called the dietitian, a skinny blonde. "But only if you bring Devin with you."

A wet, black bikini top landed with a plop at Mark's feet. He blushed fiery red, visible even under the outdoor lights. It brought Devin to his senses. However much he despised Rachel right now, he couldn't tell Mark here.

"We broke up," he said. "Do me a favor, buddy. Take her back to Auckland."

Color crept back into her pale face. *"Thank you,"* she mouthed. Turning away, she hesitated. "I have to clear one thing up. It wasn't just about…what you thought it was."

He'd thought it was about love. Devin started unbuttoning his shirt. "Yeah, well, like *you* said. No longer important." One benefit of living in the public eye was the ability to pretend you didn't give a damn. "Make room for me, ladies."

He kicked off his boots, then unbuckled his belt. Rachel looked from him to the spa, then back again. She seemed unable to move.

Unzipping his jeans, Devin dropped his pants, to whistles of appreciation from the spa, and stood in black briefs. "So, was there anything else?" he inquired impatiently.

"Yes." Her voice was a whisper. "You don't fool me." Leaving him feeling like an idiot, she turned and walked away. When she reached Mark, he put his arm around her shoulder as he glared back at Devin. *Tough.* The kid would get over it. They disappeared from sight.

A gust of wind made Devin shiver even though it wasn't cold. Briefly, he closed his eyes, then picked up his clothes and began dressing, his movements tight, economical, verging on vicious.

Heartbreaker. He'd thrown down the challenge and it had come back to haunt him with a vengeance.

"Wait a minute!" Dimity stood up in the spa, her skin as red as an overcooked lobster, her blond hair dripping. "Aren't you joining us?"

He shook his head. "Sorry, girls. Party's over."

# CHAPTER SEVENTEEN

MARK SPENT MOST OF THE taxi ride back to Devin's to pick up their bags, then to the wharf, racking his brain for something to say to make things better.

"I'll buy the tickets," he said when they got to the terminal. "You sit down."

"Will you quit worrying? I'm fine." But there was a terrible emptiness behind Rachel's "reassuring" smile. As he waited while she made the purchase, Mark decided he'd lost some respect for Devin. Stripping down for the spa was cruel when he and Rachel had just split up. It was almost like he was trying to punish her.

When she handed Mark his ticket and led the way to the ferry, brightly lit at the end of the wooden dock, Mark overrode her protests and carried her weekend bag. Someone had to look after her.

"This is my fault, isn't it?" he ventured. "The breakup." Rachel stumbled over the ridged gangplank and he caught her by the elbow to steady her.

"What makes you say that?"

"You blame Devin for letting Zander smoke dope in front of me. But what could Dev do, Rachel, wrestle it away from him?"

The wind shook the electric lanterns hanging on the rail, and light wavered on her set face. "He could have sent you away."

Mark winced. He was not a child. "Well, mostly Devin *trusted* me. I don't think it was a coincidence that he showed up when he did." Over the past five weeks they'd had frank talks about drugs and alcohol. Tonight had only confirmed that being stoned wasn't a good look—even on someone as cool as Zander.

The interior cabin was nearly deserted. Mark recognized a few partygoers. By their shrieks of laughter, they were still partying.

Rachel backed up. "Mind if we sit outside? I know it's windy but I need fresh air."

She did look pale. "Sure." They settled on a sheltered bench at the stern. The ferry chugged away from the dock; in silence they watched Waiheke's smatter of lights recede into the distance. Mark's thoughts turned to Auckland…and Trixie. First thing tomorrow he'd shake the information out of her if he had to. He shifted restlessly on the hard bench.

"Really, our breakup isn't your fault," stressed Rachel, misinterpreting his agitation.

Bracing against the bulkhead to counter the increasing swell as they hit open water, he searched for something to cheer her up. *Zander said he'd give me a job when I want one.* Nope, the guy wasn't exactly top of Rachel's hit parade. Someone at the party had even said she'd shoved him into the pool, but Mark figured that was another rumor, like Devin rejoining the—

He brightened. "Devin's not leaving, you know. You could get back together." But even as he offered the crumb, Mark wondered. There had been something ruthless about their parting, something final.

"It's over." Rachel's flat tone confirmed his suspicions. She mustered another "dead woman walking" smile.

Mark pretended to buy the smile. "You're still young…ish. What, twenty-nine, thirty?" Sheesh, that sounded old. Maybe he shouldn't have mentioned age. But to his intense relief, Rachel smiled—a real one this time.

"Actually, Mark, I'm thirty-five in another month."

He whistled. "Man, you don't look anywhere near that," he said honestly. "I mean, that's old enough to be my mother."

She was still smiling, but her expression seemed to freeze over.

Mark recoiled.

Staring down at her feet, she didn't notice.

"Listen," she began awkwardly, "there's something I need to tell you about me."

He sucked in a great lungful of air. "You're my birth mother."

Rachel lifted her gaze to his. "Yes."

Mark felt like he'd been shot. Soon it was going to hurt, but right now the shock protected him. *Rachel*…his mother?

Her cold hand covered his. "I'm sorry I didn't tell you earlier."

He looked down. Even her hands were young. Then what she'd said registered. "Wait a minute…you *knew* I was looking for you?"

"Only for a week."

"A week…" Bewildered, he stared at her then jerked away, tucking his hands under his armpits. "And you didn't tell me?" A week ago he'd gone to her house with… "Does Devin know it's you?"

"Yes." She added quickly, "But the decision not to tell you straightaway was mine. He argued against it."

Trixie had called Rachel tonight, not to ask for advice but to warn her. Everyone had betrayed him. Everyone had taken *her* side.

Rachel was still talking. "You see, I wanted you to get to know me properly before I told you, so that you'd be more open to listening to—"

"Excuses!" Shooting up from the bench, he stumbled on the lurching deck.

"No excuses." Her gaze held his, raw with regret. "I should have told you earlier."

He hated her looking at him like she cared, when she couldn't have—not and kept the secret. The engines slowed to a throb as the ferry edged against the Auckland pier. Mark regained his balance. "Can you even *imagine* what it's like to discover everything you believed about yourself is a lie?" He spat the accusation at her. "Can you?"

"No, and I'm deeply sorry." Her hands twisted together in her lap. "But please know that I had no choice but to give you up."

"Why?" Maybe understanding would somehow help. "Wouldn't your parents let you keep me?"

Momentarily, her gaze dropped. "It's…complicated."

*Complicated.* Trixie had used that word. "Screw you. I don't want to listen to anything you have to say." Picking up his bag, he stormed back inside, letting the wind slam the door behind him.

Another bang told him Rachel had followed, so he headed for the gangway, toward the people milling on the lower deck, waiting to disembark.

"Mark, please." Rachel clattered down the stairs behind him. "Let me tell you the circumstances." She became aware of the curious stares and dropped her voice. "Come back to my place."

"It doesn't matter." He didn't give a damn who

was listening. Let everybody know what she was like. "You were my age when you gave me up. If it happened to me, if I got a girl pregnant, I'd stay in that kid's life no matter what."

"Steady, mate," advised the purser, who was standing near the exit. "Calm down, eh?"

They both ignored him.

"At seventeen, you see your choices as black-and-white, right and wrong," said Rachel. "I did, too. And I thought if you didn't know you were adopted—if I broke all ties—it would be easier for both of us to get on with our lives. I was wrong, Mark."

"You think?"

The gangplank rumbled down; in relief the dozen passengers debarked, heads down in embarrassment. A couple sent back curious glances.

Mark went to follow, but Rachel barred his way. "Your parents tried to talk me out of it—until I made it a condition of the adoption. I'm just sorry that they kept their word, though it shouldn't surprise me. They're good people."

"Better than you," he said, wanting to hurt her. But she only nodded.

"That's why I chose them."

She wasn't even going to fight.

He shoved all the contempt he could into his next words. "I don't want you in my life."

Rachel seemed to shrink. "That's your choice."

Even her voice was small as she stepped aside to let him pass.

"Yes," Mark said savagely. "It is." Buoyed by righteous anger, he marched down the gangway, then turned. "How does it feel being the one rejected for a change?"

IT FELT LIKE HELL.

Except Mark was wrong. Rachel had plenty of practice at being rejected.

All the color leached out of her life. For the first time in her life she was rudderless and bereft of the capable, cheerful identity she'd built block by painful block from the age of seventeen.

Worried that Mark would quit university if she remained on campus, Rachel rang her boss first thing Sunday morning. She told him everything so he'd accept an immediate resignation. He refused to accept it and insisted she take a week's leave to think things over. Rachel didn't have the energy to argue, but knew she'd never go back. It was too hard.

And thinking things over—every scathing, scalding denouncement—was killing her.

Even hating her, Devin hadn't told Mark. How could she ever have doubted him? She'd worried that love blinded her to his faults. Instead she should have worried about how love triggered her own deep-seated insecurities.

The truth was, she'd launched into a blind attack the first excuse she got. Because she'd wanted to shut Devin down before she got hurt. It was ironic that the one time he'd tried to deceive her—stripping for the spa with Dimity—Rachel had seen right through him. He was a good man, struggling to make a new life for himself, and she'd used his imperfect past against him.

Hurt him. And hurt her son.

For the first time in five years, Rachel canceled her Sunday lunch for students. Bowed by a grief so bone-deep she couldn't cry, she spent the day hunched up in an armchair, or lying in bed staring at the ceiling.

When she'd been a scared teenager living in an Auckland youth hostel, ostracized by her parents and community, the conviction that she'd done the right thing—no matter the personal cost—had saved her. More than that, it had fueled her drive to sit up half the night studying for her library degree while working two dead-end jobs.

With that belief shaken, Rachel felt as if someone had let the air out of her.

The phone rang incessantly with voice messages from Trixie, but she didn't pick up. She had no expectation of hearing from Mark or Devin. Not only had her past lost its meaning, her future had become meaningless, too.

On Sunday night a stormy sou'wester rattled the windows and hammered on the corrugated iron roof of her cottage. Rain stripped the petals off the roses and littered the path with twigs and leaves. The world became the damp, gray chill of her childhood and adolescence, reduced to the clock ticking, light and dark, snatches of restless sleep. Blankness finally settled over her, and even that small inner voice shut up.

When she first heard the banging on the front door at six o'clock Monday night she thought the wind had shaken something loose. It persisted. Despite everything, hope propelled her out of her armchair and into the hall. But when Rachel opened the door it was Trixie standing outside, like a bed-raggled black cat. "About bloody time!"

Though her immediate impulse was to shut the door, the maternal part of Rachel wouldn't let her. "How can you go anywhere in this weather without an umbrella? Come in. I'll get you a towel." She headed toward the bathroom.

Squeezing water from her long black hair, Trixie followed. "Why haven't you answered my calls?" Her abrasive tone grated Rachel's nerves. "I've been worried sick about you, particularly after Mark's rant."

She'd forgotten that Trixie knew. In the midst of handing over a towel, Rachel paused. "Is he okay?"

"If foaming at the mouth is okay." Trixie dried

her face, her voice muffled through the towel. "He was furious with me for not telling him as soon as I found out you were his mother."

"I'm sorry." The fallout of this just went on and on, and her feeble apologies felt as useful as a Band-Aid on a severed jugular. "You two were good friends."

Emerging from the towel, Trixie said gruffly, "Why didn't *you* tell him as soon as you knew?'

"Because I'm an idiot…. Did Mark mention whether he got my message?" She didn't tell Trixie what it was. If she knew Rachel had resigned her job she'd be here arguing all night. And already Rachel was restless to be alone again.

"He didn't say," said Trixie. "He feels like you really did a number on him." There was accusation in her tone.

Rachel said nothing.

"I still can't get my head around the fact that Mark's your son or that you had a baby when you were seventeen and adopted it out. I mean, you love kids so much, I don't understand how you could have brought yourself to do it."

Again she waited for an explanation; again Rachel remained silent.

"Now if it was me, I'd understand it," Trixie continued blithely, "because I'm the hard-nosed one."

Something inside Rachel snapped. "You're a child playing at dress up. If you ever came up against real hardship you'd fold like a pack of—" She stopped, controlled her breathing. What was the use? Leading the way to the front door, she opened it. "Please go. I don't want to hurt you, too."

But Trixie stood her ground. "I'm sorry, I had no idea…. I speak without engaging my brain sometimes."

"Was Mark at university today?"

"No. Yesterday he talked about going home for a few days to spend time with his par…" Her voice trailed off.

"I'm glad," said Rachel. There was a chill to the wind blowing through the open door. She hugged herself. "At times like this, you need your family."

"What about you? Your family?"

"I'm not important. Mark is."

"Oh, Rach." Trixie stepped forward and wrapped her arms around her.

"I'm okay." Out of courtesy, Rachel waited a few seconds before she tried to free herself. Trixie only tightened her hold.

"He said you and Devin broke up, too."

"I'm okay," she insisted again, but they both knew that was a lie.

Trixie started to cry. "You're giving up, I can tell."

"No, I'm not." Giving up implied you had something *to* give up. And both Mark and Devin had made it clear she had nothing left to fight for.

Rachel's mother lived in an affluent part of Hamilton, a midsize city bisected by the Waikato River. Her house reminded Mark of his grandparents' home—his *adoptive* grandparents' home—in Cambridge.

At least fifty years old, it was brick and tile, with immaculate paintwork and ornate flowerbeds full of old people's plants—purple hydrangeas; pink and white roses, standard or climbing over freestanding arbors. Even the trees had to be flowering varieties—magnolias and camellias.

Okay, he was procrastinating again. Mark didn't give a damn about the garden. Slowly, he walked up the path to the front door and paused with his finger hovering over the bell. He'd thought telling Rachel to go to hell would be the end of it. But he still had a burning need for answers.

*It's complicated,* she'd said. What did that mean? Mark wished he'd hung around to find out, except how could he trust anything Rachel said, anyway? Last night—Sunday night, after he'd blasted Trixie—he'd got on the Internet and sourced everything he could about his birth mother. Which wasn't much. Most online references were about Rachel's dad, who'd been some big shot in Hamilton City Council before he died.

Steeling his resolve, Mark pushed the doorbell. A chime rang in the house and set his heart pounding. The idea of approaching Rachel's mother had come to him in the middle of a sleepless night. At seven this morning he'd rung her before he could chicken out. Maureen Robinson had cried when he told her who he was. Yes, she'd tell him everything he wanted to know.

So Mark had caught the afternoon bus to Hamilton, an hour and a half south, with the idea of taking another one the extra forty minutes home to Cambridge after he'd talked to Maureen. At least now he knew his parents weren't the bad guys in this.

The door opened; a plump elderly woman in a mauve housedress stared at him. She lifted her hand to her mouth.

"Hi," he said awkwardly. "I'm Mark."

"Oh, my dear." Dark eyes glistening with tears, she flung her arms around his waist. Tentatively, Mark returned her hug. She was way older then he expected, and her granny perm barely came up to his armpit.

"I wasn't going to do that…embarrass you." She released him, but brushed a hand quickly across his cheek. "Come in, Mark, come in. I have sausage rolls in the oven—I knew you'd be hungry. And a plate of queen cakes…." She bustled ahead of him. Mark had to lengthen his stride to keep up.

"Um, thanks for seeing me. It must be a shock."

She paused and looked over her shoulder. "I

prayed for this day…. Now, what would you like to drink? Tea, coffee…juice?" With one hand she opened a cupboard door, revealing cups and glasses; with the other she opened the oven. She reminded Mark of the quails at home, small and pear-shaped. Like her, they flurried.

"Juice, please. You didn't need to go to so much trouble."

Maureen reached for a glass. "You're my grandson." Pulling a tissue from a box on the bench, she dabbed at her eyes. "Ignore me, I'm…" Without finishing the sentence she waved the tissue helplessly.

"Yeah," he said, a lump in his throat.

Mark waited until she'd finished serving the food—enough for a small army—before he spoke again. "I guess I'm here to find out a couple of things, but the main one is how I came to be adopted."

"And Rachel wouldn't tell you." It was a statement, not a question. Maureen poured the juice and set it in front of him.

"She said it was complicated."

Compressing her lips, Maureen pulled out a chair and sat. "No, Mark, it was very simple. We wanted her to keep the baby, but she wouldn't consider it." His grandmother seemed to become aware of who she was talking to, and dropped her gaze in confusion. "I should have softened that—I'm sorry. This is taking awhile to sink in."

Mark managed a smile. "It's okay." *Please know that I had no choice but to give you up.* So Rachel had lied to him. Only now did he realize he'd had hope that this could still turn out all right. His cell rang, a welcome distraction. "Excuse me." Taking it out of his jacket, Mark frowned as he saw the caller ID.

Devin again. Switching it off, he put the phone back in his pocket. "No one important." That betrayal hurt the most. Devin had been his friend, the only one who guessed how much finding his birth mother had meant to him. And he'd chosen Rachel.

Mark looked back at the woman who was his grandmother. After the enthusiasm of her phone call, he'd expected to feel some kind of connection, warmth. Instead he felt more alone than ever. "You were talking about Rachel."

"She was always so compliant as a child, so good." A fleeting smile lifted the downturned corners of Maureen's mouth. "And then in her teens… well…you hear how kids change overnight, but until it happened to us… We didn't even know she'd been sneaking out at night, so her pregnancy came as a shock. It hit my husband, Gerard, particularly hard. Your grandfather was a man of some standing in the community." Her voice grew stronger. "But we never wavered, not once, in our decision to support Rachel even though the circumstances…"

Her gaze darted to Mark and shied away. She began to fidget with her wedding ring, deeply embedded in one fleshy finger. "But Rachel was determined to give you up right from the start. She was almost hysterical about it… I begged her to reconsider, and her father absolutely forbade the adoption, but she told such lies to the social worker…such lies."

Maureen's hand crept to the gold crucifix around her neck. "I still struggle to forgive her for that. You're sweating, Mark—it's probably too hot in here with the oven." She bustled to the window above the sink and opened it. Mark felt the breeze but it did nothing to cool him down.

"Anyway, you're here now. And that's all that matters. Eat up." Returning to the table, Maureen pushed the towering plates of sausage rolls and dainty cakes toward him. "I only wish your grandfather were alive to meet you. He was a wonderful man, Mark. Let me show you some pictures."

She left the room, and Mark stared at the food. A fly buzzed over the cakes, but they were still too hot to land on. The thought of eating anything made him nauseous, but he didn't want to hurt Maureen's feelings, so he hid a few in his rucksack.

His grandmother came back, hugging half a

dozen photo albums to her ample bosom. "Here we are." Mechanically, he flicked through the ones featuring his grandfather, pretending to be impressed by the faded articles Maureen had clipped from the paper over the years. His mind buzzed as fruitlessly as the fly while he tried to process what he'd heard into something other than rejection by his birth mother. With every word out of Maureen's mouth he'd felt himself diminish. Until he felt transparent. It was the strangest sensation.

Rachel had wanted to get rid of him. Except judging by the holy pictures framed in the hall and the cross around her mother's neck, he guessed her parents would never have permitted an abortion. He should consider that lucky, but right now Mark wished he'd never been born, rather than having been so unwanted.

None of the behavior Maureen was describing sounded like the Rachel he knew; but then Mark was still having trouble believing she was his mother. And she'd waited a week to tell him…and lied about having to give him up.

With difficulty, he tuned in to Maureen's prattle. "She didn't even come to her father's funeral, doesn't visit, and all I have are conscience calls…once a week."

Unable to bear any more, Mark stood. "I have to go, catch my bus back."

Maureen closed the albums. "But you'll come again?'

"I'm not sure." *No. Never.* At the door he asked his final question. "Do you know anything about my father?"

"It pains me to tell you this, Mark, but he and his parents washed their hands of responsibility when Gerard refused to discuss an abortion." She crossed herself.

When he'd finally got away Mark walked to the park across the road and stumbled down the path to the river. Had his parents known his history when they'd adopted him? *Let's take* this *baby, he's the most unwanted.* Mom would think like that, and Dad... Tears blinded Mark. Not wanting to be caught crying, he left the path and tramped through the tangle of bracken and undergrowth to the river's edge. One arm around a willow trunk, he looked at the fast-flowing, olive-brown river.

There was a vacuum inside him and his old life wouldn't fill it.

## CHAPTER EIGHTEEN

DEVIN WASN'T GOING TO quit school and run back to L.A. with his tail between his legs. Much as he wanted to. His old life was about taking the easy way out; his new one was about finishing things he'd started. Even when they were hard.

He just hadn't expected anything to be this hard.

He'd hit enough terrible lows in his life to know he would survive another, but this was a first for love. A broken heart packed its own wallop, and telling himself the librarian wasn't worth this much suffering didn't seem to make a damn bit of difference.

Fortunately, he had good reason to be away for a few days immediately following his breakup with Rachel. Zander might have agreed to play nice, but he'd renege if left to his own devices. Devin refused to let him out of his sight until they'd made their agreement legal.

That meant accompanying him to Sydney, where his brother had commitments. Devin had expected to be back in New Zealand by Tuesday, but quibbles over the fine print kept him in Australia until Wednesday night. Although he accepted the face-saving reprieve with relief, he knew he couldn't put off the real world forever.

And he was increasingly anxious to make contact with Mark. The kid hadn't returned any of his phone calls—hardly surprising given Devin's boorish behavior at the spa. Behavior he'd regretted as soon as his anger subsided.

He'd wanted to hurt Rachel, but Devin hated acting like an asshole to any woman in front of Mark. Let alone the woman he'd soon discover was his birth mother. Still, Devin was surprised when he returned to class on Thursday to learn Mark hadn't been at school this week, either.

His ego—always his strength and weakness— didn't allow him to hesitate as he entered the library. But to his immense relief Trixie told him Rachel had taken a leave of absence. Devin quashed his immediate concern for her well-being. Whether she was or wasn't okay didn't matter anymore. He decided it was probably another way to postpone telling Mark the truth. "So where's the kid?"

Trixie's dark eyebrows drew together in a frown. "You mean you haven't heard from him? He's not returning my messages, either, but I figured he was punishing me. He said he was going home for a few days."

She filled him in on Mark's reaction to Rachel's

confession and his subsequent diatribe to Trixie about "disloyalty."

So that was why Mark wasn't returning his calls. Devin scowled, a look Trixie interpreted correctly, because she said, "He'll get over it. It's not as if Rachel blamed you or me...he just—"

"Feels like he hasn't got a friend in the world." What a goddamn mess.

"Don't say that. Look, let's call him at home right now." Through directory assistance, Trixie got Mark's parents' number in Cambridge, then phoned and asked for him. Her kohl-darkened eyes widened. "Okay," she said, "well, thanks anyway. Yes, I'd appreciate the number."

Devin started to get a bad feeling. "He's not there?" he said when she hung up.

"No, and they didn't even seem to be expecting him because they told me to call him in Auckland. He canceled their visit tomorrow, too. Said he had to study for a test?"

"He's probably holed up in his apartment to study," he reassured her. *There was no test.* "Is that the phone number?" He rang it and got the answering machine, which gave Mark's cousin's cell phone number. She answered from Dubai and told him she hadn't been home for a week. Devin kept his voice casual as he asked, "What's the street address?"

When he hung up, Trixie said anxiously, "You don't think he'd—"

"No Goth overreactions," Devin interrupted, hiding his own increasing uneasiness. "My classes are finished for the day. I'll call in on the way home."

Her forehead creased in a frown. "I wish I could come, but with Rachel away we're already short-staffed."

"I'll give him your love."

That won him a smile. "Don't you dare. But phone me, won't you?" She scribbled down her number.

As soon as he was out of sight, Devin dropped the laconic stroll and whistled for a cab. Fifteen minutes later he was at the modest apartment block, hammering on Mark's ground floor door and telling himself he was every kind of idiot for worrying. No one answered. A neighbor at the next apartment poked her head out her door, pulling it back like a turtle when she caught sight of Devin.

"Ma'am," he called, "can you help me? I'm looking for Mark White. Have you seen him over the past couple days?"

Her head slowly reappeared and she scanned him from top to toe with her rheumy eyes. "Are you a drug dealer or an undercover cop?"

The right answer came instinctively. "A friend of his mother's."

"Hmm." She came out, leaning on a cane. "I don't

normally see him much but I haven't heard him for a few days…he plays the sound system loud when his cousin's not there."

Shading his eyes against the daylight, Devin peered through a chink in the curtains, and saw a light on in the lounge. "Is there any way of getting in here short of breaking the door down?"

"I have a key. Suzy, his cousin, gets me to water the plants when she's away. Mark has good intentions but he's liable to forget."

Five minutes later, when she turned the key in the lock, he stopped her from reaching for the handle. "Let me go in first."

"You're expecting something bad, son?"

"I hope not." Devin opened the door and stepped inside.

The place smelled shut up. Flies buzzed on the remains of cereal in an empty bowl. The milk had gone sour. Devin started to sweat. *This isn't the same,* he told himself. *Get a grip.*

When he was twenty, he'd lost his best friend, the band's drummer. Devin had found Jeff sprawled across his bed, the TV blaring, the paraphernalia of heroin beside him. He'd been dead for two days.

Forcing himself to walk, Devin moved from room to room until he'd checked through the whole apartment. Empty. His relief was so great he had to sit down. But it was short-lived. Where the hell was Mark?

"YOU DIDN'T PHONE on Sunday." There was accusation in her mother's voice.

She immediately felt guilty, even though there'd been nothing to stop Maureen ringing her. "I'm calling now," she said.

"Four days later."

"Mom, please…" Rachel massaged her temple. Why had she thought she might find comfort here? "This is obviously a bad time. I'll phone again when—"

"He came to see me." There was a strange satisfaction in her mother's voice.

Rachel tried to remember what they'd been talking about last week, but the world had spun on its axis too many times since then. "I'm sorry, I don't recall—"

"Your boy…Mark."

Rachel's grip tightened on the phone. "No."

"He wanted to know why he was adopted."

She went rigid. "Mom, what did you tell him?"

"The truth, of course. That your father and I wanted to keep him, but that you rejected—"

Rachel cut the connection and punched in Mark's cell phone number with trembling fingers. Trixie had told her he wasn't answering calls, but at least she could leave a message. "Mark, it's Rachel. I know you've been to see my mother. There are two sides to every story. Please call me."

She hung up. Briefly, she considered calling his parents' home, but dismissed the idea. Whether he'd told them about her or not, this was a private matter between her and Mark. And Rachel wouldn't force her way into his life without an invitation. Her son had to have some place of refuge.

Desperate to do something, she sat down at the dining room table and started writing a letter. If she posted it today, he'd get it tomorrow.

She'd only written three lines when the phone rang. Caller ID showed it was her mother. Rachel didn't trust herself to pick up. Even if she could rip through Maureen's fantasy that their life with Gerard Robinson had been normal—and right now she was angry enough to try—it would serve no purpose.

Her mother would never love her, and Rachel would only be stripping an old lady of a defense mechanism that had probably kept her sane.

*"He sets high standards, darling, and gets so disappointed when we don't follow them."*

*"Getting drunk occasionally doesn't make your father an alcoholic. He works hard and needs to vent."*

*"Oh, I always bruise easily. Goodness, I'm so clumsy."*

*And when the injuries were too obvious to
laugh off: "Darling, I'm not feeling well, I'm
staying in bed for a couple of days. You look after
your father."*

*Her father. The town councilor, the church elder,
the treasurer of the Rotary Club, the manager of a
bank…the great bloke. And in public, he always was.*

The answering machine picked up.

"Rachel, I'm disappointed in you, but not surprised," said her mother. "If you'd listened to Gerard
and me none of this would be necessary." She hung
up with a disapproving click.

Almost immediately, the phone rang again, the
library's number. Trixie had promised to ring if she
heard from Mark. Rachel snatched up the phone.
But the news only ratcheted her tension.

"What's the address?"

"Yeah, that's why I phoned…." As soon as the
call ended, Rachel ran to get her car keys. To hell
with a hands-off policy.

The front door of her son's apartment was open.
Without giving herself time for second thoughts she
tapped on it. "Mark?" Stepping inside, Rachel stalled.

Devin was checking through discarded papers on
the dining room table. Instinctively, she took a
couple of steps toward him.

"Trixie said you were coming." He didn't glance

up from what he was doing. "Mark's not here, Rachel. He hasn't been here for a few days."

Pressure tightened like a vise around her lungs, making it difficult to breathe. "Not here...then where?"

"I don't know." He gestured in frustration. "No one does, which is why I'm searching this place for clues."

"He went to see my mother in Hamilton on Monday." She started speaking faster and faster. "She told him that she and Dad didn't want to give him up for adoption. If no one's seen him since then—"

"He came back." Devin picked up the newspaper spread across the dining table in front of him. "This is Tuesday morning's paper. Wednesday's and Thursday's were still on the doormat along with his mail. It looks like some clothes are missing from his closet and there's no sign of his guitar. If he's taken that, he's still okay."

She absorbed the news and tried to think. "Is there anyone else he'd confide in, someone else he'd go to?"

"In Auckland, there was only Trixie and me." His tone held no accusation, no hint of rebuke, though they both knew she was to blame for this. His boots echoed on the linoleum as Devin entered the kitchenette. "I'm hoping he left a note for his cousin somewhere."

The internal vise wound tighter. "Why don't you just tell me it's my fault?"

"Because it won't help find him."

He was right. Rachel got a grip on herself. "Did you check his cousin's bedroom?"

"Only scanned it. Take a closer look while I search in here."

About to head in the direction he indicated, Rachel hesitated. "If I'd listened to you, or at least left you out of it, Mark would have had someone to turn to. I'm...sorry, Devin. For everything. You always had our best interests at heart."

"Apology accepted." Devin's expression was opaque; he'd completely withdrawn from her. Rachel shivered.

She searched Suzy's room but didn't find anything on the dresser or the bedside tables. About to leave, she glimpsed the corner of a white envelope poking out from under one of many pillows and bolsters piled on the double bed.

The envelope was addressed to his parents. A Post-it note attached to it read "Suz, please post this to Mom and Dad. Rent's paid until the 25th. You shouldn't have trouble finding another flatmate. Mark."

She must have made a sound because suddenly Devin was with her. Sitting her on the bed, he took the note from her nerveless fingers and read it. Then without hesitation, he ripped open the envelope and scanned the contents.

Rachel cleared her throat. "What does it say?"

"'Dear Mom and Dad, I guess I should have told you I was looking for my birth mother. Well, I found her.' There are a couple of lines scribbled out hard…he obviously doesn't want anyone deciphering them." Devin held the letter up to the light from the window and she saw that his hand, with its dragon tongue flicking across his knuckles, shook. Maybe it was the same tremor of exhaustion as hers. But Rachel didn't have time to wonder why he hadn't been sleeping. "I can only make out one word." He stopped, a hard question in his eyes as he looked at her. " 'Rejected.' "

"My mother told him I didn't want…" She shook her head, unable to finish. Tears were a luxury she wasn't entitled to.

Something like sympathy flashed in Devin's eyes, then he returned to the letter. " 'I know you're going to be disappointed but I really need some time by myself to figure out…' He's crossed out 'who I am' and replaced it with 'stuff.' " Devin frowned. " 'I will call, I promise, hopefully even before Suz comes back from Dubai and you get this letter. Don't worry, I have a job lined up already. Love, Mark.' His cousin isn't due back for another three days," Devin explained, "so he's not expecting his parents to get this until next week."

Devin frowned as a preposterous idea came to him. He pulled his cell out of his pocket. Zander had left a couple of messages in the night, which he hadn't had a chance to return. Trying not to get his hopes up—surely Mark wasn't that credulous—he rang his brother, turning to the window because he couldn't bear to look at Rachel suffering. Didn't want to be moved by it.

"Thank God," said Zander by way of greeting. "When I arrived home yesterday I found Mark on my doorstep. Apparently I told him I'd give him a job. I would cut him loose but he's like a goddamn puppy that's been kicked too many times."

"Don't! The last thing he needs is more rejection," Devin declared. Behind him, he heard Rachel gasp. "Keep him busy until I get there and don't, whatever you do, tell him I called." Devin snapped his cell shut and turned, trying to ignore the dark shadows under Rachel's eyes. She'd brought this on herself. "He's safe."

Still sitting on the bed, she dropped her head in her hands. Her long dark hair, normally glossy and thick, hung limp. "Thank God…oh, thank God."

Devin couldn't doubt the sincerity of her affection for her son. Grudgingly, he added, "He's with Zander in L.A."

She lifted her face, startled. "Why would he go there?"

Devin filled her in on Zander's throwaway invitation to Mark. "I'm going to get him."

Her throat convulsed as she stood up. "I know you hate me but—"

"Yes," he interrupted. Rachel flinched. Did she really think he could switch her off so easily? Irritated, he finished his sentence. "You can come, too."

*But I haven't forgiven you.*

RACHEL HADN'T THOUGHT about getting to L.A. beyond packing a bag and grabbing her passport. Devin had said he'd organize the flights, which she'd assumed meant traveling on a commercial jet. So it was a shock when he told her to drive her car past the international departure terminal at Auckland Airport in favor of a smaller terminal where a narrow-bodied Boeing Business Jet was being readied for takeoff, against the backdrop of a blazing West Coast sunset.

"Is that yours?" she said stupidly, pulling into the private parking lot. They'd taken her hatchback because it had a backseat, necessary for Mark. Devin had conceded when she'd made that argument. She hoped he wasn't humoring her.

"Yes, but more often than not it's subleased to other customers. Because of the short notice, we're sharing it today, but I've commandeered the bedroom for you—you need sleep." She stepped into the customs and immigration building, instinctively raising a hand to shade her gritty eyes from the bright lights and well aware she looked terrible.

Self-consciously, Rachel fumbled in her handbag and held out a wad. She'd withdrawn fourteen hundred dollars from her savings account to pay for her flight. "Obviously, it's nowhere near enough but…"

He looked at it curiously, then at her. "You'll use me to get to your son but you're coy about accepting a lift?"

"I didn't use you—" She broke off because the customs official was coming toward them. The flight, including a refueling stop in Hawaii, would be sixteen hours. Plenty of time to set the record straight.

After the formalities, Devin shepherded her aboard the aircraft. Already dazed, she found the luxurious interior only disoriented her more. While Devin went into the cockpit to talk to the captain, an attendant—Kristy—ushered Rachel past the camel-colored leather couches and armchairs, the four-seater dining room table and lavish bathroom to a smaller, private lounge, where she settled her in one of the armchairs. "I'm so sorry you're sharing the flight," she apologized.

Despite her gnawing anxiety for Mark, Rachel smiled. "That's fine," she assured her.

"Let me stow that for you." Kristy took Rachel's overnight bag and placed it in a lacquered maple cupboard. "Anything to eat or drink?"

"No, I'm not—"

"When did you last eat?" asked Devin from the

doorway. When Rachel hesitated, he turned to the attendant. "Feed her, please, Kristy." He glanced back at Rachel. "I'm assuming you don't want to join the others?"

She shook her head. Small talk was the last thing she wanted.

"Then I'll check on you later." He disappeared again, obviously unwilling to spend any time with her.

Kristy looked at Rachel, the question evident in her eyes. *What did you do?* Then, recollecting herself, she smiled, indicated the bedroom and en suite, and said she'd be back with a snack. Left alone, Rachel stared out the porthole at the last traces of smeared gold and pink streaks on the horizon.

She didn't see Devin again until halfway through the flight. By that time her thoughts were driving her mad.

He stopped at the door when he saw her. "I thought you'd be in bed."

"Don't stay away on my account."

Devin glanced over his shoulder as a burst of laughter came from the main cabin, then shrugged and stepped in, holding a briefcase. "I have work to do that needs quiet."

Rachel attempted a weak joke. "If you need help with your homework…" She'd meant schoolwork and realized too late that the comment could be read as sexual. It fell into an awful silence.

Grim-faced, Devin sat and opened his briefcase. "It's copyright paperwork on some of my early songs." Briefly, he filled her in on the reason for Zander's visit—to rub salt into the wound, Rachel suspected.

"I knew Zander had invited you to rejoin the band. I thought you were avoiding telling me because you were embarrassed about..." She stopped, picked up her cold coffee and sipped it, for something to break the sudden tension in the cabin.

"Embarrassed because I'd said I was falling in love with you and didn't mean it? No, my embarrassment came later."

"I should have trusted you." she said.

"Yeah," he said, "you should have. But it wouldn't have solved our basic problem. I was never more than a novelty toy to you, someone to play with while you waited for Mr. Right."

He'd made that accusation before. This time it wounded the part of her she'd vowed never to expose again—her heart.

"You're so wrong," she said, but he'd already stood.

"I'm going back to the other cabin."

"No!" Her anger came out of nowhere, explosively loud in the small space and catching them both by surprise. "I shouldn't have let Mark walk away without an explanation and I'm damned if you will. Sit down."

He folded his arms. "Make me."

She launched herself out of the seat and kissed him, not lightly, not tentatively, but passionately, with everything she felt for him—all the love, all the aching regret. His lips tightened under hers. His hands closed around her upper arms like steel traps as he put her away from him.

Humiliated, she returned to her seat on the couch, but Devin made no move to leave.

"Steve—Mark's father—talked me into smoking a joint the night I got pregnant." Rachel couldn't look at Devin, picking up a cushion and running her palm over the silky fabric. "I was crazy about him at this stage and he'd been teasing me about not drinking. He said it would make me happy. And oh, boy, it did. Happy and irresponsible." She choked on a laugh, looked up. "When I smelled it on Mark…well, it was easier to blame you than admit I'd failed to protect him."

Devin's eyes were grave. "It was more than that, Rachel. You wanted to believe the worst of me."

"No, that's—"

"All the qualities that made me a danger to Mark—the wildness, the bad boy history—made me safe to you. Because I'd never ask you to marry me or have children with me, never make you confront the things you'd have to if I was the right kind of guy. Like why you're so damn scared of anything approaching real intimacy. When I told you I loved you I broke the contract."

"No guy is the right guy," she cried. "I always chose men I couldn't love. You were supposed to be another one. If anyone broke faith, it was you."

"So you love me but you don't want to. Thanks, that makes me feel a whole lot better."

She had to make him understand.

"Just because I did the right thing in giving Mark up for adoption doesn't mean there aren't scars." She hugged herself, but it didn't help. "At seventeen, you think of self-sacrifice as something worthy, something good and ennobling that will carry you through the loss. You don't know that the scab will still fall off on his birthdays, that you'll still ache every time you hold a baby and smell that sweet, soft baby skin. At seventeen I made the sacrifice and at thirty-four I'm still paying. You're just the latest price."

"Rachel." Devin sat down beside her and reached for her hands; she pulled them away.

"I know what you want. You want all of me and I can't…love you like that. Giving up my baby changed me…. I can't love anybody that much again, can't risk that kind of loss. It hurt too much. It still hurts." She swallowed, forced herself to meet his gaze. "My only regret is that I hurt *you*."

For the rest of her life she'd remember the compassion in his eyes. "I'm a big boy. I can survive a few rounds in the ring with the Heartbreak Kid."

A laugh escaped her, then a sob. Ignoring her protests, he sat beside her and put his arms around her.

"I can't do this," she whispered against his shoulder, "not even for you."

"It's okay." There was nothing but comfort in his hold. "You don't need to explain. It's going to be all right."

She lifted her face. Devin had never seen such agony. "Is it? Now Mark's making me doubt the only thing I thought I got right."

Tears slid down her pale face, silent sobs shook her body. Rachel put her hands over her mouth, trying to stop.

Devin stroked her hair. "Let it go."

Shaking her head, she stood and stumbled to the adjacent bedroom, shutting the door. He followed her. She lay face down on the bed, her shoulders heaving with the effort of self-control.

He locked the door, then lay down beside her and gathered her into his arms. Rachel pushed him away, trying to curl in on herself and disappear. He pulled her arms free and put them around his waist, pushed down her bent knees and entwined their legs. He wrapped himself around her, trying to cover as much of her as he could with his body. "Let go."

Rachel stopped fighting and burrowed into him,

her nails digging into his back as she cried, jagged heartrending sobs that seemed as if they'd been held in check for seventeen years.

At last the weeping abated, her grip on him loosened and her body slowly relaxed against his, until Devin felt as if he held something ethereal, she lay so lightly in his arms. Exhausted, Rachel slept.

Releasing her, he swung his feet off the bed and stood up. Moving stiffly, his muscles still tight from absorbing her tension, he took off her shoes and pulled the covers over her inert form. She slept like the dead. Then he sat on the bed, pushed damp tendrils of hair away from her face and stared at her, his emotions mixed and powerful.

He still had the ability to minimize the damage she'd done to him, to protect himself with emotional distance.

In her sleep, Rachel sighed deeply.

Devin laid his palm against her cheek. Had anyone really loved this woman? It didn't seem so. And yet she'd still had the courage to defy her parents and do what she thought was right by her unborn baby, even at the cost of her relationship with them. She'd been alone in the world from the age of seventeen.

His life had been charmed by comparison, his losses self-indulgent. He'd been a kid in the world, too, and stumbled; but she hadn't. Not his Rachel.

Because she was his, no matter what she said. All his trials had been preparation, strengthening him to become a man capable of loving a woman who so deserved to be loved—and who might always hold something back.

He loved her anyway.

## CHAPTER NINETEEN

MARK WAS IN THE sound booth of OneRing Recording Studios, cleaning up after the latest round of coffee takeouts, when Devin strolled in on Friday morning. He started, his grip tightening on a polystyrene cup, and coffee dregs splashed the recording console.

"Watch it, dipstick!" One of the junior techs— bumped up the ranks through Mark's internship— shielded it protectively. "The VPR 60's worth more than your life."

But Mark wasn't listening. He answered his former mentor's casual greeting with a scowl. Untroubled, Devin turned to the studio technician and recording engineer. "Hey, guys, long time no see."

Both men stood to high-five and man-hug him. Even the session musicians tuning up in the isolation booth dumped their instruments to come through.

"Man, you're a sight for sore eyes."

"Good to see you! Back for good, I hope?"

Mark waited for a lull. "What are *you* doing here?"

In all that friendliness and back-thumping, his

accusatory tone struck a harshly discordant note. The other guys turned to stare at him.

"Among other things, catching up with old friends," Devin said coolly, and turned back to his buddies. Mark had imagined that when he saw Devin again, his mentor would be full of hangdog apologies, might grovel even. His first wild thought on seeing him was that Devin had come to talk him into going home. Now Mark wasn't so sure.

"So no one sent you to find me?"

Devin glanced over. "Why? Are you lost?"

Mark swallowed hard against a rush of homesickness. He'd been miserable in his week in L.A. Not because Zander mistreated him; in his own careless way the man had been kind, even getting him this job.

"No one sent me," Devin added, then looked at the studio manager. "Okay if I take Mark away for a few minutes, Tom?"

"Rehearsal room four is empty."

"We'll catch up later, guys." Devin left the sound booth, not even checking to see if Mark followed him. Mark dawdled to stress his resentment. Rehearsal room four was a large empty space with white, soundproof walls, a parquet floor and a comfortable couch. Devin sat at the grand piano—the only instrument currently in the room—running his hands lightly over the keys, seemingly unaware that he'd just been taught a lesson.

Bunching his hands in his jean pockets, Mark remained standing in the open door, trying to look aloof instead of sulky.

"Called your parents yet?"

Mark tried not to look guilty. He'd been meaning to call, except he couldn't deal with their questions or inevitable hurt. "I'm getting round to it." He had another day before Suz got home from Dubai and posted his letter.

He braced himself for criticism, but Devin only said, "What do you think of this?" and started playing.

"Sounds old-fashioned," he said impatiently.

"It came out before you were born. Listen to the lyrics."

"It's kinda schmaltzy," said Mark after a few minutes. "All this holding on through the coming years. It makes me think, get another girlfriend and get over it."

"What if the singer was female, sixteen and pregnant, and had just made the decision to adopt. What if it was a love song to her baby? Does that put a different spin on it?"

Devin sang another chorus, and suddenly Mark could feel the anguish in the song. He put his hands over his ears. "Stop."

Devin closed the lid of the piano. "It's Rachel's favorite song."

Mark clenched his hands at the mention of *her*

name. "Why did you do it, Dev? Why didn't you tell me as soon as you found out it was her?"

"Because she asked for time to get to know you." His expression softened in the same frustrated, affectionate way Dad's did when he was explaining some crazy female foible of Mom's. "She wanted you to like her first."

Mark snorted.

"It wasn't her best idea," Devin conceded, "but was she wrong to worry that you'd never give her a chance to explain?" With an effort of will, Mark held that penetrating gaze. "When she finally tried, did you listen?"

Mark clung to his righteous anger like a martyr to a hair shirt. "You know what I think? She never wanted me to find out she was my birth mother and that's why she conned you into not telling me."

"No, that's—"

"She's a liar, Dev. She said she gave me up because she had to but—" he paused to clear his throat "—her mother told me they wanted to keep me, and Rachel was the one who said no."

"What if they were both telling the truth?" Devin stood up from the piano. "Mark, you need to hear Rachel's side."

He shook his head. "If it's so damn important that I understand, then where is she? Why isn't *she* here defending herself?"

"I am here," Rachel said behind him.

MARK PALED, and tried to push past her. Heart pounding, Rachel blocked his way.

"Five minutes, then I promise you don't have to see me again."

He hesitated. To her relief he flung himself on the couch, glanced at his watch and folded his arms.

Devin got up to leave.

"Stay," she croaked, "I want you to hear this."

"And I don't want to be alone with her," Mark said savagely.

Rachel wiped her damp palms on her skirt. This was the most important conversation of her life and her mind was a blank.

Still standing by the door, she looked helplessly at Devin, trying to draw strength from his smile of encouragement as he joined Mark on the couch.

"This is a waste of time," said Mark.

"The only time Dad ever hit me was when I told him I was pregnant," she said. Rachel looked at her hands. "It was the only time Mom let him, although when the body blows started she intervened. I think that's why I made contact after he died, but…" She glanced at Mark. "Did she show you the photo albums?"

He nodded.

Rachel went over to sit at the piano stool. "My father was influential in council, in the community, in our church…. I don't think there was a charity he wasn't involved in. He never had any problem knowing exactly the right thing to do, the right way to dress and speak, the right opinions to have." She grimaced. "Of course, he spent his life constantly disappointed in other, more fallible, people."

She wasn't seeing Mark anymore, seeing only the past.

"In our home everything revolved around Dad. He was a secret drinker, always brooding over some slight, real or imagined. It infuriated him when he wasn't given the respect he deserved, and he'd take out his frustrations on my mother. The meal wasn't hot enough, the house not clean enough, she was letting herself go…letting him down."

Discordant notes echoed through the room; inadvertently, she'd leaned on the piano keys. Carefully Rachel closed the lid. "And my mother always agreed that it was her fault, always made excuses for him even when he'd hit her. Even now, when she's finally free of him, he's still a saint in her memory."

She moved restlessly on the stool. "I couldn't raise you on my own, but I couldn't let them raise you, either. For a while I put my hopes in an open adoption, but I couldn't trust Dad to leave you alone. So I canceled it." Her words were coming out all wrong—bald and harsh—but if she gave way to emotion now, she wouldn't finish what she had to say.

Rachel became aware that she was dusting the piano lid, over and over with the sleeve of her silk blouse, and stopped. "All I could give you was a future—parents who would raise you with stability, security and love. I'm sorry, but I can't regret that."

She'd promised five minutes. Rachel started to go.

"Devin said you wanted me to like you first and that's why you delayed telling me," Mark murmured.

*Silly, so silly.* "I'm sorry," she repeated. He was looking down, kicking the toe of his sneaker against the floor. The lace was untied.

"My real dad wanted you to have an abortion?"

"Yes." Rachel swallowed hard. "But I never considered it, not for a minute." She looked to Devin for more unspoken support.

Mark bent down and tied his shoe. "Still," he said gruffly, "three parents who wanted me isn't so bad."

Rachel smiled.

Her son lifted his face. There were tears in his eyes. "And I do like you," he said.

Her own vision blurred.

# CHAPTER TWENTY

IT TAKES AWHILE to believe that the person you started out thinking was all wrong for you is the one you're meant to be with.

But he was a patient man, her friend, Devin Freedman.

"I'm not going to push this," he'd said when they had a private moment on board the flight home. "But I'm not going away, either. I'm backing off until you get used to the idea that I love you. Because I'm damned if I'm doing the 'panic and dump' scenario you put the last two guys through. We're friends until you decide you're ready for more. And by more I mean love, marriage, kids—the whole shebang."

"And if I can't?" Because it wasn't a matter of won't any longer.

He'd simply smiled at her with all his lazy rock star arrogance. How could he be so confident? So sure of what he wanted? "Oh, and one more thing. Start something with me—a flirtation, anything that crosses the friendship boundary—and I'll take it as a yes." He'd leaned closer, so close Rachel felt his body heat, like a faint promise of a long, hot summer. "Because a kiss is not just a kiss, Heartbreaker, it's a commitment."

They all settled back into university life. Rachel met Mark's parents, taking Devin with her and trying not to think about how much she needed him at her back. She fought for and won an increase in her departmental budget. She got to know her son—relishing the slow, natural growth of his affection. She resumed her Sunday lunches and said no to a tattoo—a present from Trixie on her thirty-fifth birthday. And she regained her equilibrium in a very different world.

A world with family in it, even if she hadn't approved one of them yet.

She knew she was testing Devin; after all, the man had two failed marriages and a lot of wildness behind him. But over the next three months she came to trust his feelings. And hers.

And still she made him wait.

KATHERINE FREEDMAN MARRIED Matthew Bennett on a wet, blustery day at the end of June when the winter whitecaps caused more than one guest arriving by the Waiheke ferry to heave with the boat.

Standing beside Mark, watching Devin and

Zander walk their mother to her groom's side, Rachel's stomach fluttered nervously. It was a small wedding, only fifty close friends and family, and today she intended to signify her readiness to move from the former into the latter.

Outside, a cold wind shook the bare grapevines in the fields surrounding the mud-brick restaurant. Inside, it was as snug as a hobbit's burrow.

Tall tapers flickered in candelabras on two oak barrels by the arched window where they were to exchange vows. Tea candles lined the long tables, drawing the eye like landing lights on a runway. Overhead, fairy lights spiraled the rough-hewn beams.

A fire crackled in the stone hearth, roaring back at the weather every time a gust came down the chimney.

In a soft apricot suit, Katherine made a beautiful bride. Her sons had dressed to match the wedding party, in conventional dark suits, but to Rachel's relief nothing could civilize Devin's dramatic good looks. His hair would never play nice and the two brothers' diamond cuff links, diamond ear studs and chunky rings threatened to out-bling the bride's. Amid the cops that made up many of the groom's guests, they looked like two elegant thugs waiting for the right moment to pull machine guns out of their guitar cases.

"...to have and to hold," said Katherine, "to love and to cherish..."

Devin captured Rachel's gaze. Normally the fire

in his eyes was banked, though it always smoldered under the guise of friendship. Today it blazed.

But then she had dressed provocatively. Lifting her chin, she sent back a sweet, innocuous smile, reminding him who was in charge here. With her doubts settled, there was something fun, something dizzyingly, deliciously female in being the object of unrequited desire. In making Mr. Have-Any-Woman-He-Wanted wait.

His eyes glinted. Suddenly hot, Rachel undid some of the buttons of her 1950s Dior brocade swing coat, tempted to take it off.

The color of raspberries, patterned with gold starbursts, the matching sheath underneath had a deep V in the back, which closed to a large flat bow above the curve of her bottom.

"Sexy as hell," Devin had said when he'd given it to her for her birthday. "But think of the coat like a matador's cape. Only take it off if you want trouble."

Okay, she'd deliberately stoked the fires by wearing this outfit today. But was she ready for this much Toro Bravo? She wavered.

"I now pronounce you man and wife," intoned the celebrant. The reflected light burnished the smiles of the guests and illuminated the glow of the bridal couple. Matthew kissed his bride with a tenderness that softened Devin's expression. Taking a deep breath, Rachel reached for the last button.

As the applause and conversation restarted, Mark said beside her, "You next. Devin's already asked me to be his best man."

Rachel moved the hand on the button to her hip. "What?"

"When the time comes."

"I think he's getting a little ahead of himself," she said tartly. Maybe she'd make him wait *another* three months.

"I said I'd have to ask you first in case you might, you know—" her son's shrug couldn't quite hide his shyness "—like me to walk you down the aisle or something."

Tears sprang to Rachel's eyes, the offer was so unexpected, so moving.

Mark grinned. "I guess that's a yes?"

Blinking hard, she nodded and hugged him. "I'll keep you posted," she said gruffly. He felt so good, her son, hugging her back.

Devin joined them. "Can I have one of those, Heartbreaker?"

"A hug or a yes?" said Mark. The innocence of his query suggested a conspiracy.

"Both."

Releasing her traitorous son, Rachel glared in mock anger. "You said you'd be patient," she reminded Devin.

"Heartbreaker, you made up your mind weeks

ago." His eyes were very green. "Now you're playing me."

"Well, you are fun to play with," she said reasonably, and escaped to congratulate the bridal couple. Dried lavender strewed the flagstones underfoot, its astringent scent mingling with those of the guests. In future she would always associate the old-fashioned fragrance with an anticipatory thrill.

Katherine and Matthew welcomed her with open arms.

"The celebrant's here for another half an hour, Rachel," hinted the bride.

"Why is everyone ganging up on me today?"

"Because I don't want to be the only normal person in this crazy family," said Matthew.

"So what number wife would that make you?" teased Zander, who was already hauling off his tie. He still hadn't entirely forgiven her for the swimming pool incident.

"The last," said Devin as he joined them with Mark.

Rachel frowned. "Excuse me, but I still haven't said yes yet."

"First a cop in the family, now a librarian?" Zander shook his head. "God help my image."

"Musicians are as much geeks as petrol heads and computer nerds," retorted Rachel, "but to repeat, I haven't said yes yet."

Zander turned to his brother. "You do know she'll be teaching you big words like *virtuous* and *respectable.*"

"I was working on those anyway," said Devin. "No, what the librarian's done is extend my emotional vocabulary." The teasing left his voice. "Taught me what love means."

Rachel stared at him. "Oh, you're not playing fair," she whispered.

He picked up her hand. "I know where I belong. With you. Now take off the coat, Rachel."

She dropped his hand, trying not to laugh. "You're incorrigible."

"So put me in my place again, Heartbreaker."

Rachel laid a hand over her heart, palm open, and tapped it gently. Devin's gaze followed the gesture then lifted swiftly, all the teasing gone.

He kissed her, right there among the guests, and it wasn't a chaste public kiss but a toe-curling, carnal one that left her disheveled and breathless. They broke apart amid laughter and cheers.

"Let's get out of here," he said huskily.

They'd started walking before she came to her senses. "We can't, we're at your mother's wedding."

"That's right," Katherine called across the room. "Mark, go stop the celebrant from leaving." He tore out.

Rachel's heart started to pound. "That's crazy."

"You can't stay on the kids' carousel forever," said Devin. "It's time for the roller coaster."

She could barely breathe for the hammering against her ribs. She wanted to say yes but... Helplessly, she stared at him. "Devin..."

He pulled her aside. "Tell me," he said gently.

"How do you know this is different...from the others?"

"Those relationships started with a bang—literally—followed by rapid disillusionment. With you, the feelings only get stronger."

She remembered their first encounter and smiled. "You thought of me as a fossilized conservative—"

"Who transformed not herself, but me," he said seriously.

Mark returned, panting. "The celebrant's coming back."

Devin held out his hand to her, the dragon's tongue flicking the tip of that one knuckle. Outside, the clouds broke; rays of sunlight shimmered through the sheets of rain, tinting the bleak gray mist with gold, streaming in the window to burnish his smile, his hair, his eyes. "Be my wife," he said, "my one true love."

Rachel shrugged off her coat and handed it to her son, then took Devin's hand. "Yes."

Maybe she would get that birthday tattoo Trixie offered. Perhaps a tiny sword-wielding female knight on her rump. It was a joke that Devin would appreciate.

\* \* \* \* \*

*Harlequin offers a romance for every mood!*
*See below for a sneak peek*
*from our paranormal romance line,*
*Silhouette® Nocturne™.*
*Enjoy a preview of REUNION by USA TODAY*
*bestselling author Lindsay McKenna.*

Aella closed her eyes and sensed a distinct shift, like movement from the world around her to the unseen world.

She opened her eyes. And had a slight shock at the man standing ten feet away. He wasn't just any man. Her heart leaped and pounded. He reminded her of a fierce warrior from an ancient civilization. Incan? She wasn't sure but she felt his deep power and masculinity.

*I'm Aella. Are you the guardian of this sacred site?* she asked, hoping her telepathy was strong.

Fox's entire body soared with joy. Fox struggled to put his personal pleasure aside.

*Greetings, Aella. I'm the assistant guardian to this sacred area. You may call me Fox. How can I be of service to you, Aella?* he asked.

*I'm searching for a green sphere. A legend says that the Emperor Pachacuti had seven emerald spheres created for the Emerald Key necklace. He had seven of his priestesses and priests travel the world to hide these spheres from evil forces. It is said that when all seven spheres are found, restrung and worn, that Light will return to the Earth. The fourth sphere is here, at your sacred site. Are you aware of it?* Aella held her breath. She loved looking at him, especially his sensual mouth. The desire to kiss him came out of nowhere.

Fox was stunned by the request. *I know of the Emerald Key necklace because I served the emperor at the time it was created. However, I did not realize that one of the spheres is here.*

Aella felt sad. Why? Every time she looked at Fox, her heart felt as if it would tear out of her chest. *May I stay in touch with you as I work with this site?* she asked.

*Of course.* Fox wanted nothing more than to be here with her. To absorb her ephemeral beauty and hear her speak once more.

Aella's spirit lifted. What *was* this strange connection between them? Her curiosity was strong, but she had more pressing matters. In the next few days, Aella knew her life would change forever. How, she had no idea....

*Look for REUNION*
*by USA TODAY bestselling author*
*Lindsay McKenna,*
*available April 2010,*
*only from Silhouette® Nocturne™.*

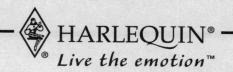

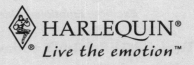

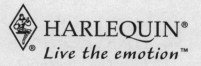

# HARLEQUIN®
# INTRIGUE®

## BREATHTAKING ROMANTIC SUSPENSE

Shared dangers and passions lead to electrifying
romance and heart-stopping suspense!

Every month, you'll meet six new heroes
who are guaranteed to make your spine tingle
and your pulse pound. With them you'll enter
into the exciting world of Harlequin Intrigue—
where your life is on the line
and so is your heart!

### THAT'S INTRIGUE—
### ROMANTIC SUSPENSE
### AT ITS BEST!

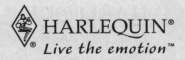

HARLEQUIN®
*Live the emotion*™

## Harlequin® Historical
### Historical Romantic Adventure!

*Imagine a time of chivalrous
knights and unconventional ladies,
roguish rakes and impetuous
heiresses, rugged cowboys
and spirited frontierswomen—
these rich and vivid tales will
capture your imagination!*

*Harlequin Historical . . .
they're too good to miss!*

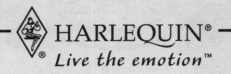